Praise for *How to Fracture a Fairy Tale*

"This collection is Jane Yolen at her best, telling stories you've never seen before but have known all your life, and stories as familiar as your left hand that you barely recognize, spun from shadows and moonlight and breathed through silvered glass. This is magic."
—Patricia C. Wrede, author of the *Enchanted Forest Chronicles*

"Yolen's deftly-flowing prose highlights each unique perspective or imaginative speculation. Her tales, once fractured, don't splinter—they sparkle."
—Alex Flinn, author of *Beastly* and *Beheld*

"A master storyteller at her best. I've been a fan of Jane Yolen and fractured fairytales for years and this collection doesn't disappoint."
—Chanda Hahn, author of *Reign (An Unfortunate Fairy Tale)*

"*How to Fracture a Fairy Tale* is a fascinating exploration of how old stories we all think we know can become fresh and new and stunning in the hands of the masterful Jane Yolen. So many of Yolen's stories here are like origami—with expert snips and twists and turns, she transforms the ordinary into fantastic art. This book can be read just for sheer pleasure or as a study for other writers in what is possible."
—Margaret Peterson Haddix, author of *The Missing* series and *The Shadow Children* series

"Ever the master storyteller, Jane Yolen weaves and spins and fractures her way through a far-ranging, culturally diverse array of fairy-tales. Ranging from the comic (various famous fairy tale wolves kvetching in an Old Wolves Home) to the disturbing (a take on Cinderella involving incest) to the poetic (a lovely version of the Native American tale 'The Woman Who Loved a Bear'), each tale is a finely crafted gemstone. Readers will be filled with

wonder and delight, pain and joy, and may even be inspired to try their own hand at fracturing a fairy tale. I particularly loved Yolen's explanatory 'How I Fractured These Stories' section at the end, identifying the origin tale, each one accompanied by a luminous poem."
—Edith Pattou, author of *West* and *East*

Praise for Jane Yolen

"One of the treasures of the science-fiction community."
—Brandon Sanderson, author of *Mistborn*

"There is simply no better storyteller working in the fantasy field today. She's a national treasure."
—Terri Windling, author of *The Wood Wife*

"The Aesop of the twentieth century."
—*New York Times*

"Jane Yolen is a gem in the diadem of science fiction and fantasy."
—*Analog*

"The Hans Christian Andersen of America."
—*Newsweek*

Praise for *The Emerald Circus*

"Jane Yolen facets her glittering stories with the craft of a master jeweller. Everything she writes, including *The Emerald Circus*, is original and timeless, deliciously creepy and disturbingly lovely."
—Elizabeth Wein, author of *Code Name Verity*

"Jane Yolen's *The Emerald Circus* is full of marvels. She turns toads into witches, Sir Lancelot into a 600-year-old monk, Dorothy into

a tightrope walker, and Emily Dickinson into a spacefarer. From Snow Queen to spaceship, *The Emerald Circus* is a delight."
—Patricia A. McKillip, author of *The Riddle-Master of Hed*

"★ These delightful retellings of favorite stories will captivate newcomers and fans of Yolen as she once again delivers the magic, humor, and lovely prose that has attracted readers for years."
—*Library Journal*, starred review

"★ These highly entertaining retellings are perfect for teen fans of fairy tales and classic literature, though they are easily enjoyed without any background knowledge."
—*School Library Journal*, starred review

"★ *The Emerald Circus* dances at the border between bucking tradition and paying homage to the great stories and figures of ages past. The result is a brilliant assemblage of narratives with the potential to leave an audience spellbound."
—*Foreword*, starred review

"Ever the wordsmith, Yolen dazzles with her first short story collection for adults in years."
—*Booklist*

"Jane Yolen is a consummate storyteller, weaving old and new threads to create tales rich in wisdom and depth. *The Emerald Circus* is an utter delight."
—Juliet Marillier, award-winning author of the Sevenwaters series

"Jane Yolen's collection *The Emerald Circus* is pure delight for anyone who craves inspired retellings of classics from literature, or re-imaginings of the lives of real literary figures. 5/5 stars."
—*YA Books Central*

Also by Jane Yolen

Novels
The Wizard of Washington Square (1969)
Hobo Toad and the Motorcycle Gang (1970)
The Magic Three of Solatia (1974)
The Transfigured Hart (1975)
The Mermaid's Three Wisdoms (1978)
The Acorn Quest (1981)
The Stone Silenus (1984)
Cards of Grief (1985)
The Devil's Arithmetic (1988)
The Dragon's Boy (1990)
Wizard's Hall (1991)
Briar Rose (1992)
The Wild Hunt (1995)
The Sea Man (1997)
Boots and the Seven Leaguers (2000)
Sword of the Rightful King (2003)
The Young Merlin Trilogy: Passager, Hobby, and Merlin (2004)
Except the Queen (with Midori Snyder, 2010)
Snow in Summer (2011)
Curse of the Thirteenth Fey (2012)
Centaur Rising (2014)
A Plague of Unicorns (2014)
Trash Mountain (2015)
Mapping the Bones (2018)
Finding Baba Yaga (verse novel, 2018)
Magic Three of Solatia (TBD)

The Pit Dragons Chronicles
Dragon's Blood (1982)
Heart's Blood (1984)
A Sending of Dragons (1987)
Dragon's Heart (2009)

Great Alta Books
Sister Light, Sister Dark (1989)
White Jenna (1989)
The One-Armed Queen (1998)

Tartan Magic Series
The Wizard's Map (1999)
The Pictish Child (1999)
The Bagpiper's Ghost (2002)

Rock & Roll Fairy Tales
Pay the Piper (with Adam Stemple, 2005)
Troll Bridge (with Adam Stemple, 2006)
B. U. G. (Big Ugly Guy) (with Adam Stemple, 2013)

Young Heroes Series
Odysseus in the Serpent Maze (with Robert J. Harris, 2001)
Hippolyta and the Curse of the Amazon (with Robert J. Harris, 2002)

Atalanta and the Arcadian Beast (with Robert J. Harris, 2003)
Jason and the Gorgon's Blood (with Robert J. Harris, 2004)

The Seelie Wars Trilogy
The Hostage Prince (with Adam Stemple, 2013)
The Last Changeling (with Adam Stemple, 2014)
The Seelie King's War (with Adam Stemple, 2016)

Collections
The Girl Who Cried Flowers and Other Tales (1974)
The Moon Ribbon (1976)
The Hundredth Dove and Other Tales (1977)
Dream Weaver (1979)
Neptune Rising: Songs and Tales of the Undersea People (1982)
Tales of Wonder (1983)
The Whitethorn Wood and Other Magicks (1984)
Dragonfield and Other Stories (1985)
Merlin's Booke (1986)
The Faery Flag (1989)
Storyteller (1992)
Here There Be Dragons (1993)
Here There Be Unicorns (1994)
Here There Be Witches (1995)
Among Angels (with Nancy Willard, 1995)
Here There Be Angels (1996)
Here There Be Ghosts (1998)
Twelve Impossible Things Before Breakfast (1997)
Sister Emily's Lightship and Other Stories (2000)
Not One Damsel in Distress (2000)
Mightier Than the Sword (2003)
Once Upon A Time (She Said) (2005)
The Last Selchie Child (2012)
Grumbles from the Forest: Fairy-Tales Voices with a Twist (with Rebecca Kai Dotlich, 2013)
The Emerald Circus (2017)

Graphic Novels
Foiled (2010)
The Last Dragon (2011)
Curses! Foiled Again (2013)
Stone Man Mysteries (with Adam Stemple):
Stone Cold (2016)
Sanctuary (2018)

HOW TO FRACTURE A FAIRY TALE
JANE YOLEN

WITHDRAWN

WITHDRAWN

tachyon | san francisco

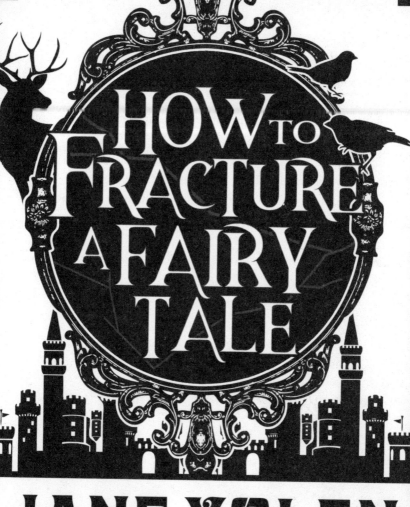

HOW TO FRACTURE A FAIRY TALE

JANE YOLEN

Introduction copyright © 2018 by Marissa Meyer
"How to Fracture a Fairy Tale" copyright © 2018 by Jane Yolen
Interior and cover design by Elizabeth Story

Pages 300-304 constitute an extension of this copyright page

Tachyon Publications LLC
1459 18th Street #139
San Francisco, CA 94107
415.285.5615
www.tachyonpublications.com
tachyon@tachyonpublications.com

Series Editor: Jacob Weisman
Project Editor: Jill Roberts

Print ISBN: 978-1-61696-306-4
Digital ISBN: 978-1-61696-307-1

First Edition: 2018
9 8 7 6 5 4 3 2 1

CONTENTS

How I Fractured These Stories: Notes and Poems

INTRODUCTION
MARISSA MEYER

O ne of the fascinating things about fairy tales that has captured countless imaginations is the breadth of possibility these stories have to offer. We may think we know a particular tale—from Grimm, Andersen, or even Disney—but once we start to uncover its sweeping history, we learn that there is so much more to it than a beautiful princess, a mean stepmother, or a happily ever after. There is a history of tales told and retold that spans centuries—even millennia—and reaches to all corners of the globe. To trace that history reveals just how much the stories have been changed with time . . . and also, interestingly, how much they have stayed the same.

And that doesn't even begin to touch on the library of fairy tale retellings and fractured legends that have been amassed from an endless array of contemporary storytellers, of which Jane Yolen is, of course, one of the most beloved. This collection of her works clearly exemplifies why Yolen has been called a modern-day Hans Christian Andersen.

In the pages that follow, Yolen demonstrates the vast potential contained within these classic tales. Nothing is sacred.

Everything can be altered according to a writer's whims and imagination—the time period, the location, the protagonist, the point of view . . . even the *ever after* bit, whether happily or otherwise. Fairy tales are a living thing. They are meant to be adapted for each new generation. They are meant to grow and morph along with their tellers and their listeners (who are sometimes children . . . but certainly not always). These modified versions of the familiar are sometimes dark and haunting, sometimes witty and satirical, but always as universal and worthy of telling as any of their predecessors.

With their basis in well-known fairy tales, legends, and myths, the stories contained here *are* familiar, but only to a point. Some have been altered in ways that are subtle, yet profound. Others have been smashed into pieces and glued back together. They have been reimagined, reworked, and, now, retold.

The result?

Poetry. Wishes. Heartache. Dreams.

And oh yes, a few nightmares, too.

Expect to be greeted with characters that are both well-known and forgotten, and more often than not, changed, as in the case of a wolf who fights for animal welfare, and a modern-day pied piper in a small tourist town. Prepare to have your long-held opinions put to the test, as with a sleeping princess with a cruel heart, or even Death herself, whose own tragedies are as poignant as they are sympathetic. You might even meet a character who is exactly what you *wanted* them to be, all this time, as was the case for me when I read the story of the plump Cinderella and her awkward prince (to which the plump teenager of my past gave a resounding cheer—*finally!*).

In the course of all that, you will be transported.

To a rookery off the shores of Scotland and a temple off the coast of Japan and even World War II concentration camps—as horrific and cruel in these altered tales as any historical account. You will be swept away to caves at the tops of mountains and grottos beneath the sea. To castles and palaces and, naturally, a few cottages in the woods. Though the stories found inside those unassuming walls may not be the stories of your childhood. For these are stories of lust, betrayal, and sorrow, as much as they are of love, longing, and magic. These are stories that have been mined from a wealth of traditions, chiseled and polished to once again reveal their universal truths, and—ultimately—fractured.

—Marissa Meyer
Tacoma, Washington, 2018

HOW TO FRACTURE A FAIRYTALE

A fracture is a break, usually in the bone, but also can mean a crack in the earth, an interruption of the norm. It can be a fault line, a fissure, a split, breach, disruption, splintering, fissure—oh, and a breakup. It sounds explosive, can hurt like a sprain or reveal like a geode being split apart to show the jewels within.

As a writer, I find all those possibilities both fascinating and freeing.

As a *fairy tale* writer, it means I can have fun with old stories, breaking them open to pull out the insides, reveal them to the light, and make prophesies, aka stories. A combination of academic, Aztec priest, griot, seeress, and hardworking author.

These old stories, from way back in human history, have already been told and retold in many different ways. They are guised and disguised.

Of course, when a writer or storyteller rewrites and refines them for the world we now live in, magic happens. Sometimes the fracture reveals beauty, sometimes suppurating flesh. Sometimes it causes an itch or discloses a deep wound. Sometimes it makes the reader gasp or laugh, or give a fist bump to other readers. Sometimes that fracture makes a difference in a life.

As a teacher of writing, I also ask—how does a writer fracture a fairy tale? Use a bludgeon? Sometimes. A scalpel—other times. Or a good sensible piece of dark chocolate to tease out the meanings—also good. But first read the old story in as many incarnations as you can. Because, honestly, you may already be reading one that has been seriously fractured in just the way you'd planned.

Then you have to figure out what kind of fracture you're attempting. A small sprain or the calving of glaciers? Do you want to subvert the story's paradigm entirely, or just make a joke? I have done both. In "Allerleirauh," using a *Cinderella* variant, I show the bitter truth of incest. In "Sleeping Ugly" I tell *Sleeping Beauty* as a joke.

Do you want to write the story from a different point of view? For example, I have told "The Three Billy Goats Gruff" from the bridge's point of view. Taken several incarnations of the Big Bad Wolf stories and placed them into a nursing home for old wolves.

How about setting a story that is well known, like *Rumpelstiltskin*, in a different time and place? I read the story as an anti-Semitic tale, and set it in a make-believe Middle European kingdom (sort of Poland but not actually) where the spinner of straw into gold becomes a money-changer. His widow is known as "Granny Rumple."

Just fracturing an old tale is fun. Occasionally it takes courage. Sometimes the story sells. What more can a writer ask for?

Fame, a large house, many awards.

Well—like the old witch in the woods of hundreds of old fairy tales—let me give you this piece of advice: be careful what you wish for. One of my awards set my good coat on fire. That may sound like a fairy tale well fractured, but it really happened.

—Jane Yolen, Phoenix Farm, 2018

SNOW IN SUMMER

They call that white flower that covers the lawn like a poplin carpet Snow in Summer. And because I was born in July with a white caul on my head, they called me that, too. Mama wanted me to answer to Summer, which is a warm, pretty name. But my Stepmama, who took me in hand just six months after Mama passed away, only spoke the single syllable of my name, and she didn't say it nicely.

"Snow!" It was a curse in her mouth. It was a cold, unfeeling thing. "Snow, where are you, girl? Snow, what have you done now?"

I didn't love her. I couldn't love her, though I tried. For Papa's sake I tried. She was a beautiful woman, everyone said. But as Miss Nancy down at the postal store opined, "Looks ain't nothing without a good heart." And she was staring right at my Stepmama when she said it. But then Miss Nancy had been Mama's closest friend ever since they'd been little ones, and it nigh killed her, too, when Mama was took by death.

Papa was besot with my Stepmama. He thought she couldn't do no wrong. The day she moved into Cumberland he said she was the queen of love and beauty. That she was prettier than a summer night. He praised her so often, she took it ill any day he left off complimenting, even after they was hitched. She would have rather heard those soft nothings said about her than to talk of any of the things a husband needs to tell his wife: like when is dinner going to be ready or what bills are still to be paid.

I lived twelve years under that woman's hard hand, with only Miss Nancy to give me a kind word, sweet pop, and a magic story when I was blue. Was it any wonder I always went to town with a happier countenance than when I had to stay at home?

And then one day Papa said something at the dinner table, his mouth greasy with the chicken I had cooked and his plate full with the taters I had boiled. And not a thing on that table that my Stepmama had made. Papa said, as if surprised by it, "Why Rosemarie" . . . which was my Stepmama's Christian name . . . "why Rosemarie do look at what a beauty that child has become."

And for the first time my Stepmama looked—really looked—at me.

I do not think she liked what she saw.

Her green eyes got hard, like gems. A row of small lines raised up on her forehead. Her lips twisted around. "Beauty," she said. "Snow," she said. She did not say the two words together. They did not fit that way in her mouth.

I didn't think much of it at the time. If I thought of myself at all those days, it was as a lanky, gawky, coltish child. Beauty was for horses or grown women, Miss Nancy always said. So I just laughed.

"Papa, you are just fooling," I told him. "A daddy *has* to say such things about his girl." Though in the thirteen years I had been alive he had never said any such over much. None in fact that I could remember.

But then he added something that made things worse, though I wasn't to know it that night. "She looks like her Mama. Just like her dear Mama."

My Stepmama only said, "Snow, clear the dishes."

So I did.

But the very next day my Stepmama went and joined the Holy Roller Mt. Hosea Church, which did snake handling on the fourth Sunday of each month and twice on Easter. Because of the Bible saying "Those who love the Lord can take up vipers and they will not be killed," the Mt. Hosea folk proved the power of their faith by dragging out rattlers and copperheads from a box and carrying them about their shoulders like a slippery shawl. Kissing them, too, and letting the pizzen drip down on their checks.

Stepmama came home from church, her face all flushed and her eyes all bright and said to me, "Snow, you will come with me next Sunday."

"But I love Webster Baptist," I cried. "And Reverend Bester. And the hymns." I didn't add that I loved sitting next to Miss Nancy and hearing the stories out of the Bible the way she told them to the children's class during the Reverend's long sermon.

"Please Papa, don't make me go."

For once my Papa listened. And I was glad he said no. I am feared of snakes, though I love the Lord mightily. But I wasn't sure any old Mt. Hosea rattler would know the depth of that love. Still, it wasn't the snakes Papa was worried about. It was, he said, those Mt. Hosea boys.

My Stepmama went to Mt. Hosea alone all that winter, coming home later and later in the afternoon from church, often escorted by young men who had scars on their cheeks where they'd been snakebit. One of them, a tall blond fellow who was almost handsome except for the meanness around his eyes, had a tattoo of a rattler on his bicep with the legend "Love Jesus Or Else" right under it.

9

My Papa was not amused.

"Rosemarie," he said, "you are displaying yourself. That is not a reason to go to church."

"I have not been doing this for myself," she replied. "I thought Snow should meet some young men now she's becoming a woman. A *beautiful* woman." It was not a compliment in her mouth. And it was not the truth, either, for she had never even introduced me to the young men nor told them my true name.

Still, Papa was satisfied with her answer, though Miss Nancy, when I told her about it later, said, "No sow I know ever turned a boar over to her litter without a fight."

However, the blond with the tattoo came calling one day and he didn't ask for my Stepmama. He asked for me. For Snow. My Stepmama smiled at his words, but it was a snake's smile, all teeth and no lips. She sent me out to walk with him, though I did not really want to go. It was the mean eyes and the scars and the rattler on his arm, some. But more than that, it was a feeling I had that my Stepmama wanted me to be with him. And that plum frightened me.

When we were in the deep woods, he pulled me to him and tried to kiss me with an open mouth and I kicked him in the place Miss Nancy had told me about, and while he was screaming, I ran away. Instead of chasing me, he called after me in a voice filled with pain. "That's not even what your Stepmama wanted me to do to you." But I kept running, not wanting to hear any more.

I ran and ran even deeper into the woods, long past the places where the rhododendron grew wild. Into the dark places, the boggy places, where night came upon me and would not let me go. I was so tired from all that running, I fell asleep right on a tussock of grass. When I woke there was a passel of strangers staring down at me. They were small, humpedbacked men, their skin blackened by coal dust, their eyes curious. They were ugly as an unspoken sin.

"Who are you?" I whispered, for a moment afraid they might be more of my Stepmama's crew.

They spoke together, as if their tongues had been tied in a knot at the back end. "Miners," they said. "On Keeperwood Mountain."

"I'm Snow in Summer," I said. "Like the flower."

"Summer," they said as one. But they said it with softness and a kind of dark grace. And they were somehow not so ugly anymore. "Summer."

So I followed them home.

And there I lived for seven years, one year for each of them. They were as good to me and as kind as if I was their own little sister. Each year, almost as if by magic, they got better to look at. Or maybe I just got used to their outsides and saw within. They taught me how to carve out jewels from the black cave stone. They showed me the secret paths around their mountain. They warned me about strangers finding their way to our little house.

I cooked for them and cleaned for them and told them Miss Nancy's magic stories at night. And we were happy as can be. Oh, I missed my Papa now and then, but my Stepmama not at all. At night I sometimes dreamed of the tall blond man with the rattler tattoo, but when I cried out one of the miners would always comfort me and sing me back to sleep in a deep, gruff voice that sounded something like a father and something like a bear.

Each day my little men went off to their mine and I tidied and swept and made up the beds. Then I'd go outside to play. I had deer I knew by name, grey squirrels who came at my bidding, and the sweetest family of doves that ate cracked corn out of my hand. The garden was mine, and there I grew everything we needed. I did not mourn for what I did not have.

But one day a stranger came to the clearing in the woods. Though she strived to look like an old woman, with cross-eyes and a mouth full of black teeth, I knew her at once. It was my Stepmama in disguise. I pretended I did not know who she was, but when she inquired, I told her my name straight out.

"Summer," I said.

I saw "Snow" on her lips.

I fed her a deep-dish apple pie and while she bent over the table shoveling it into her mouth, I felled her with a single blow of the fry pan. My little men helped me bury her out back.

Miss Nancy's stories had always ended happy-ever-after. But she used to add every time: "Still, you must make your own happiness, Summer dear."

And so I did. My happiness—and hers.

I went to the wedding when Papa and Miss Nancy tied the knot. I danced with some handsome young men from Webster and from Elkins and from Canaan. But I went back home alone. To the clearing and the woods and the little house with the eight beds. My seven little fathers needed keeping. They needed my good stout meals. And they needed my stories of magic and mystery. To keep them alive.

To keep me alive, too.

THE BRIDGE'S COMPLAINT

rit-trot, trit-trot, trit-trot, all day long. You'd think their demned hooves were made of iron. It fair gives me a headache, it does. Back and forth, back and forth. As if the grass were actually greener on one side one day, on the other the next. Goats really are a monstrous race.

It makes me long for the days of Troll.

We never were on more than a generic-name basis. He was Troll. I was Bridge. It takes trolls—and bridges, for that matter—a long time to warm up to full introductions. So I never had a chance to know his first name before he was . . . well . . . gone. But he was a pleasant sort, for a troll. Knew a lot of stories. Troll stories, of course, are full of blood and food, food and blood. But they were good stories, for all that. Told loudly and with great passion. I really do miss them.

Not that I don't have a few good stories of my own to tell. I mean, I wasn't always a Goat Bridge. Long before that demned tribe arrived to foul my planking, I was a Bridge of Some Consequence. Mme. D'Aulnoy herself traversed my boards. And her friend Mme. le Prince du Beaumont. Ah—the sound of wheels rolling. There is a memory to treasure.

None of this *trit-trot, trit-trot* business.

But then the dear ladies were gone and the meadows, once pied with colorful flowers, were sold to a goat merchant, M. de Gruff. He pastured his demned beasties on both sides of my river. They sharpened their horns on my railings, pawed deep into the earthen slopes, and ate up every last one of the flowers. The grass in the meadows was gnawed down to nubbins by those voracious creatures. In other words, they made a desert out of an Eden.

Trit-trot, trit-trot, indeed.

So you can imagine how thrilled I was when Troll showed up, pushing his way upstream from the confluence of the great rivers below.

He wasn't much to look at when he arrived, being young and quite thin. Of course he had the big bran-muffin eyes and the sled-jump nose and the gingko-leaf ears that identify a troll immediately. And when he smiled, there were those moss green teeth, filed to points. But otherwise he was a quite unprepossessing troll.

Trolls are territorial, you know, and when food gets scarce, the young are pushed out by the older, bigger, meaner trolls. Or so my Troll told me, and I have no reason to disbelieve him. He said, "Me dad gave a shove when he got hungry. I had to go. Been on the move awhile."

That was an understatement. Actually he had been wading through miles of river before he found me unoccupied. He must have thought it paradise when he saw all those goats.

Not that he could have run across the fields after them. It is a well-kept secret that trolls must have one foot in the water at times. Troll told me this one night when we were trading tales. They call it *water-logging*. Troll even sang me a song about it that went something like this:

*Two feet wet
None on shore,
You will live
Evermore.*

*One foot wet,
One foot dry,
You will never
Need to cry.*

*Two feet dry—
Say good-bye.*

Well, trolls are actually better at stories than poems. You want good poetry, you have to hang out with boggles or sprites.

Of course the whole thing is a secret and I only tell you this because there are no longer many trolls about. It is a shame, actually. M. Darwin wrote of this disappearing phenomenon, and I, for one, believe it.

So trolls must wait by a river's bank for some creature to cross if they want to eat. That's why trolls and bridges have such an affinity. A bridge means a crossing place, and we are much more stable than fords. Trolls, while not having particularly scientific minds, long ago figured this much out.

So there we were, Troll and I, he dining on M. de Gruff's billy goats, large and small and in-between. And after each meal, after he had a round of belching and farting—which trolls consider good form—he favored me with a troll tale.

He told me about trolls in love and trolls at war—which to the untutored ear can sound much the same.

He told me a tale about a troll who lived in the waters near Nôtre-Dame, eating fish and fishermen. But that troll conceived an unlikely passion for the cathedral. He desired to talk to the gargoyles, whom he thought must be cousins of his. He began to waste away with longing for just a single word with his stone kin. So he pulled himself up out of the water and started across the land. After three steps he died, of course. The Parisians used his bones for soup and built a monument where he fell. But he died happy—or so Troll said.

He told me about a troll who had been interviewed by a journalist, and when I asked what paper the piece had appeared in, he giggled, an unlikely sound coming from such a large source. The silly troll, he said, had eaten the man *before* he wrote the story, not after. We had a good laugh about that!

And then he told me about his mother, about the good times before his father had given him a shove. We cried together. After all, that's what friends are for.

He was so delighted with my company, he tried to compose a troll song to the beauty of my span, but he got lost in rhymes about tans/fans/bans and never did finish it. But he was a good teller of tales.

And I am the consummate listener.

I must admit that—except for the day Mme. d'Aulnoy and Mme. le Prince du Beaumont traded stories sitting on the banks of my stream, their *petite* picnic spread out on a blanket—I was never happier.

But the sad fact is that trolls are not very smart. Good storytellers, yes. Pleasant companions, quite. Undemanding friends, absolutely. But they lack upstairs what they have elsewhere. Breadth. They are—alas—really quite stupid. They do not have the slightest understanding of diplomatic dissembling. They do not know how to prevaricate—or to put it more succinctly, they cannot tell a lie. Even with my coaching, Troll would not move downstream a ways and take goats from different parts of the river just to fool them.

"I like it here with you," he said. "Besides, this is my place."

And not being a troll myself, I couldn't shove him off.

So the day came when the goats stopped crossing the bridge because it had become too notably dangerous. For a month not a single one went over my span. And while I was delighted to be rid of that constant, demned *trit-trot, trit-trot*, it worried me to see my friend grow so thin and wan. It got so one could almost read a book through him. He had not even the energy to tell stories.

So I did what I could. Bridges are not a flighty tribe. We are solid and stolid. We stay put. But we have our wiles for all that. One does not arch over a river for so many years without learning something.

I waited until one rather silly young goat strayed a bit too close to my embankments and I called to him.

"Come here, little goat."

He looked about cautiously. "Are you a troll?"

"A troll? Do I look like a troll?"

"Well, actually you look like a bridge."

"And have you ever *seen* a troll?"

He shook his little nubbined head.

"But you *have* seen a bridge?"

He giggled. I knew then that I had him.

"So if you have never seen a troll, how do you know they exist?"

"My mother warned me about them."

I allowed myself a deprecating little laugh. "Mothers! I bet she also warned you about eating tins and paper products and staying out too late at night."

He nodded.

"I am just a bridge," I said. "Immobile and proper. And of course, on my side is . . ."

"A green meadow?" he said.

"Greener than any you have ever seen," I said.

That did it. He upped and started over. *Trit-trot, trit-trot.*

Of course, halfway there, Troll came up and grabbed the

fool off and had his first good dinner in a month. Well, *good* dinner is perhaps an exaggeration. It was only a very little goat. Practically a kid.

If only he had been content with the one. But the next goat I snared for him with my promise of greener pastures was middle-sized.

"Let this one go over," I whispered to Troll, "and you will soon have the entire herd wanting to follow." Even though I mentally cringed at the idea of so many *trits* and so many *trots*, I did not want my friend to die.

But that smacked too much of planning, something trolls have no sense about. And lying, which they know nothing of at all.

"Hungry *now!*" Troll complained, and ate the middle-sized de Gruff goat right then and there.

So when the big goat followed, with horns as sharp as gaffing hooks and a sly twist of mind, it is no wonder that my dear Troll was taken in.

It was not the fall that killed him, of course. It was when the big billy goat of M. de Gruff lifted him out of the water. Troll was dead long before he hit the ground.

My own fault then, you will say, that I must endure this *trit-trot, trit-trot* all day long. I do not, myself, accept blame. Life is like a river: forever changing. Sometimes it is at flood stage, and sometimes not.

But if you should hear of another troll who is looking for a home, tell him there is a Bridge of Slight Consequence placed between two green meadows not far from Avignon. Fish abound in the water, and goats gambol on the hills. And if he is not too greedy a troll, he can make a good living here. Besides, he will have an excellent listener to his tales. What troll could resist that?

THE MOON RIBBON

There was once a plain but good-hearted girl named Sylva whose sole possession was a ribbon her mother had left her. It was a strange ribbon, the color of moonlight, for it had been woven from the grey hairs of her mother and her mother's mother and her mother's mother's mother before her.

Sylva lived with her widowed father in a great house by the forest's edge. Once the great house had belonged to her mother, but when she died, it became Sylva's father's house to do with as he willed. And what he willed was to live simply and happily with his daughter without thinking of the days to come.

But one day, when there was little enough to live on, and only the great house to recommend him, Sylva's father married again, a beautiful widow who had two beautiful daughters of her own.

It was a disastrous choice, for no sooner were they wed than it was apparent the woman was mean in spirit and meaner in tongue. She dismissed most of the servants and gave their chores over to Sylva, who followed her orders without complaint. For simply living in her mother's house with her loving father seemed enough for the girl.

After a bit, however, the old man died in order to have some peace and the house passed on to the stepmother. Scarcely two days had passed or maybe three, when the stepmother left off mourning the old man and turned on Sylva. She dismissed the last of the servants without their pay.

"Girl," she called out, for she never used Sylva's name, "you will sleep in the kitchen and do the charring." And from that time on it was so.

Sylva swept the floor and washed and mended the family's clothing. She sowed and hoed and tended the fields. She ground the wheat and kneaded the bread, and she waited on the others as though she were a servant. But she did not complain.

Yet late at night, when the stepmother and her own two daughters were asleep, Sylva would weep bitterly into her pillow, which was nothing more than an old broom laid in front of the hearth.

One day, when she was cleaning out an old desk, Sylva came upon a hidden drawer she had never seen before. Trembling, she opened the drawer. It was empty except for a silver ribbon with a label attached to it. *For Sylva* read the card. *The Moon Ribbon of Her Mother's Hair.* She took it out and stared at it. And all that she had lost was borne in upon her. She felt the stars start in her eyes, and so as not to cry she took the tag off and began to stroke the ribbon with her hand. It was rough and smooth at once and shone the rays of the moon.

At that moment her stepsisters came into the room.

"What is that?" asked one. "Is it nice? It is mine."

"I want it. I saw it first," cried the other.

The noise brought the stepmother to them. "Show it to me," she said.

Obediently, Sylva came over and held the ribbon out to her. But when the stepmother picked it up, it looked like no more than strands of grey hair woven together unevenly. It was prickly to the touch.

"Disgusting," said the stepmother, dropping it back into Sylva's hand. "Throw it out at once."

"Burn it," cried one stepsister.

"Bury it," cried the other.

"Oh, please. It was my mother's. She left it for me. Please let me keep it," begged Sylva.

The stepmother looked again at the grey strand. "Very well," she said with a grim smile. "It suits you." And she strode out of the room, her daughters behind her.

Now that she had the silver ribbon, Sylva thought her life would be better. But instead it became worse. As if to punish her for speaking out for the ribbon, her sisters were at her to wait on them both day and night. And wheareas before she'd had to sleep by the hearth, she now had to sleep outside with the animals. Yet she did not complain or run away, for she was tied by her memories to her mother's house.

One night, when the frost was on the grass turning each blade into a silver spear, Sylva threw herself to the ground in tears. And the silver ribbon, which she had tied loosely about her hair, slipped off and lay on the ground before her. She had never seen it in the moonlight. It glittered and shone and seemed to ripple.

Sylva bent over to touch it and her tears fell upon it. Suddenly the ribbon began to grow and change, and as it changed the air was filled with a woman's soft voice speaking these words:

> *"Silver ribbon, silver hair,*
> *Carry Sylva with great care.*
> *Bring my daughter home."*

And there at Sylva's feet was a silver river that glittered and shone and rippled in the moonlight.

There was neither boat nor bridge, but Sylva did not care. She thought the river would wash away her sorrows, and without a single word, she threw herself in.

But she did not sink. Instead she floated like a swan and the river bore her on, on past houses and hills, past high places and low. And strange to say, she was not wet at all.

At last she was carried around a great bend in the river and deposited gently on a grassy slope that came right down to the water's edge. Sylva scrambled up onto the bank and looked about. There was a great meadow of grass so green and still, it might have been painted on. At the meadow's rim, near a dark forest, sat a house that was like and yet not like the one in which Sylva lived.

Surely someone will be there who can tell me where I am and why I have been brought here, she thought. So she made her way across the meadow and only where she stepped down did the grass move. When she moved beyond, the grass sprang back and was the same as before. And though she passed larkspur and meadowsweet, clover and rye, they did not seem like real flowers, for they had no smell at all.

Am I dreaming? she wondered, *or am I dead?* But she did not say it out loud, for she was afraid to speak into the silence.

Sylva walked up to the house and hesitated at the door. She feared to knock and yet feared equally not to. As she was deciding, the door opened of itself and she walked in.

She found herself in a large, long, dark hall with a single crystal door at the end that emitted a strange glow the color of moonlight. As she walked down the hall, her shoes made no clatter on the polished wood floor. And when she reached the door, she tried to peer through into the room beyond, but the crystal panes merely gave back her own reflection twelve times.

Sylva reached for the doorknob and pulled sharply. The glowing crystal knob came off in her hand. She would have wept then, but anger stayed her; she beat her fist against the door and it suddenly gave way.

Inside was a small room lit only by a fireplace and a round, white globe that hung from the ceiling like a pale, wan moon. Before the fireplace stood a tall woman dressed all in white. Her silver-white hair was unbound and cascaded to her knees. Around her neck was a silver ribbon.

"Welcome, my daughter," she said.

"Are you my mother?" asked Sylva wonderingly, for what little she remembered of her mother, she remembered no one as grand as this.

"I am if you make me so," came the reply.

"And how do I do that?" asked Sylva.

"Give me your hand."

As the woman spoke, she seemed to move away, yet she moved not at all. Instead the floor between them moved and cracked apart. Soon they were separated by a great chasm which was so black it seemed to have no bottom.

"I cannot reach," said Sylva.

"You must try," the woman replied.

So Sylva clutched the crystal knob to her breast and leaped, but it was too far. As she fell, she heard a woman's voice speaking from behind her and before her and all about her, warm with praise.

"Well done, my daughter. You are halfway home."

Sylva landed gently on the meadow grass, but a moment's walk from her house. In her hand she still held the knob, shrunk now to the size of a jewel. The river shimmered once before her and was gone, and where it had been was the silver ribbon, lying limp and damp in the morning frost.

The door to the house stood open. She drew a deep breath and went in.

"What is that?" cried one of the stepsisters when she saw the crystalline jewel in Sylva's hand.

"I want it," cried the other, grabbing it from her.

"I will take that," said the stepmother, snatching it from them all. She held it up to the light and examined it. "It will fetch a good price and repay me for my care of you. Where did you get it?" she asked Sylva.

Sylva tried to tell them of the ribbon and the river, the tall woman and the black crevasse. But they laughed at her and did not believe her. Yet they could not explain away the jewel. So they left her then and went off to the city to sell it. When they returned, it was late. They thrust Sylva outside to sleep and went themselves to their comfortable beds to dream of their riches.

Sylva sat on the cold ground and thought about what had happened. She reached up and took down the ribbon from her hair. She stroked it, and it felt smooth and soft and yet hard, too. Carefully she placed it on the ground.

In the moonlight, the ribbon glittered and shone. Sylva recalled the song she had heard, so she sang it to herself:

> "Silver ribbon, silver hair,
> Carry Sylva with great care,
> Bring my daughter home."

Suddenly the ribbon began to grow and change, and there at her feet was a silver highway that glittered and glistened in the moonlight.

Without a moment's hesitation, Sylva got up and stepped out onto the road and waited for it to bring her to the magical house.

But the road did not move.

"Strange," she said to herself. "Why does it not carry me as the river did?"

Sylva stood on the road and waited a moment more, then tentatively set one foot in front of the other. As soon as she had set off on her own, the road set off, too, and they moved together past fields and forests, faster and faster, till the scenery seemed to fly by and blur into a moon-bleached rainbow of yellows, greys, and black.

The road took a great turning and then quite suddenly stopped, but Sylva did not. She scrambled up the bank where the road ended and found herself again in the meadow. At the far rim of the grass, where the forest began, was the house she had seen before.

Sylva strode purposefully through the grass, and this time the meadow was filled with the song of birds, the meadowlark and the bunting and the sweet *jug-jug-jug* of the nightingale. She could smell fresh-mown hay and the pungent pine.

The door of the house stood wide open, so Sylva went right in. The long hall was no longer dark but filled with the strange moonglow. And when she reached the crystal door at the end, and gazed at her reflection twelve times in the glass, she saw her own face set with strange grey eyes and long grey hair. She put her hand up to her mouth to stop herself from crying out. But the sound came through, and the door opened of itself. Inside was the tall woman, all in white, and the globe above her was as bright as a harvest moon.

"Welcome, my sister," the woman said.

"I have no sister," said Sylva, "but the two stepsisters I left at home. And you are none of those."

"I am if you make me so."

"How do I do that?"

"Give me back my heart, which you took from me yesterday."

"I did not take your heart. I took nothing but a crystal jewel."

The woman smiled. "It was my heart."

Sylva looked stricken. "But I cannot give it back. My step-mother took it from me."

"No one can take unless you give."

"I had no choice."

"There is always a choice," the woman said.

Sylva would have cried then, but a sudden thought struck her. "Then it must have been your choice to give me your heart."

The woman smiled again, nodded gently, and held out her hand.

Sylva placed her hand in the woman's, and there glowed for a moment on the woman's breast a silvery jewel that melted and disappeared.

"Now will you give me your heart?"

"I have done that already," said Sylva, and as she said it, she knew it to be true.

The woman reached over and touched Sylva on her breast and her heart sprang out onto the woman's hand and turned into two fiery jewels. "Once given, twice gained," said the woman. She handed one of the jewels back to Sylva. "Only take care that you give each jewel with love."

Sylva felt the jewel warm and glowing in her hand, and at its touch felt such comfort as she had not in many days. She closed her eyes and a smile came on her face. And when she opened her eyes again, she was standing on the meadow grass not two steps from her own door. It was morning, and by her feet lay the silver ribbon, limp and damp from the frost.

The door to her house stood open.

Sylva drew in her breath, picked up the ribbon, and went in.

"What has happened to your hair?" asked one stepsister.

"What has happened to your eyes?" asked the other.

For indeed Sylva's hair and eyes had turned as silver as the moon.

But the stepmother saw only the fiery red jewel in Sylva's hand. "Give it to me," she said, pointing to the gem.

At first Sylva held out her hand, but then quickly drew it back. "I *can*not," she said.

The stepmother's eyes became hard. "Girl, give it here."

"I *will* not," said Sylva.

The stepmother's eyes narrowed. "Then you shall tell me where you got it."

"That I shall, and gladly," said Sylva. She told them of the silver ribbon and the silver road, of the house with the crystal door. But strange to say she left out the woman and her words.

The stepmother closed her eyes and thought. At last she said, "Let me see this wondrous silver ribbon, that I may believe what you say."

Sylva handed her the ribbon, but she was not fooled by her stepmother's tone.

The moment the silver ribbon lay prickly and limp in the stepmother's hand, she looked up triumphantly at Sylva. Her face broke into a wolfish grin. "Fool," she said, "the magic is herein. With this ribbon there are jewels for the taking." She marched out of the door and the stepsisters hurried behind her.

Sylva walked after them, but slowly, stopping in the open door.

The stepmother flung the ribbon down. In the early morning sun it glowed as if with a cold flame.

"Say the words, girl," the stepmother commanded.

From the doorway Sylva whispered:

"Silver ribbon, silver hair,
Lead the ladies with great care,
Lead them to their home."

The silver ribbon wriggled and writhed in the sunlight, and as they watched, it turned into a silvered stair that went down into the ground.

"Wait," called Sylva. "Do not go." But it was too late.

With a great shout, the stepmother gathered up her skirts and ran down the steps, her daughters fast behind her. And before Sylva could move, the ground had closed up after them and the meadow was as before.

On the grass lay the silver ribbon, limp and dull. Sylva went and picked it up. As she did so, the jewel melted in her hand and she felt a burning in her breast. She put her hand up to it, and she felt her heart beating strongly beneath. Sylva smiled, put the silver ribbon in her pocket, and went back into her house.

After a time, Sylva's hair returned to its own color, except for seven silver strands, but her eyes never changed back. And when she was married and had a child of her own, Sylva plucked the silver strands from her own hair and wove them into the silver ribbon, which she kept in a wooden box. When Sylva's child was old enough to understand, the box with the ribbon was put into her safekeeping, and she has kept them for her own daughter to this very day.

GODMOTHER DEATH

You think you know this story. You do not.
You think it comes from Ireland, from Norway, from Spain.
It does not. You have heard it in Hebrew, in Swedish, in German.
You have read it in French, in Italian, in Greek.

It is not a story, though many mouths have made it that way.
It is true.

How do I know? Death, herself, told me. She told me in that
whispery voice she saves for special tellings. She brushed her
thick black hair away from that white forehead, and told me.

I have no reason to disbelieve her. Death does not know how
to lie. She has no need to.

It happened this way, only imagine it in Death's own soft
breeze of a voice. Imagine she is standing over your right shoulder speaking this true story in your ear. You do not turn to look
at her. I would not advise it. But if you do turn, she will smile
at you, her smile a child's smile, a woman's smile, the grin of a
crone. But she will not tell *her* story anymore. She will tell yours.

It happened this way, as Death told me. She was on the
road, between Cellardyke and Crail. Or between Claverham

and Clifton. Or between Chagford and anywhere. Does it matter the road? It was small and winding; it was cobbled and potholed; it led from one place of human habitation to another. Horses trotted there. Dogs marked their places. Pig drovers and cattle drovers and sheepherders used those roads. So why not Death?

She was visible that day. Sometimes she plays at being mortal. It amuses her. She has had a long time trying to amuse herself. She wore her long gown kirtled above her knee. She wore her black hair up in a knot. But if you looked carefully, she did not walk like a girl of that time. She moved too freely for that, her arms swinging. She stepped on her full foot, not on the toes, not mincing. She could copy the clothes, but she never remembered how girls really walk.

A man, frantic, saw her and stopped her. He actually put his hand on her arm. It startled her. That did not happen often, that Death is startled. Or that a man puts a hand on her.

"Please," the man said. "My Lady." She was clearly above him, though she had thought she was wearing peasant clothes. It was the way she stood, the way she walked. "My wife is about to give birth to our child and we need someone to stand godmother. You are all who is on the road."

Godmother? It amused her. She had never been asked to be one. "Do you know who I am?" she asked.

"My Lady?" The man suddenly trembled at his temerity. Had he touched a high lord's wife? Would she have him executed? No matter. It was his first child. He was beyond thinking.

Death put a hand up to her black hair and pulled down her other face. "Do you know me now?"

He knew. Peasants are well acquainted with Death in that form. He nodded.

"And want me still?" Death asked.

He nodded and at last found his voice. "You are greater than God or the Devil, Lady. You would honor us indeed."

His answer pleased her, and so she went with him. His wife was couched under a rowan tree, proof against witches. The babe was near to crowning when they arrived.

"I have found a great lady to stand as godmother," the man said. "But do not look up at her face, wife." For suddenly he feared what he had done.

His wife did not look, except out of the corner of her eye. But so seeing Death's pale, beautiful face, she was blinded in that eye forever. Not because Death had blinded the woman, that was not her way. But fear—and perhaps the sugar sickness—did what Death would not.

The child, a boy, was born with a caul. Death ripped it open with her own hand, then dropped the slimed covering onto the morning grass where it shimmered for a moment like dew.

"Name him Haden," Death said. "And when he is a man I shall teach him a trade." Then she was gone, no longer amused. Birth never amused her for long.

Death followed the boy's progress one year closely, another not at all. She sent no gifts. She did not stand for him at the church font. Still, the boy's father and his half-blind mother did well for themselves; certainly better than peasants had any reason to expect. They were able to purchase their own farm, able to send their boy to a school. They assumed it was because of Death's patronage, when in fact she had all but forgotten them and her godson. You cannot expect Death to care so about a single child, who has seen so many.

Yet on the day Haden became a man, on the day of his majority, his father called Death. He drew her sign in the sand, the same that he had seen on the chain around her neck. He said her name and the boy's.

And Death came.

One minute the man was alone and the next he was not.

Death was neither winded nor troubled by her travel, though she still wore the khakis of an army nurse. She had not bothered to change from her last posting.

"Is it time?" she asked, who was both in and out of time. "Is he a man, my godson?" She knew he was not dead. *That* she would have known.

"It is time, Lady," the man said, carefully looking down at his feet. *He* was not going to be blinded like his wife.

"Ah." She reached up and took off the nurse's cap and shook down her black hair. The trouble with bargains, she mused, was that they had to be kept.

"He shall be a doctor," she said after a moment.

"A doctor?" The man had thought no further than a great farm for his boy.

"A doctor," Death said. "For doctors and generals know me best. And I have recently seen too much of generals." She did not tell him of the Crimea, of the Dardanelles, of the riders from beyond the steppes. "A doctor would be nice."

Haden was brought to her. He was a smart lad, but not overly smart. He had strong hands and a quick smile.

Death dismissed the father and took the son by the hand, first warming her own hand. It was an effort she rarely made.

"Haden, you shall be a doctor of power," she said. "Listen carefully and treat this power well."

Haden nodded. He did not look at her, not right at her. His mother had warned him, and though he was not sure he believed, he believed.

"You will become the best-known doctor in the land, my godson," Death said. "For each time you are called to a patient, look for me at the bedside. If I stand at the head of the bed, the patient will live, no matter what you or any other doctor will do. But if I stand at the foot, the patient will die. And there is nought anyone can do—no dose and no diagnoses—to save him."

Haden nodded again. "I understand, Godmother."
"I think you do," she said, and was gone.

In a few short years, Haden became known throughout his small village, and a few more years and his reputation had spread through the county. A few more and he was known in the kingdom. If he said a patient would live, that patient would rise up singing. If he said one would die, even though the illness seemed but slight, then that patient would die. It seemed uncanny, but he was *always* right. He was more than a doctor. He was—some said—a seer.

Word came at last to the king himself.

Ah—now you think I have been lying to you, that this is only a story. It has a king in it. And while a story with Death might be true, a story with a king in it is always a fairy tale. But remember, this comes from a time when kings were as common as corn. Plant a field and you got corn. Plant a kingdom and you got a king. It is that simple.

The king had a beautiful daughter. Nothing breeds as well as money, except power. Of course a king's child would be beautiful.

She was also dangerously ill, so ill in fact that the king promised his kingdom—not half but all—to anyone who could save her. The promise included marriage, for how else could he hand the kingdom off. She was his only child, and he would not beggar her to save her life. That was *worse* than death.

Haden heard of the offer and rode three days and three nights, trading horses at each inn. When he came to the king's palace he was, himself, thin and weary from travel; there was dirt under his fingernails. His hair was ill kempt. But his reputation had preceded him.

"Can she be cured?" asked the king. He had no time or temper for formalities.

"Take me to her room," Haden said.

So the king and the queen together led him into the room.

The princess's room was dark with grief and damp with crying. The long velvet drapes were pulled close against the light. The place smelled of Death's perfume, that soft, musky odor. The tapers at the door scarcely lent any light.

"I cannot see," Haden said, taking one of the tapers. Bending over the bed, he peered down at the princess and a bit of hot wax fell on her cheek. She opened her eyes and they were the color of late wine, a deep plum. Haden gasped at her beauty.

"Open the drapes," he commanded, and the king himself drew the curtains aside.

Then Haden saw that Death was sitting at the foot of the great four-poster bed, buffing her nails. She was wearing a black shift, cut entirely too low in the front. Her hair fell across her shoulders in black waves. The light from the windows shone through her and she paid no attention to what was happening in the room, intent on her nails.

Haden put his finger to his lips and summoned four serving men to him. Without a word, instructing them only with his hands, he told them to turn the bed around quickly. And such was his reputation, they did as he bade.

Then he walked to the bed's head, where Death was finishing her final nail. He was so close, he might have touched her. But instead, he lifted the princess's head and helped her sit up. She smiled, not at him but through him, as if he were as transparent as Death.

"She will live, sire," Haden said.

Both Death and the maiden looked at Haden straight on, startled, Death because she had been fooled, and the princess because she had not noticed him before. Only then did the princess smile at Haden, as she would to a footman, a servingman, a cook. She smiled at him, but Death did not.

"A trick will not save her," said Death. "I will have all in the end." She shook her head. "I do not say this as a boast. Nor as a promise. It simply is what it is."

"I know," Haden said.

"What do you know?" asked the king, for he could not see or hear Death.

Haden looked at the king and smiled a bit sadly. "I know she will live and that if you let me, I will take care of her the rest of her life."

The king did not smile. A peasant's son, even though he is a doctor, even though he is famous throughout the kingdom, does not marry a princess. In a story, perhaps. Not in the real world. Unlike Death, kings do not have to keep bargains. He had Haden thrown into the dungeon.

There Haden spent three miserable days. On the fourth he woke to find Godmother Death sitting at his bedfoot. She was dressed as if for a ball, her hair in three braids that were caught up on the top of her head with a jeweled pin. Her dress, of some white silken stuff, was demurely pleated and there were rosettes at each shoulder. She looked sixteen or sixteen hundred. She looked ageless.

"I see you at my bedfoot," Haden said. "I suppose that means that today I die."

She nodded.

"And there is no hope for me?"

"I can be tricked only once," Death said. "The king will hang you at noon."

"And the princess?"

"Oh, I am going to her wedding," Death said, standing and pirouetting gracefully so that Haden could see how pretty the dress was, front and back.

"Then I shall see her in the hereafter," Haden said. "She did not look well at all. Ah—then I am content to die."

Death, who was a kind godmother after all, did not tell him that it was not the princess who was to die that day. Nor was the king to die, either. It was just some old auntie for whom the excitement of the wedding would prove fatal. Death would never lie to her godson, but she did not always tell the entire truth. Like her brother Sleep, she liked to say things on the slant. Even Death can be excused just one weakness.

At least, that is what she told me, and I have no reason to doubt the truth of it. She was sitting at my bedfoot, and—sitting there—what need would she have to lie?

Dedicated to the memory of
Charles Mikolaycak

HAPPY DENS

OR
A DAY IN THE OLD WOLVES' HOME

Nurse Lamb stood in front of the big white house with the black shutters. She shivered. She was a brand-new nurse and this was her very first job.

From inside the house came loud and angry growls. Nurse Lamb looked at the name carved over the door: HAPPY DENS. But it didn't sound like a happy place, she thought, as she listened to the howls from inside.

Shuddering, she knocked on the door.

The only answer was another howl.

Lifting the latch, Nurse Lamb went in.

No sooner had she stepped across the doorstep than a bowl sped by her head. It splattered against the wall. Nurse Lamb ducked, but she was too late. Her fresh white uniform was spotted and dotted with whatever had been in the bowl.

"*Mush!*" shouted an old wolf, shaking his cane at her. "Great howls and thorny paws. I can't stand another day of it. The end of life is nothing but a big bowl of mush."

Nurse Lamb gave a frightened little bleat and turned to go

back out the door, but a great big wolf with two black ears and one black paw barred her way. "Mush for breakfast, mush for dinner, and more mush in between," he growled. "That's all they serve us here at Happy Dens, Home for Aging Wolves."

The wolf with the cane added: "When we were young and full of teeth it was never like this." He howled.

Nurse Lamb gave another bleat and ran into the next room. To her surprise it was a kitchen. A large, comfortable-looking pig wearing a white hat was leaning over the stove and stirring an enormous pot. Since the wolves had not followed her in, Nurse Lamb sat down on a kitchen stool and began to cry.

The cook put her spoon down, wiped her trotters with a stained towel, and patted Nurse Lamb on the head, right behind the ears.

"There, there, lambkin," said the cook. "Don't start a new job in tears. We say that in the barnyard all the time."

Nurse Lamb looked up and snuffled. "I . . . I don't think I'm right for this place. I feel as if I have been thrown to the wolves."

The cook nodded wisely. "And, in a manner of speaking, you have been. But these poor old dears are all bark and no bite. Toothless, don't you know. All they can manage is mush."

"But no one told me this was an old wolves' home," complained Nurse Lamb. "They just said 'How would you like to work at Happy Dens?' And it sounded like the nicest place in the world to work."

"And so it is. And so it is," said the cook. "It just takes getting used to."

Nurse Lamb wiped her nose and looked around. "But how could someone like you work here. I mean . . ." She dropped her voice to a whisper. "I heard all about it at school. The three little pigs and all. Did you know them?"

The cook sniffed. "And a bad lot they were, too. As we say in the barnyard, 'There's more than one side to every sty.'"

"But I was told that the big bad wolf tried to eat the three little pigs. And he huffed and he puffed and . . ." Nurse Lamb looked confused.

Cook just smiled and began to stir the pot again, lifting up a spoonful to taste.

"And then there was that poor little child in the woods with the red riding hood," said Nurse Lamb. "Bringing the basket of goodies to her sick grandmother."

Cook shook her head and added pepper to the pot. "In the barnyard we say, 'Don't take slop from a kid in a cloak.'" She ladled out a bowlful of mush.

Nurse Lamb stood up. She walked up to the cook and put her hooves on her hips. "But what about that boy Peter? The one who caught the wolf by the tail after he ate the duck. And the hunters came and—"

"Bad press," said a voice from the doorway. It was the wolf with the two black ears. "Much of what you know about wolves is bad press."

Nurse Lamb turned and looked at him. "I don't even know what bad press means," she said.

"It means that only one side of the story has been told. There is another way of telling those very same tales. From the wolf's point of view." He grinned at her. "My name is Wolfgang and if you will bring a bowl of that thoroughly awful stuff to the table"—he pointed to the pot—"I will tell you my side of a familiar tale."

Sheepishly, Nurse Lamb picked up the bowl and followed the wolf into the living room. She put the bowl on the table in front of Wolfgang and sat down. There were half a dozen wolves sitting there.

Nurse Lamb smiled at them timidly.

They smiled back. The cook was right. Only Wolfgang had any teeth.

Wolfgang's Tale

Once upon a time (began the black-eared wolf) there was a thoroughly nice young wolf. He had two black ears and one black paw. He was a poet and a dreamer.

This thoroughly nice wolf loved to lay about in the woods staring at the lacy curlings of fiddlehead ferns and smelling the wild roses.

He was a vegetarian—except for lizards and an occasional snake, which don't count. He loved carrot cake and was partial to peanut-butter pie.

One day as he lay by the side of a babbling brook, writing a poem that began

> *Twinkle, twinkle, lambkin's eye,*
> *How I wish you were close by . . .*

he heard the sound of a child weeping. He knew it was a human child because only they cry with that snuffling gasp. So the thoroughly nice wolf leaped to his feet and ran over, his hind end waggling, eager to help.

The child looked up from her crying. She was quite young and dressed in a long red riding hood, a lacy dress, white stockings, and black patent-leather Mary Jane shoes. Hardly what you would call your usual hiking-in-the-woods outfit.

"Oh, hello, wolfie," she said. In those days, of course, humans often talked to wolves. "I am quite lost."

The thoroughly nice wolf sat down by her side and held her hand. "There, there," he said. "Tell me where you live."

The child grabbed her hand back. "If I knew that, you silly growler, I wouldn't be lost, would I?"

The thoroughly nice wolf bit back his own sharp answer and asked her in rhyme:

Where are you going
My pretty young maid?
Answer me this
And I'll make you a trade.

The path through the forest
Is dark and it's long,
So I will go with you
And sing you a song.

The little girl was charmed. "I'm going to my grandmother's house," she said. "With this." She held up a basket that was covered with a red-checked cloth. The wolf could smell carrot cake. He grinned.

"Oh, poet, what big teeth you have," said the child.

"The better to eat carrot cake with," said the thoroughly nice wolf.

"My granny hates carrot cake," said the child. "In fact, she hates anything but mush."

"What bad taste," said the wolf. "I made up a poem about that once:

If I found someone
Who liked to eat mush
I'd sit them in front of it,
Then give a . . .

"*Push!*" shouted the child.

"Why, you're a poet, too," said the wolf.

"I'm really more of a storyteller," said the child, blushing prettily. "But I do love carrot cake."

"All poets do," said the wolf. "So you must be a poet as well."

"Well, my granny is no poet. Every week when I bring the

carrot cake over, she dumps it into her mush and mushes it all up together and then makes me eat it with her. She says that I have to learn that life ends with a bowl of mush."

"Great howls!" said the wolf, shuddering. "What a terribly wicked thing to say and do."

"I guess so," said the child.

"Then we must save this wonderful carrot cake from your grandmother," the wolf said, scratching his head below his ears.

The child clapped her hands. "I know," she said. "Let's pretend."

"Pretend?" asked the wolf.

"Let's pretend that you are Granny and I am bringing the cake to you. Here, you wear my red riding hood and we'll pretend it's Granny's nightcap and nightgown."

The wolf took her little cape and slung it over his head. He grinned again. He was a poet and he loved pretending.

The child skipped up to him and knocked upon an imaginary door.

The wolf opened it. "Come in. Come in."

"Oh, no," said the child. "My grandmother never gets out of bed."

"Never?" asked the wolf.

"Never," said the child.

"All right," said the thoroughly nice wolf, shaking his head. He lay down on the cool green grass, clasped his paws over his stomach, and made a very loud pretend snore.

The child walked over to his feet and knocked again.

"Who is it?" called out the wolf in a high, weak, scratchy voice.

"It is your granddaughter, Little Red Riding Hood," the child said, giggling.

"Come in, come in. Just lift the latch. I'm in bed with aches and pains and a bad case of the rheumaticks," said the wolf in the high, funny voice.

The child walked in through the pretend door.

"I have brought you a basket of goodies," said the child, putting the basket by the wolf's side. She placed her hands on her hips. "But you know, Grandmother, you look very different today."

"How so?" asked the wolf, opening both his yellow eyes wide.

"Well, Grandmother, what big eyes you have," said the child.

The wolf closed his eyes and opened them again quickly. "The better to see you with, my dear," he said.

"Oh, you silly wolf. She never calls me dear. She calls me *Sweetface*. Or *Punkins*. Or her *Airy Fairy Dee*."

"How awful," said the wolf.

"I know," said the child. "But that's what she calls me."

"Well, I can't," said the wolf, turning over on his side. "I'm a poet, after all, and no self-respecting poet could possibly use those words. If I have to call you that, there's no more pretending."

"I guess you can call me dear," said the child in a very small voice. "But I didn't know that poets were so particular."

"About *words* we are," said the wolf.

"And you have an awfully big nose," said the child.

The wolf put his paw over his nose. "Now that is uncalled-for," he said. "My nose isn't all that big—for a wolf."

"It's part of the game," said the child.

"Oh, yes, the game. I had forgotten. The better to smell the basket of goodies, my dear," said the wolf.

"And Grandmother, what big teeth you have."

The thoroughly nice wolf sat up. "The better to eat carrot cake with," he said.

At that, the game was over. They shared the carrot cake evenly and licked their fingers, which was not very polite but certainly the best thing to do on a picnic in the woods. And the wolf sang an ode to carrot cake which he made up on the spot:

Carrot cake, O carrot cake
The best thing a baker ever could make,
Mushy or munchy
Gushy or crunchy
Eat it by a woodland lake.

"We are really by a stream," said the child.

"That is what is known as poetic license," said the wolf. "Calling a stream a lake."

"Maybe you can use your license to drive me home."

The wolf nodded. "I will if you tell me your name. I know it's not really Little Red Riding Hood."

The child stood up and brushed crumbs off her dress.

"It's Elisabet Grimm," she said.

"Of the Grimm family on Forest Lane?" asked the wolf.

"Of course," she answered.

"Everyone knows where that is. I'll take you home right now," said the wolf. He stretched himself from tip to tail. "But what will you tell your mother about her cake?" He took her by the hand.

"Oh, I'm a storyteller," said the child. "I'll think of something."

And she did.

"She did indeed," said Nurse Lamb thoughtfully. She cleared away the now empty bowls and took them back to the kitchen. When she returned, she was carrying a tray full of steaming mugs of coffee.

"I told you I had bad press," said Wolfgang.

"I should say you had," Nurse Lamb replied, passing out the mugs.

"Me, too," said the wolf with the cane.

"You, too, what?" asked Nurse Lamb.

"I had bad press, too, though my story is somewhat different.

By the by, my name is Oliver," said the wolf. "Would you like to hear my tale?"

Nurse Lamb sat down. "Oh, please, yes."

Oliver Wolf's Tale

Once upon a time there was a very clever young wolf. He had an especially broad, bushy tail and a white star under his chin.

In his playpen he had built tall buildings of blocks and straw.

In the schoolyard he had built forts of mud and sticks.

And once, after a trip with his father to the bricklayer's, he had made a tower of bricks.

Oh, how that clever young wolf loved to build things.

"When I grow up," he said to his mother and father not once but many times, "I want to be an architect."

"That's nice, dear," they would answer, though they wondered about it. After all, no one in their family had ever been anything more than a wolf.

When the clever little wolf was old enough, his father sent him out into the world with a pack of tools and letters from his teachers.

"*This* is a very clever young wolf," read one letter.

"Quite the cleverest I have ever met," said another.

So the clever young wolf set out looking for work.

In a short while he came to a crossroads and who should be there but three punk pigs building themselves houses and making quite a mess of it.

The first little pig was trying to build a house of straw.

"Really," said the clever wolf, "I tried that in the playpen. It won't work. A breath of air will knock it over."

"Well, if you're so clever," said the pig, pushing his sunglasses back up his snout, "why don't you try and blow it down."

The wolf set his pack by the side of the road, rolled up his shirt-sleeves, and huffed and puffed. The house of straw collapsed in a twinkling.

"See," said the clever wolf.

The little pig got a funny look on his face and ran one of his trotters up under his collar.

The wolf turned to the second little pig, who had just hammered a nail into the house he was trying to build. It was a makeshift affair of sticks and twigs.

"Yours is not much better, I'm afraid," said the clever wolf.

"Oh, yeah?" replied the pig. "Clever is as clever does." He thumbed his snout at the wolf. "Let's see you blow *this* house down, dog-breath."

The wolf sucked in a big gulp of air. Then he huffed and puffed a bit harder than before. The sticks tumbled down in a heap of dry kindling, just as he knew they would.

The second little pig picked up one of the larger pieces and turned it nervously in his trotters.

"Nyah, nyah nyah, nyah nyah!" said the third little pig, stretching his suspenders and letting them snap back with a loud twang. "Who do you think's afraid of you, little wolf? Try your muzzle on this pile of bricks, hair-face."

"That won't be necessary," said the clever wolf. "Every good builder knows bricks are excellent for houses."

The third little pig sniffed and snapped his suspenders once again.

"However," said the wolf, pointing at the roof, "since you have asked my opinion, I think you missed the point about chimneys. They are supposed to go straight up, not sideways."

"Well, if you're so clever . . ." began the first little pig.

"And have such strong breath . . ." added the second little pig.

"And are such a know-it-all and tell-it-ever . . ." put in the third little pig.

"Why don't you go up there and fix it yourself!" all three said together.

"Well, thank you," said the clever wolf, realizing he had just been given his very first job. "I'll get to it at once." Finding a ladder resting against the side of the brick house, he hoisted his pack of tools onto his back and climbed up onto the roof.

He set the bricks properly, lining them up with his plumb line. He mixed the mortar with care. He was exacting in his measurements and careful in his calculations. The sun was beginning to set before he was done.

"There," he said at last. "That should do it." He expected, at the very least, a thank-you from the pigs. But instead all he got was a loud laugh from the third little pig, a snout-thumbing from the second, and a nasty wink from the first.

The clever wolf shrugged his shoulders. After all, pigs will be pigs and he couldn't expect them to be wolves. But when he went to climb down he found they had removed the ladder.

"Clever your way out of this one, fuzz-ball," shouted the third little pig. Then they ran inside the house, turned up the stereo, and phoned their friends for a party.

The only way down was the chimney. But the wolf had to wait until the bricks and mortar had set as hard as stone. That took half the night. When at last the chimney was ready, the wolf slowly made his way down the inside, his pack on his back.

The pigs and their friends heard him coming. And between one record and the next, they shoved a pot of boiling mush into the hearth. They laughed themselves silly when the wolf fell in.

"That's how things end, fur-tail," the pigs shouted.

"With a bowl of mush."

Dripping and unhappy, the wolf ran out the door. He vowed never to associate with pigs again. And to this day—with the exception of the cook—he never has. And being a well-brought-up wolf, as well as clever, he has never told his side of the story until today.

"Well, the pigs sure talked about it," said Nurse Lamb, shaking her head. "The way they have told it, it is quite a different story."

"Nobody listens to pigs," said Oliver Wolf. He looked quickly at the kitchen door.

"I'm not so sure," said a wolf who had a patch over his eye. "I'm not so sure."

"So you're not sure," said Oliver. "Bet you think you're pretty clever, Lone Wolf."

"No," said Lone Wolf. "I never said I was clever. You are the clever little wolf."

Wolfgang laughed. "So clever he was outwitted by a pack of punk pigs."

The other wolves laughed.

"You didn't do so well with one human child," answered Oliver.

"Now, now, now," said the cook, poking her head in through the door. "As we say in the barnyard, 'Words are wood, a handy weapon.'"

"No weapons. No fighting," said Nurse Lamb, standing up and shaking her hoof at the wolves. "We are supposed to be telling stories, not getting into fights."

Lone Wolf stared at her. "I never in my life ran from a fight. Not if it was for a good cause."

Nurse Lamb got up her courage and put her hand on his shoulder. "I believe you," she said. "Why not tell me about some of the good causes you fought for?"

Lone Wolf twitched his ears. "All right," he said at last. "I'm not boasting, you understand. Just setting the record straight."

Nurse Lamb looked over at the kitchen door. The old sow winked at her and went back to work.

Lone Wolf's Tale

Once upon a time there was a kind, tender, and compassionate young wolf. He had a black patch over one eye and another black patch at the tip of his tail. He loved to help the under-dog, the under-wolf, the under-lamb, and even the under-pig.

His basement was full of the signs of his good fights. Signs like LOVE A TREE and HAVE YOU KISSED A FLOWER TODAY? and PIGS ARE PEOPLE, TOO! and HONK IF YOU LOVE A WEASEL.

One day he was in the basement running off petitions on his mimeo machine when he heard a terrible noise.

KA-BLAAAAAAAM KA-BLOOOOOOOIE.

It was the sound a gun makes in the forest.

Checking his calendar, the kind and tender wolf saw with horror that it was opening day of duck-hunting season. Quickly he put on his red hat and red vest. Then he grabbed up the signs he had made for that occasion: SOME DUCKS CAN'T DUCK and EAT CORN NOT CORN-EATERS and DUCKS HAVE MOTHERS, TOO. Then he ran out of his door and down the path as fast as he could go.

KA-BLAAAAAAAM KA-BLOOOOOOOIE.

The kind and tender wolf knew just where to go. Deep in the forest was a wonderful pond where the ducks liked to stop on their way north. The food was good, the reeds comfortable, the prices reasonable, and the linens changed daily.

When the kind and tender wolf got to the pond, all he could see was one small and very frightened mallard duck in the middle and thirteen hunters around the edge.

"Stop!" he shouted as the hunters raised their guns.

This did not stop them.

The kind and tender wolf tried again, shouting anything he could think of. "We shall overcome," he called. "No smoking. No nukes. Stay off the grass."

Nothing worked. The hunters sighted down their guns. The wolf knew it was time to act.

He put one of the signs in the water and sat on it. He picked up another sign as a paddle. Using his tail as a rudder, he pushed off into the pond and rowed toward the duck.

"I will save you," he cried. "We are brothers. Quack."

The mallard looked confused. Then it turned and swam toward the wolf. When it reached him, it climbed onto the sign and quacked back.

"Saved," said the kind and tender wolf triumphantly, neglecting to notice that their combined weight was making the cardboard sign sink. But when the water was up to his chin, the wolf suddenly remembered he could not swim.

"Save yourself, friend," he called out, splashing great waves and swallowing them.

The mallard was kind and tender, too. It pushed the drowning wolf to shore and then, hidden by a patch of reeds, gave the well-meaning wolf beak-to-muzzle resuscitation. Then the bird flew off behind the cover of trees. The hunters never saw it go.

But they found the wolf, his fur all soggy.

"Look!" said one who had his name, PETER, stenciled on the pocket of his coat. "There are feathers on this wolf's jaws and in his whiskers. He has eaten *our* duck."

And so the hunters grabbed up the kind and tender wolf by his tail and slung him on top of the remaining sign. They marched him once around the town and threw him into jail for a week, where they gave him nothing to eat but mush.

"Now, wolf," shouted the hunter Peter when they finally let him out of jail, "don't you come back here again or it will be mush for you from now till the end of your life."

The kind and tender wolf, nursing his hurt tail and his aching teeth, left town. The next day the newspaper ran a story that read: PETER & THE WOLF FIGHT/PETER RUNS FOR MAYOR. VOWS TO KEEP WOLF FROM DOOR. And to this day no one believes the kind and tender wolf's side of the tale.

"I believe it," said Nurse Lamb, looking at Lone Wolf with tears in her eyes. "In fact, I believe all of you." She stood up and collected the empty mugs.

"Hurray!" said the cook, peeking in the doorway. "Maybe this is one young nurse we'll keep."

"Keep?" Nurse Lamb suddenly looked around, all her fear coming back. Lone Wolf was cleaning his nails. Three old wolves had dozed off. Wolfgang was gazing at the ceiling. But Oliver grinned at her and licked his chops. "What do you mean, keep?"

"Do you want our side of the story?" asked Oliver, still grinning. "Or the nurses'?"

Nurse Lamb gulped.

Oliver winked.

Then Nurse Lamb knew they were teasing her. "Oh, you big bad wolf," she said and patted him on the head. She walked back into the kitchen.

"You know," she said to the cook, "I think I'm going to like it here. I think I can help make it a real *happy* HAPPY DEN. I'll get them to write down their stories. And maybe we'll make a book of them. Life doesn't *have* to end with a bowl of mush."

Stirring the pot, the cook nodded and smiled.

"In fact," said Nurse Lamb loudly, "why don't we try chicken soup for lunch?"

From the dining room came a great big cheer.

GRANNY RUMPLE

She was known as Granny Rumple because her dress and face were masses of wrinkles, or at least that's what my father's father's mother used to say. Of course, the Yolens being notorious liars, it might not have been so. It might simply have been a bad translation from the Yiddish. Or jealousy, Granny Rumple having been a great beauty in her day.

Like my great-grandmother, Granny Rumple was a money-lender, one of the few jobs a Jew could have in the Ukraine that brought them into daily contact with the *goyim*. She could have had one of the many traditional women's roles—a match-maker, perhaps, or an *opshprekherin* giving advice and remedies, or an herb vendor. But she was a moneylender because her husband had been one, and they had no children to take over his business. My great-grandmother, on the other hand, had learned her trade from her father, and when he died and she was a widow with a single son to raise, she followed in her father's footsteps. *A sakh melokhes un vynik brokhes*: "Many trades and little profit." It was a good choice for both of them.

If Granny Rumple's story sounds a bit like another you have

heard, I am not surprised. My father's father used to entertain customers at his wife's inn with a rendition of *Romeo and Juliet* in Yiddish, passing it off as a story of his own invention. And what is folklore, after all, but the recounting of old tales. We Yolens have always borrowed from the best.

Great-grandmother's story of Granny Rumple was always told in an odd mixture of English and Yiddish, but I am of the generation of Jews who never learned the old tongue. Our parents were ashamed of it, the language of the ghetto. They used it sparingly, for punchlines of off-color jokes or to commiserate with one another at funerals. So my telling of Granny Rumple's odd history is necessarily my own. If I have left anything out, it is due neither to the censorship of commerce nor art, but the inability to get the whole thing straight from my aging relatives. As a Yolen ages, he or she remembers less and invents more. It is lucky none of us is an historian.

As a girl, Granny Rumple's name was Shana and she had been pursued by all the local boys. Even a Cossack or two had knocked loudly at her door of an evening. Such was her beauty, she managed to turn even them away with a smile. When she was finally led under the wedding canopy, the entire village was surprised, for she married neither the chief rabbi's son, a dark-eyed scholar named Lev, nor the local butcher, who was a fat, ribald widower, nor the half dozen others who had asked her. Instead she chose Shmuel Zvi Bar Michael, the moneychanger. No one was more surprised than he, for he was small, skinny, and extremely ugly, with his father's large nose spread liberally across his face. Like many ugly people, though, he was also gentle, kind, and intensely interested in the happiness of others.

"Why did you marry him?" my great-grandmother had wondered.

"Because he proposed to me without stuttering," Shana had replied, stuttering being the one common thread in the other suits. It was all the answer she was ever to give.

By all accounts, it was a love match and the expected children would have followed apace—with Shana's looks, her mother had prayed—but Shmuel was murdered within a year of the wedding.

It is the telling of that murder, ornamented by time, that my great-grandmother liked to tell. Distance lends a fascination to blood tales. It runs in our family. I read murder mysteries; my daughter is a detective.

There was, you see, a walled Jewish ghetto in the town of Ykaterinislav and beyond it, past the trenches where the soldiers practiced every spring, the larger Christian settlement. The separate Jewish quarters are no longer there, of course. It is a family joke: What the Cossacks and Hitler only began, Chernobyl finished.

Every day Shmuel Zvi Bar Michael would say his prayers in his little stone house, donning *tefillin* and giving thanks he was not a woman—but secretly giving thanks as well that he had a woman like Shana in his bed each night. He was not a man unmindful of his blessings and he only stuttered when addressing the Lord G-d.

Then he would make his way past the gates of the ghetto, past the trenches, and onto the twisting cobbled streets of Ykaterinislav proper. He secreted gold in various pockets of his black coat, and sewed extra coins and jewels into the linings of his vest. But of course everyone knew he had such monies on him. He was a changer, after all.

Now one Friday he was going along the High Street where the shops of the merchants leaned despondently on one another. Even in Christian Ykaterinislav recessions could not be ignored and the czar's coinage did not flow as freely there as it did in the great cities. As he turned one particular corner, he heard rather loud weeping coming from beside the mill house. When he stopped in—his profession and his extreme ugliness allowing him entree other Jews did not have—he saw the miller's daughter sobbing messily into her apron. It was a white apron embroidered with gillyflowers on the hem; of such details legends are made real. Shmuel knew the girl, having met her once or twice when doing business with her father, for the miller was always buying on margin and needing extra gold. As a miller's wares are always in demand, Shmuel had no fear that he would not be repaid. *Gelt halt zikh nor in a grobn zak*: Money stays only in a thick sack. The miller's sack, Shmuel knew, was the thickest.

The girl's name was Tasha-Tana to her family—and as pretty as her blond head was, it was empty. If she thought something, she said it, true or not. And she agreed with her father in everything. She would have been beaten otherwise. She was not smart—but she was not *that* stupid.

"Na-na, Tana," Shmuel said, using her familiar name to comfort her. "What goes?"

In between the loud snuffles and rather muffled sobs, she offered up the explanation. Her father had boasted to the mayor of Ykaterinislav that Tana could spin miracles of flax and weave cloth as beautiful as the gold coats of the Burgundian seamstresses.

"And where is Burgundian anyway?" Tana asked, sniffling.

"A long way from here," replied Shmuel. It was little comfort.

"I am a poor spinner at best," Tana confessed. She whispered it for it was nothing to boast of. "And I cannot weave at all. But I *can* cook."

"Na-na, Tana," Shmuel said, "but what is the *real* problem?"

"The real problem?"

"Why are you *really* crying?"

"Oh!" She took a deep breath. "Unless I can spin and sew such a cloth, my father's boast will lose us both our heads."

"This sounds like a fairy tale to me," said Shmuel, though of course he did not use the *fairy*, that being a French invention.

He said "It sounds like a story of the *leshy*." But if I had said that, you would not have understood. And indeed, I did not either, until it was explained to me by an aunt.

"But it is *true!*" she wailed and would be neither comforted nor moved from her version of the facts.

"Then I shall lend you the money—and at no interest—to buy such a cloth and you can give that to your father, who can offer it to the mayor in place of your own poor work."

"*At no interest!*" Tana exclaimed, that in itself such a miraculous event as to seem a fairy story.

"In honor of a woman as dark as you are fair, but equally beautiful," Shmuel said.

"Who is that?" asked Tana, immediately suspecting sorcery.

"My new bride," Shmuel reported proudly.

At which point she knew it to be devil's work indeed, for where would such an ugly little man get a beautiful bride except through sorcery. But so great was her own perceived need, she crossed herself surreptitiously and accepted his loan.

Shmuel found her a gold coin in the right pocket of his coat and made a great show of its presentation. Then he had her sign her X on a paper, and left certain he had done the right thing.

Tana went right out to the market of a neighboring town, where she bought a piece of gold-embroidered cloth from a tinker. It was more intricate than anything either she or her father could have imagined, with the initials T and L cunningly intertwined beneath the body of a dancing bear.

The mayor of Ykaterinislav was suitably impressed, and he immediately introduced his son Leon to Tana. The twined initials were not lost upon them. The son, while not as smart as his father, was handsome, and he was heir to his father's fortune as well. Dreaming of another fortune to add to the family's wealth, he proposed.

Good husband that he was, Shmuel reported all his dealings to Shana. He was extremely uxorious; nothing pleased him more than to relate the day's business to her.

"They would not have killed her for a story," she said. "Probably her father had wagered on it."

"Who knows what the *goyim* will do," he replied. "Trust me, Shana, I deal with them every day. They do not know story from history. It is all the same to them."

Shana shrugged and went back to her own work; but as she said the prayers over the Sabbath candles that evening, she added an extra prayer to keep her beloved husband safe.

Who says the Lord G-d has no sense of humor? Just a week went by and Shmuel once again passed along the High Street and heard the miller's daughter sobbing.

"Na-na, Tana," he said. "What goes this time?"

"I am to be married," she said.

"That is not an institution to be despised. I myself have a beautiful bride. Happiness is in the marriage bed."

This time she did not bother to hide her genuflection, but Shmuel was used to the ways of the *goy.*

"My father-in-law-to-be, the mayor, insists that I produce the wedding costume, and the costumes of my attending maidens besides."

"But of course," Shmuel agreed. "Even beyond the gates . . ." —and he gestured toward the ghetto walls—"even there the bride's family supplies . . ."

"Myself!" she cried. "I am to make each myself. And embroider them with my own hands. *And I cannot sew!*" She proceeded to weep again into her apron, this time so prodigiously, the gillyflowers would surely have grown from the watering had the Lord G-d been paying attention as in the days of old.

"A-ha!" Shmuel said, reaching into his pockets and jangling

several coins together. "I understand. But my dear, I have the means to help you, only . . ."

"Only?" She looked up from the soggy apron.

"Only this time, as you have prospects of a rich marriage . . ." —for gossip travels through stone walls where people themselves cannot pass; it is one of the nine metaphysical wonders of the world—number three actually.

"Only?" To say the girl was two platters and a bottle short of a banquet is to do her honor.

"Only this time you must pay interest on the loan," Shmuel said. He was a businessman after all, not just a Samaritan. And Samaria—like Burgundy—was a long way from there.

Tana agreed at once and put her X to a paper she could not read, then gratefully pocketed three gold pieces. It would buy the services of many fine seamstresses with—she reckoned quickly—enough left over for a chain for her neck and a net for her hair. She could not read but, like most of the girls of Ykaterinislav, she *could* count.

"I do not like such dealings," Shana remarked that evening. "The men at least are honorable in their own way. But the women of the *goyim* . . ."

"I am a respected moneylender," Shmuel said, his voice sharp. Then afraid he might have been *too* sharp, he added, "Their women are nothing like ours; and *you* are a queen of the ghetto."

If she was appeased, she did not show it, but that night her prayers were even longer over the candles, as if she were having a stern talking-to with the Lord G-d.

Ah—you think you know the tale now. And perhaps you are right. But, as Shmuel noted, some do not know story from history. Perhaps you are one of those. Story tells us that the little devil, the child stealer, the black imp was thwarted. Of such blood libels good rousing pogroms are made.

Still, history has two sides, not one. Here is the other.

Tana and her Leon were married, of course. Even without the cloth it was a good match. The miller's business was a thriving one; the mayor was rich on graft. It was a merger as well as a marriage. Properties were exchanged along with the wedding pledges. Within the first month Tana was with child. So she was cloistered there, in the lord mayor's fine house, while her own new house was being built, and therefore did not see Shmuel again.

And then the interest on the loan came due.

A week after Tana's child was delivered, she had a visitor.

It was not Shmuel, of course. He would never have been allowed into the woman's section of a Christian house, never allowed near the new infant.

It was Shana.

"Who are you?" asked Tana, afraid that in her long and difficult pregnancy her husband had taken a Jewish concubine, for such was not unheard of. The woman before her was extraordinarily beautiful.

"I am the wife of Shmuel Zvi Bar Michael."

"Who is that?" asked Tana. For her, one Jewish name was as unpronounceable as another.

"Shmuel Zvi Bar Michael," Shana explained patiently, as to a child. "The moneylender. Who lent you money for your wedding."

"My father paid for my wedding," Tana said, making the sign of the cross as protection for herself and the child in her arms.

Shana did not even flinch. This puzzled Tana a great deal and frightened her as well. "What do you want?"

"Repayment of the loan," Shana said, adding under her breath in Yiddish: "*Vi men brokt zikh ayn di farjl, azoy est men zey oyf,*" which means "The way your *farjl* is cut, that's how you'll eat it." In other words, "You made your bed, now you'll lie in it." *Trust me,* you don't want to ask about *farjl.*

"I borrowed nothing from you," Tana said.

Talking as if to an idiot or to one who does not understand the language, Shana said, "You borrowed it from my husband." She took a paper from her bosom and shoved it under Tana's nose.

Tana shrank from the paper and covered the child's face with a cloth as if the paper would contaminate it, poor thing. Then she began to scream: "Demon! Witch! Child stealer!" Her screams would have brought in the household if they had not all been about the business of the day.

But a Jew—any Jew—knows better than to stay where the charge of blood libel has been laid. Shana left at once, the paper still fluttering in her hand.

She went home but said nothing to her husband. When necessary, Shana could keep her own counsel.

Still, the damage had been done. Terrified she would have to admit her failures, Tana told her husband a fairy tale indeed, complete with a little, ugly black imp with an unpronounceable name who had sworn to take her child for unspeakable rites. And as it was springtime, and behind the ghetto walls the Jewish community of Ykaterinislav was preparing for Passover, Tana's accusations of blood libel were believed, though it took her a full night of complaining to convince Leon.

Who but a Jew, after all, was little and dark—never mind that half of the population both in front of and behind the walls were tall and blond thanks to the Vikings who had settled their trade center in Kiev generations before. Who but a Jew had an unpronounceable name—never mind that the local goyish names did not have a sufficiency of vowels. Who but a Jew would steal a Christian child, slitting its throat and using the innocent blood in the making of matzoh—never mind that it was the Jews, not the gentiles, who had been on the blade end of the killing knife all along.

Besides, it had been years since the last pogrom. Blood calls for blood, even if it is just a story. Leon went to his friends, elaborating on Tana's tale.

What happened next was simple. Just as the *shammes* was going around the ghetto, rapping with his special hammer on the shutters of the houses and calling out "Arise, Jews, and serve the Lord! Arise and recite the psalms!" the local bullyboys were massing outside the ghetto walls.

In house after house, Jewish men rose and donned their *tefillin* and began their prayers; the women lit the fires in the stoves.

Then the wife of Gdalye the butcher—his new wife—went out to pull water from the well and saw the angry men outside the gate. She raised the alarm, but by then it was too late. As they hammered down the gate, the cries went from the streets to Heaven, but if the Lord G-d was home and listening, there was no sign of it.

The rabble broke through the gates and roamed freely along the streets. They pulled Jews out of their houses and measured them against a piece of lumber with a blood-red line drawn halfway up. Any man found below the line was beaten, no matter his age. And all the while the rabble chanted "Little black imp!" and "Stealer of children!"

By morning's end the count was this: two concussions, three broken arms, many bruises and blackened eyes, a dislocated jaw, the butcher's and baker's shops set afire, and one woman raped. She was an old woman. The only one they could find. By pogrom standards it was minor stuff, and the Jews of Ykaterinislav were relieved. They knew, even if the *goyim* did not, that this sort of thing is easier done in the disguise of night.

One man only was missing—Shmuel Zvi Bar Michael, the moneylender. He was the shortest and the ugliest and the blackest little man the crowd of sinners could find.

Of course the rest of the Jews were too busy to look for him. The men were trying to save what they could of Gdalye the butcher's shop and Avreml the baker's house. The women were too busy binding up the heads of Reb Jakob and his son Lev, and the arms of three men and one ten-year-old boy, and the jaw of Moyshe the cobbler, and tending to the old woman. Besides, Shana had been too guilt-ridden to press them into the search.

It was not until the next day that she found his body—or the half of it that remained—in the soldiers' trenches.

At the funeral she tore her face with her fingernails and wept until her eyes were permanently reddened. Her hair turned white during the week she sat shiva. And it was thus that Granny Rumple was born of sorrow, shame, and guilt. At least that was my great-grandmother's story. And while details in the middle of the tale had a tendency to change with each telling, the ending was always tragic.

But the story, you say, is too familiar for belief? *Belief!* Is it less difficult to believe that a man distributed food to thousands using only a few loaves and fishes? Is it less difficult to believe the Red Sea opened in the middle to let a tribe of wandering desert dwellers through? Is it less difficult to believe that Elvis is alive and well and shopping at Safeway?

Look at the story you know. Who is the moral center of it? Is it the miller who lies and his daughter who is complicitous in the lie? Is it the king who wants her for commercial purposes only? Or is it the dark, ugly little man with the unpronounceable name who promises to change flax into gold—and does exactly what he promises?

Stories are told one way, history another. But for the Jews—despite their long association with the Lord G-d—the endings have always been the same.

ONE OX, TWO OX, THREE OX,
AND THE DRAGON KING

There was once a poor farmer who had but a small farm and no beasts to help him plow. When his wife gave birth to a son, the farmer insisted on calling the boy One Ox. "For," the farmer said, "someday he will work with me in the field."

When his wife gave birth a year later to a second son, the boy was called Two Ox.

And a year after that, their third son was named Three Ox.

But before the boys were old enough to help, the farmer died, leaving the poor farm to his wife. She worked hard and the farm managed to support the four of them, but barely. And when the boys were big enough, they worked harder still.

Each evening after toiling all day in the fields, the boys would sit by the fire eating their rice and drinking their tea. To make them laugh and to teach them of the great wide world, their mother would tell them stories. Some of the stories were of wizards and some of the stories were of warriors; some of the stories were of kinship and some of the stories were of kings.

But at the end of each tale, she would sigh and say, "Alas that all I have to give to you, my sons, are these tales. The farm is so small and so poor, it cannot be shared. Only one of you can inherit it when I die."

"Which one?" they would ask every night.

But each night her answer was the same: "Whoever works the hardest."

"And the one who works the hardest—that one you love the best?" they would ask.

"How can I choose between my dear sons?" she always answered. "I love you each the best." And with that answer, they had to be content.

Now one year the farmer's wife caught a chill, grew sick, and all but died. The boys went without rice in order to pay for a doctor. But after he examined her, the old potion-maker shook his head. "Nothing in the world can save her."

"If nothing *in* the world can save her," said One Ox, "then is there something *out* of it?"

"Name it and we will find it," said Two Ox.

"Though we must go to the ends of the earth," added Three Ox. "For just so much do we love our mother."

"Only the Waters of Life can save her now," the doctor said.

"And where can the waters be found?" the three boys asked together.

"In the cave of the Dragon King," the old man answered, packing up his potions and pins, "is a ring of power. Put that ring in a glass of clear water, and when it is drunk, the sick are made well."

"Where is this cave?" asked One Ox.

"And who is the Dragon King?" asked Two Ox.

Three Ox was silent.

"As to the cave," the old doctor said, "it is beyond the farthest mountains and then one mountain farther And as to the Dragon King, I would not want to meet him myself. His name

65

is Lung-Wang, and he is said to be more than a *li* in length— five hundred yards. He has horns on top of his head, and he is covered with scales. It is bad enough to meet one of the lesser kings, the Nagas. Do not seek out Lung-Wang if you value your lives."

Only then did Three Ox speak. "Our mother's life *is* our lives, and you have said only the Waters of Life will save her."

The doctor pulled his long beard and looked both sad and wise. "That is merely a way of saying that she is beyond help, my son."

"Nevertheless," said Three Ox, "we will help her. We could do nothing for our father when he died for we were too young. But now we are older and stronger. We will find these waters or die."

"Then," the doctor said solemnly, "you may very well die. Lung-Wang will not give up the Waters of Life, his most precious gift, just for the asking. He will demand three magical objects in trade. To get one is difficult; to get two is nearly impossible; to get three is beyond belief."

One Ox looked sad.

Two Ox looked puzzled.

"Nevertheless," said Three Ox, "it will be done." And his brothers nodded quickly. They commended their mother to the doctor's good care and set out within the hour.

Following the sun, the boys walked toward the nearest mountains. Each had but a single coin in his pocket; the rest of the family's small savings had been left to pay the doctor's fee.

They had not been gone but an hour past noon when One Ox turned to his brothers.

"The doctor has said we need three magical objects to trade, but he did not say which three, nor where they might be found. Perhaps we should separate and each search for one. That way our chances will be tripled. We could meet back here in seven days."

Two Ox nodded. "A fine plan, my brother, but for this one thing: our dear mother is much too weak to last that long. I propose we meet back in five days."

Three Ox likewise nodded, adding, "There is, of course, still the Dragon King's cave to find. Perhaps we should meet back here in three days, not five, else our dear mother will be in her grave and all the Waters of Life will not save her then."

So they agreed on three, and at a triple fork in the road, One Ox went east, Two Ox went west, and Three Ox went forward toward the nearest hills. They did not even take the time to wave good-bye.

To the east were the high towers of the city of Kai-lung. It was the city in which the Master of Masters, the magician Kuang-li, lived. It was said of her that if she called a man blind, that man would become blind in an instant; if she called him emperor, he would be crowned within the week.

One Ox walked toward Kai-lung until his feet ached and his stomach proclaimed its emptiness, but he did not dare rest. He thought only of his sick mother and the magic gift he might find within the city walls.

It was near dark when he reached Kai-lung and full night before he found a place to sleep in a narrow niche within a wall. "In the morning," he told himself, "I will seek out a magician and see if I can beg a gift of him."

The morning dawned early and One Ox looked out from the niche, seeing for the first time how a city stirs in the light. Carters pulled and pushed their creaking wagons; vendors began to call out their wares; and a little flower girl, no more than five years old, stood below the window of the tallest of the tall towers crying up, "Peonies for the Master of Masters. Flowers for the Dragon of Kai-lung."

A hand with nails as long as knives extended out of the

tower window and lowered a willow basket on a rope. When the basket settled on the ground, the child knelt down, extracted a single coin from it, and placed a bunch of flowers in the coin's stead. Then she pulled three times on the rope. Slowly the long-nailed hand drew up the rope and basket to the window and, with a wink, rope, basket, and all were gone.

One Ox stood and brushed his dark hair back with his hands. Going over to the child, he asked, "Who is this Master of Masters? Who is this Dragon of Kai-lung?"

The girl looked surprised. "Everyone knows that."

"I am not everyone," said One Ox. "And I assure you that I do not know."

The child looked guilelessly into his eyes. "Kuang-li is one of the Nagas, a dragon master of the highest degree. If Kuang-li calls you by your true name, you will belong to the Master forever."

"Then I shall not say my name," said One Ox, "for I have no time to remain in this city for more than a single day and surely not forever. But I *would* like to purchase a piece of this Master's magic."

"Then," the child said before turning away, "you will have to get into the tower, though it has no stairs, for Kuang-li does not come out during the day, and at night in dragon form flies over our city, guarding it from the dangers of the dark."

One Ox thought long and hard about this, and by evening he had an idea. With his single coin, he purchased a bunch of flowers from another flower seller. Then, just before the sun went down, he stood directly under the tower so that he could not be seen from above, and cried out in imitation of the child, "Peonies for the Master of Masters. Flowers for the Dragon of Kai-lung."

For a long moment he waited, wondering if his coin had been spent in vain. But at last the hand with the long nails extended out of the tower window, lowering the willow basket.

One Ox did not take time even to extract the coin inside. Instead, placing the flowers in the basket, he grabbed hold of the rope and quickly, hand over hand, climbed up the tower wall. Once at the window, he flung himself over the sill.

"You look little like a peony, my eager friend," said a voice as old and cracked as leather.

When One Ox looked up, there was a serving woman whose face was as lined as a map, but whether amusement or condemnation was written there, he could not tell. She turned from him and brought up the basket, then took the flowers out and placed them in a blue-glazed jar.

Only when she was done did she turn to him again. "Come, speak quickly, tell me what you want."

"Old mother, I wish to speak to your master, the Master of Masters," One Ox said. "I wish to speak to Kuang-li."

"Are you not afraid of the dragon?" asked the old woman.

"My need is greater than my fear," said One Ox.

"And your ignorance exceeds them both," said the old woman. "But I will forgive you this once."

One Ox stood, towering over the old woman. "I ask you again, mother of mothers, take me to Kuang-li."

"And I will forgive you twice," said the old woman. "But not once more. Do you speak to all mothers this way?"

Suddenly remembering his manners, One Ox bowed his head.

"Forgive me, but it is because my own mother lies sick that I must see the Dragon of Kai-lung."

"Then listen well, son of a dying mother, *I* am the Master of Masters. *I* am the Dragon of Kai-lung. And when the sun goes down and I become the Naga in truth, I will be much tempted by the meat in your young arms and thighs still warm from the heat of the sun." She reached out with her long nails and pinched his arm as she spoke.

One Ox shivered. "O mighty dragon," he began, terrified at

how badly he had started and not at all sure there was any way to change what had begun. "The doctor says that my mother is beyond all help save that of the Waters of Life. But we cannot get the waters without three magical objects in exchange. My brothers and I have each gone out on the road to find such pieces of magic to trade with the Dragon King."

"And you thought . . ." the old woman said, turning her head to look out of the window, where the sun was fast fading behind the hills, "that I would give you such a thing."

"I was hoping . . ." One Ox said, his head bowed low.

"And what will you give *me*?" she asked, her voice beginning to roughen. When One Ox dared to look up, he saw she had sprouted a horn on each side of her head.

"I have . . . I have only myself," he said, looking down again quickly. "But you may have that if it will save my mother. I will give you myself—and my name. I am called One Ox."

"Good answer," the old woman said. "I will not eat you now." Only this time, her tongue stuck out as she spoke, and it was red and forked. She reached into her pocket and pulled out a tiny folded packet, not quite paper and not quite skin. "When you get to the ground unfold this. It is a bit of magic that even the Dragon King will envy. And when your mother is well again, come back to Kai-lung."

She handed him the packet. "I will work you hard for a year."

"I am not afraid of hard work," One Ox said, his eyes on the ground.

"But be afraid of me," came the response.

When One Ox looked up, a dragon the blue-black of midnight stood before him.

"Be very afraid." Its silver teeth glittered like stars in that night sky.

One Ox's knees trembled and there was a bitter taste in his mouth. As he watched, the dragon shook out its great blue-black wings, arched its back, and ran its claws along the floor. The claws drew runnels like rivers in the wood. Then the dragon leaped through the tower window and was gone.

One Ox drew in a long breath, and by the time he had let it out again, the full moon had risen over the hills. He could see the silhouette of the dragon as it sailed across the sky, as clean and crisp as if cut from paper.

The dragon will not return until morning, One Ox thought. I should leave at once. But when he looked around the tower room, his old habits claimed him. He found a broom and swept away the petals from the peonies that had fallen in the rush of air from the dragon's wings. He washed out a teacup. He straightened the dragon's bed. What with one thing and another, he was not finished in the tower until almost dawn and was so tired he lay down on the floor and fell fast asleep. He did not see the dragon return, nor did he see it change back into the old woman. He woke only when she touched his arm.

"Come, my good worker, come," she said. "You have pleased me well. But now you must go. Your brothers will be waiting." And she held the rope for him so that he might reach the ground in safety.

No sooner did his feet touch the street than the Master of Masters pulled up the rope and basket and they disappeared in a wink.

One Ox took the packet from his pocket. It weighed hardly an ounce. Slowly he began to unfold it, one piece at a time. He was halfway through the unfolding before he realized it was a tiny pony made of cloth as brown as earth, with a foam-colored mane and tail. When the last fold lay flat in his hand, the pony gave a high-pitched whinny. This so startled One Ox that he dropped it to the ground.

The minute it touched the ground, the tiny pony began to grow. Bigger and bigger it grew until it was the size of a large horse. One Ox put his hand on its back, and the horse turned its head toward him. Its eyes were like black gems with a red fire at each center.

Though he had never ridden a horse before, One Ox had seen men ride by the farm, and he knew just what to do. Leaping onto its back, he threaded his fingers into its foam-colored mane. The horse reared once, then raced down the road, swift as the east wind, to the place of the three forks.

In the meanwhile, Two Ox had gone west, and to the west was the sea, down in whose depths lived the Master of Masters, the wizard Kuang-jun. It was said of Kuang-jun that if he called a man old, that man would wither as the words were spoken; and if he called a man living, even a corpse would kick up its heels.

Two Ox walked toward the Western Sea until his feet ached and his stomach proclaimed its emptiness, but he did not dare rest. He thought only of his sick mother and the magic gift he might find on the banks of the sea.

It was near dark when he reached the shore, and he stood a long time watching the waves as they stretched and flattened upon the sand. He saw no one near and no one far away, so he lay down and slept on a gray rock.

The morning dawned early and Two Ox looked up from the rock, seeing for the first time how a beach stirs in the morning's light. Crabs scuttled across the sand; gulls dived down to pick them up; and a little fisher lad, no more than five years old, threw an orange net filled with gray stones into the sea, crying, "Silver coins for silver cockles, O Master of Masters. Silver coins for silver fish, O Dragon of the Western Sea." When he drew in his net, it was filled with cockleshells and tiny fish leaping up as if on the boil. But of the silver stones there was no sign.

Two Ox stood up and smoothed down his shirt and pants. Going over to the child, he asked, "Who is this Master of Masters? Who is the Dragon of the Western Sea?"

The boy looked surprised. "Everyone knows that."

"I am not everyone," said Two Ox. "And I assure you I do not know."

The boy looked innocently into Two Ox's eyes. "Kuang-jun is one of the Nagas, a dragon master of the highest degree. If Kuang-jun calls you by your true name, you will belong to the Master forever."

"Then I shall not say my name," said Two Ox, "for I do not have time to remain by the sea for more than this one day, and surely not forever. But I *would* like to purchase a piece of this Master's magic."

The child spread out his net to dry in the sun. "Then you will have to throw yourself into the water and learn to breathe it, for Kuang-jun lives beneath the waves. Except at night, when he flies in dragon form up and down the western shore, he does not come up out of the sea."

Two Ox thought long and hard about this. At last he said to the child, "I have but a single coin. If you would give me the loan of your net for the rest of this day and this night, I will give the coin to you. Tomorrow, whatever my fate, you will have your net back."

The child nodded solemnly, took the coin, picked up his fish basket, and went away.

Two Ox contemplated the ocean all that afternoon, but at last he knew there was no other way. Wrapping himself in the net, with silver beach stones for weights, he waded out into the ocean. The water was cold and final around his legs.

Then, in imitation of the child, he cried out, "Silver coins for silver cockles, O Master of Masters. Silver coins for silver fish, O Dragon of the Western Sea." His voice seemed to sink down, down, down into the dark water and he flung himself after it.

The waves tumbled him over and over, stripping away the netting and his shirt and trousers and shoes. It scoured his skin

73

and the shells of his ears, it rubbed away and scrubbed away all thoughts of the shore. And when it was done with him, it dumped him down upon a broad white road underneath the sea. He took a deep breath and, surprised to find it was air, opened his eyes. At the end of the road was a castle made of shells. He pushed his way through the water toward it and, upon entering, found himself face to face with an old, old serving man in a bright red robe. The man's face was the color of weak tea, and his shoulders were bowed with age.

"Old man," Two Ox began, the words as round as bubbles, "I wish to speak to your master, the Master of Masters. I wish to speak to Kuang-jun."

"Are you not afraid of the dragon?" asked the old man.

"My need is greater than my fear," said Two Ox.

"And your foolishness exceeds them both," said the old man. "But I will forgive you this once."

Two Ox drew himself up. He towered over the old man. "Do not confuse my nakedness with unpreparedness, old father. Take me to this Kuang-jun."

"And I will forgive your bad manners twice," said the old man. He handed Two Ox a ceremonial robe the color of the sea.

Suddenly ashamed of his behavior, Two Ox put on the robe and bowed his head. "Forgive me, but it is because my mother lies ill and would have died already to see me in such fashion. It is for her sake that I must see the Dragon of the Western Sea."

"Then listen well, son of a dying mother: *I* am the Master of Masters. *I* am the Dragon of the Western Sea. And when the sun goes down, darkening even these dark waters, I become the Naga in truth. Then I will be much tempted by the meat in your arms and thighs, now salted to my taste by the waves." He reached out and pinched Two Ox on the arm.

Two Ox shivered, though the robe was warm. "O mighty

dragon," he began, "the doctor says that my mother is beyond all help save that of the Waters of Life. But to get the waters my brothers and I need three magical objects to trade. We have each gone out on the road to find such pieces of magic to tempt the Dragon King."

The old man smiled, looking up toward the top of the waves which were, even then, beginning to darken. When he looked down again, bubbles formed around his head like horns. "And you thought I would just *give* you such a thing."

"I was hoping beyond hope . . ." Two Ox said, his head bowed low.

"And what will you give me in exchange?" the old man asked. His voice grew rough, and when Two Ox looked again he saw that green scales were beginning to form on the old man's face.

"I had but a single coin," Two Ox said, "with which I purchased the use of the net. And my clothes were all stripped away by the waves. All I have left to give you is myself"—he hesitated for a moment—"and my name." He took a deep breath and tasted salt in his mouth. "I am called Two Ox."

"Good answer," the old man said. "I will not eat you now." But when he spoke, his tongue stuck out and it was black and forked. He reached into the pocket of his robe and pulled out a silver hairpin. "When you are once again on land," he said, "use this when need is great. This is a piece of magic even the Dragon King will envy. And when your mother is once again well, come back to the Western Sea." He handed the hairpin to Two Ox. "I will work you hard for a year."

"I am not afraid of hard work," Two Ox said.

"But be very afraid of me," came the response. And as Two Ox watched, the old man changed completely into a dragon the green-black of the sea, its silver teeth glittering like the tops of waves.

Two Ox's knees trembled, and he let out a soft moan. As he

watched, the green-black dragon shook out its great green-black wings, lashed its mighty tail like a rudder, and sailed off through the water in a cascade of foam.

When the bubbles at last subsided, Two Ox thought to himself, "The dragon will not return until morning. I should leave at once." But when he looked around the shell castle, he saw that everything had been greatly disturbed by the dragon's leaving, and his old land habits claimed him. He picked up the bright red robe and hung it on a peg. He straightened the matting on the floor. He tidied up the dishes. And what with one thing and another, he was not done in the sea castle until the first waves of light had filtered down from above. And then he was so tired, he fell asleep on the floor and so did not see the dragon return, or see it change back into the old man. He woke only when he was shaken.

"Come, my good worker, come," the old man said. "You have already pleased me well. But now you must go. Your brothers will be waiting." He took Two Ox's ceremonial robe and handed him trousers, shirt, shoes, and the child's netting. Then he gave Two Ox a push that was so hard, Two Ox was propelled straight through the water and onto the shore.

No sooner did Two Ox's feet touch the beach than he got dressed. He found the hairpin stuck into the waistband of his trousers. Spreading the fisher lad's netting out to dry, Two Ox removed the hairpin and looked at it. It caught the sunlight and shimmered. When he touched the tip, it pricked his finger and he cried out, dropping the pin to the sand. No sooner did it touch the sand than a fountain of water sprang up.

Two Ox bent down, picked up the pin by the head, and drew its point along the sand. A river of silver water tumbled into the groove, and a silver boat bounced up and down on the waves. Two Ox climbed into the boat and, using the hairpin as a rudder, steered himself down the stream toward the road and the three forks.

Meanwhile, Three Ox had gone forward into the hills. There were no Nagas in the hills, only spirits like elves and ghosts and worst of all the *wang-liang*, ogres whose bodies are covered with coarse hair and who devour any human being whole.

Three Ox walked into the hills until his feet ached and his stomach proclaimed its emptiness, but he did not dare rest. He thought only of his sick mother and the magic gift he might find somewhere in the hills.

But as the way grew steeper and darker, Three Ox decided to cut himself a stick—pointed at one end, it would help him with the walking; pointed at the other, it could serve as a weapon.

No sooner had he done this than he heard a noise and, turning, saw a strange creature following him. Head to foot it was covered with coarse orange-brown hair, and when it smiled its teeth were sharp and long.

"Who are you?" Three Ox asked.

"Give me a coin and you may pass," the creature said.

"I have already passed," said Three Ox.

"Give me a coin and I shall not eat you," said the creature.

"I will not make much of a meal," said Three Ox.

"Give me a coin," said the creature, "and my magic is yours."

Three Ox dug into his pocket and pulled out the single coin. He tossed it to the ogre. The ogre bit into the coin, swallowed it, and laughed.

"I lied!" the ogre cried. "You will still be mine." It leaped.

Three Ox held the stick in front of him, one point at his own breast, one at the ogre, for he thought, "If the ogre is to eat me, at least I will not be alive to suffer it." But unaccountably the ogre hesitated in the air, as if held there by invisible ties.

"O mortal," the ogre screamed, "how did you know only such a pointed stick at your breast and mine would stop me?"

Three Ox hadn't known, but he thought he should not tell that to the ogre. "Everyone knows such tricks," he said.

"O mortal," the monster cried, "let me go and I promise I will not harm you. "

Three Ox thought to himself that such a promise was bought too cheaply. "What more will you give me?"

"I will give you back your coin," the ogre cried.

"That's one," Three Ox said.

"I will give you my boot," said the ogre. "Have you not heard of such boots? They can run many miles." The ogre smiled.

Three Ox did not like the ogre's smile or the way the coarse hair blew in and out of its mouth as it spoke. Then he remembered an old story his mother had told.

"The boot you offer me is a coffin. If I take it from you, I will lie in it forever."

The ogre gnashed its teeth and spoke curses that blued the air.

"Then will you take my hat!"

Three Ox did not like the eager way the ogre spoke, or that the nails on the hands offering the hat were the color of a storm-stirred pond. He remembered another story his mother had told.

"The hat you offer me is a funeral fire," he said. "If I take it I will be burned to ashes."

The *wang-liang* gnashed its awful teeth and roared until the grass wilted in three circles around it. "Then what will you have?"

Three Ox smiled. He remembered still another story his mother had recited. "I will have my coin," he said. Then while the monster spit up the money, he added, "And I will have your face!"

The *wang-liang* screamed until the trees near them shivered and lost their bark, but Three Ox was not moved. And so the ogre had to strip the very skin from its face with its muddy brown nails.

"Remember your promise," said Three Ox, slipping the face into his pocket. Then he set down the pointed stick.

The *wang-liang* whimpered, and holding its hands in front of its blank face, wandered away into the forest leaving a trail of ashes wherever it stepped.

Three Ox found a cozy cave in which to shelter for the night and in the morning headed back down the way he had come.

As Three Ox had a full day on his brothers, he arrived at the place of the three forks first. There he sat down with his back to a tree, and flipping the coin, thought about the ogre's face in his pocket. His mother's story had said such a face made the wearer invisible.

"But the *wang-liang* himself wore the face, and he could be seen," he reminded himself. It was a puzzle. Still it was worth trying. So he pulled the face from his pocket and drew it over his head.

He looked down at his hands. They were no longer there.

He looked down at his feet. *They* were no longer there.

He picked up a leaf. It disappeared.

He touched the tree. Where his fingers met the bark, the bark disappeared. But the rest of the branch and root and buds and leaves were there to see.

Smiling, he drew off the face and put it back into his pocket.

"Here is a piece of magic that the Dragon King will envy," he said to himself. He spent the rest of the day looking for food and feasting on berries. The night passed quickly, and in the morning of the third day he knew it was time for his brothers to arrive.

"I can surprise them," he said as he pulled the *wang-liang's* face down over his. Invisible, he sat down and waited.

Suddenly by his invisible feet a river began to run, glittering silver in the morning light. Three Ox stared up the river and saw a silver boat bobbing along the current. Sitting in the back and steering with a silver rudder was Two Ox, smiling to himself.

The boat reached the river's end, and Two Ox got out. He took the silver rudder from its lock, and it became a silver pin. At the same moment, both boat and river disappeared. Smiling even more broadly, Two Ox stuck the pin through the waistband of his trousers and sat down to rest.

"As I am the first," he said aloud, "I must now wait; and as I had little time for sleep at the dragon's home, I will take a rest." He lay down and was soon snoring.

Invisible, Three Ox watched his brother for some time, and when he was sure nothing would wake Two Ox, he drew out the silver pin from his brother's waistband. Then he waited to see what more would happen.

Soon the sounds of horse's hooves came to his ears. And as he watched, a brown horse with a foam-colored mane and tail came galloping to the place of the three forks. Atop its back was One Ox, grinning broadly. When One Ox saw Two Ox asleep by the roadside, he dismounted and patted the horse on its flank. Then he pulled the horse's head until its nose touched its neck, pushed the horse onto its knees, and wrapped the tail up over its back. The horse gave a tiny whinny and shrank and shrank and shrank until it was the size of a folded letter. He slipped it into the pocket of his shirt.

"If my brother can sleep, so can I," One Ox whispered. "For I got little rest in the dragon's house." And he lay down by Two Ox's side. Within minutes he too was snoring.

When Three Ox was certain nothing would wake his brothers, he knelt beside them and drew out the folded horse from One Ox's pocket. Then he stood and waited to see what else would happen.

After many minutes the two brothers awoke.

"I was the first!" said Two Ox.

"Indeed you were," said One Ox. "And I the second. But

where is that laggard youngest brother of ours?" For, as Three Ox still wore the *wang-liang's* face, he was invisible. "Once he is here, I shall show you both the great piece of magic I have." One Ox tapped his pocket but there was no crackling sound. He reached into his pocket. There was nothing there. Turning on his brother, he shouted, "You have stolen my piece of magic while I slept!" He raised his fist.

"Wait, I too was asleep," said Two Ox. "And what need have I for your magic when I have magic of my own? I will show it to you."

He felt along the waistband of his trousers. There was no pin. "Aieee, my brother, you have taken what is mine!" He raised his own fist.

Just then Three Ox laughed, and the brothers, hearing the sound but seeing no one, grew very afraid.

"Who is it?" they cried as one. "Who is there?" And they stood back to back, ready to defend one another.

Three Ox drew off the *wang-liang's* face and was visible at once. Stuffing the mask into his pocket, he handed the folded horse to One Ox, the silver hairpin to Two Ox. "Brothers, we must trust one another," he said, "but trust no one else. The two of you went to sleep and anyone—man or monster—could have stolen your magic. What then would our poor mother do? Come, we must take our three pieces of power and make our way to the Dragon King."

Ashamed, One Ox and Two Ox bowed their heads, for they knew Three Ox was right. And taking what was theirs, they followed their youngest brother along the road.

They went beyond the mountains and there, as the doctor had said, was one mountain farther. Neither horse nor boat could help them now, for the way was too rough for the horse, and what rivers could be made to spring up along the crags flowed downward.

Three Ox showed them how to take a stick and sharpen both ends, in case of ogres, but none came to trouble them on their climb. Indeed, the mountain was strangely still. No birds, no frogs, no bears called out. It was as if a great magic had silenced them all. Even the three brothers had trouble speaking as they climbed.

At last, after many hours of effort, they saw a cave.

"Should we go in?" asked One Ox.

"Dare we go in?" asked Two Ox.

"How can we not?" asked Three Ox, so they entered.

A cold wind seemed to blow through the cave, carrying with it a fine fragrance, something like jasmine, something like rain. A thin fragment of sound was carried in the wind as well, like the ringing of silver bells.

"This must be the cave of the Dragon King," said Three Ox.

"Be kind to old serving women," cautioned One Ox.

"Be kind to old serving men," added Two Ox.

The wind's fragrance turned to dust and ashes; the sound of the bells became a roar. One Ox and Two Ox turned to face the oncoming wind, holding their hands over their eyes. They did not see Three Ox slip the *wang-liang*'s face over his own and disappear.

"Who has dared enter the palace of the Dragon King?" came a voice out of the wind, a soft voice that was somehow more terrible than a scream.

"We are sons of a poor farmer, O Master of Masters," One Ox and Two Ox said together.

The wind swirled suddenly in the center of the cave, kicking up dirt and sticks and tiny stones which suddenly formed into the shape of a very large man. He had a long beard and mustaches drooping down either side of his mouth like twin waterfalls of hair. His gown was gray-green, like old moss, and emblazoned with dark green dragons. He did not smile.

"What do two farm boys have to do with me?" the man asked.

"For I am Lung-Wang, King of all the Dragons." Though he asked a question, he did not look at them but stared at the ring on his hand, the center of which contained a shiny pearl as large as a pea.

"Two?" whispered One Ox.

"Two?" whispered Two Ox.

Then they mentioned it no more, guessing their youngest brother had some plan in mind.

"O mighty Lung-Wang," said One Ox bowing low, "our mother is desperately ill." He did not dare look up.

"And needs to drink of the Waters of Life," said Two Ox, bowing even lower.

"Yes, yes, I know all this," said Lung-Wang, his voice sounding bored. "My sister Kuang-li, the dragon who enlarges good, and my brother Kuang-jun, the dragon who enlarges favor, have told me all about you when we flew together in the night. I expected you long before this. You must have slept on the way."

"Never," said One Ox.

"Never," Two Ox said.

"Do not lie to me," said the Dragon King.

"We slept," they admitted.

"Good, good," the Dragon King murmured, his voice like water over stone. "And what pieces of magic have you for me! Not that tiresome folded pony of my sister's! It always returns home to her.

"And not that silly silver hairpin of my brother's. The waters only flow downhill." He twisted the ring once more around his finger, then polished it on his robe.

The two brothers held up the disfavored gifts. "Alas, they are all we have."

The Dragon King took the gifts and, putting his head back, roared with laughter. The sound filled the cave until the two brothers had to put their hands over their ears or be drowned in it.

Lung-Wang threw down the gifts at their feet and stopped laughing.

In the sudden silence, the silver pin made a little tinkling noise on the rock floor and the packet whinnied painfully.

"Well, my two fine fellows, if this is all you have, then your mother will surely die."

They were about to answer him, to tell him about their brother Three Ox and the *wang-liang*'s face, when invisible fingers touched their lips and an invisible mouth whispered into their ears. "Trust no one else."

"What did you say?" the Dragon King asked suspiciously.

"Nothing, O great and mighty Lung-Wang," said One Ox.

"We just sighed," said Two Ox.

"Just so, just so," said Lung-Wang. "But if I ever suspect that you have lied to me, it will not go well with you. Since you have nothing more to offer me, you shall sit in my dungeon until I am ready to eat you. Perhaps at the end of this night. Or the next. Or even the one after that. The mountain climb has toughened you—but I like my meat that way. I am in no hurry, after all, dragons live a very long time." He picked them up by the back of their shirts, as if they weighed no more than chicks, and raised them until their heads nearly touched the roof. They were sure they would hear the sound of his great tail sweeping along behind.

The Dragon King's dungeon was of rock and stone and so far beneath the ground it was lit only by the phosphorescence in the rock. There was no need for bars on the door, for the door was but a hole in the roof high above them, down which they had been flung. When the brothers looked up, they could not see the hole for the dark.

"Three Ox, brother," they called up at last, "can you help us?"

"I will help, brothers," he called back down, "when I can. And see what I have in my hand."

"We can see nothing in the dark, brother," said One Ox.

"And even if we could," Two Ox added, "what you hold in your invisible hand becomes invisible itself."

"Just so," replied Three Ox. "Then I shall tell you. I have both the pocket beast and the pin."

"And what will you do now?" the brothers called up to him.

"What must be done," he answered, and was gone.

While One Ox and Two Ox waited in the cold and dark of their stone prison, Three Ox made his way back along the twisting tunnels of the cave, following the path swept clean by the dragon's tail. At last he found himself in a great room whose ceiling was lined with panels of obsidian and jade and whose walls were encrusted with pearl. In the center stood Lung-Wang, now more dragon than man. His shoulders, as green as the jade, were fiercely scaled; his eyes and teeth were the black of jet; and down from his back ran a sinuous, twisting green tail. But his hands were still a man's, and as the invisible boy watched, the Dragon King removed the ring from his own finger, reciting this charm:

Ring of power, ring of life,
Ring that neither blade nor knife
Nor ax nor sword can sever from me,
Swallow now so I become me!

Then the Dragon King threw the ring into the air and opened his mighty jaws to receive it

In the second that the ring was thrown into the air, Three Ox remembered what the doctor had said. The ring was the guardian of the Waters of Life. It was also—clearly—the guardian of the Dragon King. He could not be transformed back into a man without it. Even as the ring was tumbling back down, the transformation into the King of All Dragons was complete.

Three Ox ran forward and leaped high into the air. With his invisible hand he snatched the ring before it could fall into the dragon's waiting jaws. Then in one swift, silent movement, he dived, somersaulted, and stood again, the ring now invisible in his closed hand.

For a moment more the Dragon King waited for the ring to fall into his open mouth. When it did not, he snapped his jaws shut with a sound as resounding as an executioner's ax.

"Where is it?" he cried. "Where is the Dragon King's own ring?" Falling on all fours, he began to sniff and snort and root around the room, lighting every crack and crevice with his fiery breath.

Three Ox did not wait for the Dragon King's search to be over. Swiftly and silently he made his way down the tunnels to the dungeon. There he stripped off his shirt and dangled it through the hole that served as the dungeon door. As the shirt was no longer on his body, it was visible to the point where it met his hand.

"Quickly, my brothers," he called, "grab hold of the shirt and I will pull you up. We have little time. Soon the dragon will stop searching for the ring alone and follow my scent."

But the shirt did not reach far enough down into the hole to help. So One Ox put Two Ox on his shoulders and then Two Ox was able to reach the shirt. With a mighty effort, Three Ox pulled him up. Then Two Ox took off his own shirt and tied it to Three Ox's. This way they had a long enough line to reach One Ox and pull him to safety. Then hand in hand in invisible hand they ran out of the cave.

Once outside, Three Ox stripped off the *wang-liang's* face and held up the ring. "Here is the very thing that contains the Waters of Life. But unless we can escape the anger of the Dragon King we will not be able to bring it to our mother." He pulled the hairpin from his waistband. "Two Ox, you must get us down the mountainside with your river and boat."

"Gladly," said Two Ox, drawing the pin along the path. As he did so, a river began to bubble before them and there was the boat, bobbing gently in the current. "Climb in, my brothers, and I will bring us to the mountain's foot."

They climbed in, and using the silver pin as a rudder, Two Ox steered them with great skill down the steep mountainside. Behind them they heard the sound of a dragon roaring.

When they came to the bottom of the mountainside, the river stopped and so did the boat. They climbed out and Two Ox quickly took the rudder from the lock so that the boat and river became a pin once more. Then he stuck the pin in his waistband.

There was a full moon overhead and in the cool of the night all three boys shuddered.

"What now?" Two Ox asked.

"Now we must ride more swiftly than the dragon flies," Three Ox said, handing the packet to One Ox. "If we keep to the trees, we will be safe."

One Ox placed the packet on the ground. Then he unfolded it one piece at a time. As they watched, the horse grew and grew until it was large enough for three. They got on, One Ox in front, his fingers threaded through the horse's foam-colored mane. Behind him sat Two Ox, his arms around his brother's waist. And at the back sat Three Ox, clutching his brother's shirt.

The horse galloped swiftly beneath the trees all the night through, and so long as they remained hidden under the leafy boughs, the dragon could not get to them. But soon there lay ahead of them only farmland, and their mother's poor farm on the farther side.

"What can we do now?" asked One Ox.

"Dismount, my brothers," said Three Ox.

"How will that help?" asked Two Ox.

"I alone will ride to the farm, with the *wang-liang's* face over my own, invisible. All the dragon will know is that a horse gallops swiftly below him. But you, my brothers, will not be riding." And as he spoke, he drew the *wang-liang*'s face down over his own. In a moment he could not be seen.

One Ox and Two Ox dismounted and hid themselves behind the largest tree at the forest's edge. As they watched, the horse shrank to fit a single rider, then pounded across the furrowed fields, heading straight toward their mother's farm. But the rider and part of the horse's back and mane could not be seen.

The dragon strained across the lightening sky, and when it saw the strange riderless horse, its anger was renewed. It pursued the horse with hot fury and hotter breath and soon flames singed the horse's tail. Still the horse galloped on and on; if anything, fire added to its speed. Within minutes it was at the farmhouse where the mother of One Ox, Two Ox, and Three Ox lay dying.

Hearing the commotion, the old woman tottered out of bed. And when she looked out into the growing dawn, she saw a horse galloping toward her with a great jade dragon behind it. She put her hand to her heart and cried out, "My son!" for though Three Ox was invisible to everyone else, he could not fool his mother's eyes.

Then the Dragon King understood how he had been deceived, and like a stooping hawk he cleaved his great jade wings to his sides and dived toward the running horse.

Just then the sun rose full over the farthest mountains, and its red eye burned into the dragon's jet eyes. The Dragon King gave an awful cry, remembering only at that moment that he had to be home by dawn. Then he burst like a series of bright skyrockets in the air; the light of it was seen as far away as the city of Kai-lung and down into the depths of the Western Sea. The ashes settled over the entire farm more than a *li* in length.

One Ox and Two Ox ran from the sheltering trees and joined their mother and brother in a mighty embrace by the farmhouse door. Then they dipped the Dragon King's ring into a glass of clear springwater. When their mother drank it down, she felt well again. In fact she felt better than she had in years.

Once the new crop was planted, One Ox went off to the city of Kai-lung to serve his dragon master for a year. And Two Ox went off to the Western Sea to serve his. But Three Ox stayed home to take care of his mother and tend the farm.

The farm flourished as never before because the ashes of the Dragon King made the soil rich and strong. When the two older brothers returned, there was more than enough for them all.

"Which is just as well," said their mother, "for I could never choose among my dear sons. I love each of you the best."

And indeed she did. For many years to come she played in the flowering orchards with her many grandchildren, giving them rides on the pocket pony, or floating with them in the silver boat, where she told them story after story after story just like the one I have just told you.

BROTHER HART

Deep in a wood, so dark and tangled few men dared enter it, there was a small clearing. And in that clearing lived a girl and her brother Hart.

By day, in his deer shape, Brother Hart would go out and forage on green grass and budlings while his sister remained at home.

But whenever dusk began, the girl Hinda would go to the edge of the clearing and call out in a high, sweet voice:

> Dear heart, Brother Hart,
> Come at my behest.
> We shall dine on berry wine
> And you shall have your rest.

Then, in his deer heart, her brother would know the day's enchantment was at an end and run swiftly home. There, at the lintel over the cottage door, he would rub between his antlers until the hide on his forehead broke bloodlessly apart. He would rub and rub further still until the brown hide skinned back along both sides and he stepped out a naked man.

His sister would take the hide and shake it out and brush and comb it until it shone like polished wood. Then she hung the hide up by the antlers beside the door, with the legs dangling down. It would hang there until the morning, when Brother Hart donned it once again and raced off to the lowland meadows to graze.

What spell or sorcerer had brought them there, deep in the wood, neither could recall. Their faces mirrored one another, and their lives were twinned. Their memories, like the sorcerer, had vanished. The woods, the meadow, the clearing, the deer hide, the cottage door, were all they knew.

Now one day in late spring, Brother Hart had gone as usual to the lowland meadows, leaving Hinda at home. She had washed and scrubbed the little cottage until it was neat and clean. She had put new straw in their bedding. But as she stood by the window brushing out her long dark hair, an unfamiliar sound greeted her ears: a loud, harsh calling, neither bird nor jackal nor good grey wolf.

Again and again the call came. So Hinda went to the door, for she feared nothing in the wood. And who should come winded to the cottage but Brother Hart. He had no words to tell her in his deer form, but blood beaded his head like a crown. It was the first time she had ever seen him bleed. He pushed past her and collapsed, shivering, on their bed.

Hinda ran over to him and would have bathed him with her tears, but the jangling noise called out again, close and insistent. She ran to the window to see.

There was a man outside in the clearing. At least she thought it was a man. Yet he did not look like Brother Hart, who was the only man she knew.

He was large where Brother Hart was slim. He was fair where Brother Hart was dark. He was hairy where Brother Hart was smooth. And he was dressed in animal skins that hung from his shoulders to his feet. About the man leaped fawning wolves, some spotted like jackals, some tan and some white. He pushed them from him with a rough sweep of his hand.

"I seek a deer," he called when he glimpsed Hinda's face, a pale moon, at the window.

But when Hinda came out of the door, closing it behind her to hide what lay inside, the man did not speak again. Instead he took off his fur hat and laid it upon his heart, kneeling down before her.

"Who are you?" asked Hinda. "What are you? And why do you seek the deer?" Her voice was gentle but firm.

The man neither spoke nor rose but stared at her face.

"Who are you?" Hinda asked again. "Say what it is you are."

As if she had broken a spell, the man spoke at last. "I am but a man," he said. "A man who has traveled far and who has seen much, but never a beauty such as yours."

"If it *is* beauty, and beauty is what you prize, you shall not see it again," said Hinda. "For a man who hunts the deer can be no friend of mine."

The man rose then, and Hinda marveled at the height of him, for he was as tall as the cottage door and his hands were grained like wood.

"Then I shall hunt the deer no more," he said, "if you will give me leave to hunt that which is now all at once dearer to me."

"And what is that?"

"You, dear heart," he said, reaching for her. Startled, Hinda moved away from him but, remembering her brother inside the cottage, found voice to say, "Tomorrow." She reached behind her and steadied herself on the door handle. She thought she heard the heavy breathing of Brother Hart through the walls. "Come tomorrow."

"I shall surely come." He bowed, turned, and then was gone, walking swiftly, a man's stride, through the woods. His animals were at his heels.

Hinda's eyes followed him down the path until she counted even the shadows of trees as his own. When she was certain he was gone, she opened the cottage door and went in.

The cottage was suddenly dark, filled with the musk of deer.

Brother Hart lay on their straw bed. When he looked up at her, Hinda could not bear the twin wounds of his eyes. She turned away and said, "You may go out now. It is safe. He will not hunt you again."

The deer rose heavily to his feet, nuzzled open the door, and sprang away to the meadows.

But he was home again at dark.

When he stepped out of his skin and entered the cottage, he did not greet his sister with his usual embrace. Instead he said, "You did not call me to the clearing. You did not say my name. Only when I was tired and the sun had almost gone, did I know it was time to come home."

Hinda could not answer. She could not even look at him. For even more than his words, his nakedness suddenly shamed her. She put their food on the table and they ate their meal in silence. Then they lay down together and slept without dreams like the wild creatures of the wood.

When the sun called Brother Hart to his deerskin once again, Hinda opened the door. Silently she ushered him outside, silently watched him change, and sent him off on his silent way to the meadows without word of farewell. Her thoughts were on the hunter, the man of the wolves. She never doubted he would come.

And come he did, neither silently nor slowly, but with loud, purposeful steps. He stood for a moment at the clearing's edge, looking at Hinda, measuring her with his eyes. Then he smiled and crossed to her.

He stayed all the day with her and taught her wonders she had never known. He told her tales of kingdoms she had never seen. He sang songs she had never heard before, singing them

93

softly into her ears. He spoke again and again of his love for her, but he touched no more than her hand.

"You are as innocent as any creature in the woods," he said over and over in amazement.

So passed the day.

Suddenly it was dusk, and Hinda looked up with a start. "You must go now," she said.

"Nay, I must stay."

"No no, you must go," Hinda said again. "I cannot have you here at night. If you love me, go." Then she added softly, her dark eyes on his, "But come again in the morning."

Her sudden fear puzzled him, but it also touched him, so he stood and smoothed down the skins of his coat. "I will go. But I will return."

He whistled his animals to him, and left the clearing as swiftly as he had come.

Hinda would have called after him then, called after and made him stay, but she did not even know his name. So she went instead to the clearing's edge and cried:

> Dear Heart, Brother Hart,
> Come at my bidding.
> We shall dine on berry wine
> And dance at my wedding.

And hearing her voice, Brother Hart raced home.

He stopped at the clearing's edge, raised his head, and sniffed. The smell of man hung on the air, heavy and threatening. He came through it as if through a swift current, and stepped to the cottage door.

Rubbing his head more savagely than ever on the lintel, as if to rip off his thoughts with his hide, Brother Hart removed his skin.

"The hunter was here," he said as he crossed the threshold of the door.

"He does not seek you," Hinda replied.

"You will not see him again. You will tell him to go."

"I see him for your sake," said Hinda. "If he sees me, he does not see you. If he hunts me, he does not hunt you. I do it for you, brother dear."

Satisfied, Brother Hart sat down to eat. But Hinda was not hungry. She served her brother and watched as he ate his fill.

"You should sleep," she said when he was done. "Sleep, and I will rub your head and sing to you."

"I *am* tired," he answered. "My head aches where yesterday he struck me. My heart aches still with the fear. I tremble all over. You are right. I should sleep."

So he lay down on the bed and Hinda sat by him. She rubbed cinquefoil on his head to soothe it and sang him many songs, and soon Brother Hart was asleep.

When the moon lit the clearing, the hunter returned. He could not wait until the morning. Hinda's fear had made him afraid, though he had never known fear before. He dared not leave her alone in the forest. But he moved quietly as a beast in the dark. He left his dogs behind.

The cottage in the clearing was still except for a breath of song, wordless and longing, that floated on the air. It was Hinda's voice, and when the hunter heard it, he smiled for she was singing a tune he had taught her.

He moved out into the clearing, more boldly now. Then suddenly he stopped. He saw a strange shape hanging by the cottage door. It was a deerskin, a fine buck's hide, hung by the antlers and the legs dangling down.

Caution, an old habit, claimed him. He circled the clearing, never once making a sound. He approached the cottage from the side, and Hinda's singing led him on. When he reached the window, he peered in.

Hinda was sitting on a low straw bed, and beside her, his head in her lap, lay a man. The man was slim and naked and dark. His hair was long and straight and came to his shoulders. The hunter could not see his face, but he lay in sleep like a man who was no stranger to the bed.

The hunter controlled the shaking of his hands, but he could not control his heart. He allowed himself one moment of fierce anger. With his knife he thrust a long gash on the left side of the deerskin that hung by the door. Then he was gone.

In the cottage Brother Hart cried out in his sleep, a swift sharp cry. His hand went to his side and suddenly, under his heart, a thin red line like a knife's slash appeared. It bled for a moment. Hinda caught his hand up in hers, and at the sight of the blood she grew pale. It was the second time she had seen Brother Hart bleed.

She got up without disturbing him and went to the cupboard, where she found a white linen towel. She washed the wound with water. The cut was long, but it was not deep. Some scratch he had got in the woods perhaps. She knew it would heal before morning. So she lay down beside him and fitted her body to the curve of his back. Brother Hart stirred slightly but did not waken. Then Hinda, too, fell asleep.

In the morning Brother Hart rose, but his movements were slow. "I wish I could stay," he said to his sister. "I wish this enchantment were at an end."

But the rising sun summoned him outside. He donned the deerskin and leaped away.

Hinda stood at the door and raised her hand to shade her eyes. The last she saw of him was the flash of white tail as he sped off into the woods.

She did not go back into the cottage to clean. She stood waiting for the hunter to come. Her eyes and ears strained for the signs of his approach. There were none.

She waited through the whole of the long morning, until the

sun was high overhead. Not until then did she go indoors, where she threw herself down on the straw bedding and wept.

At dusk the sun began to fade and the cottage darkened. Hinda got up. She went out to the clearing's edge and called:

> Dear heart, Brother Hart,
> Come at my crying.
> We shall dine on berry wine
> And . . .

But she got no further. A loud sound in the woods stayed her. It was too heavy for a deer. And when the hunter stepped out of the woods on the very path that Brother Hart usually took, Hinda gave a gasp, part delight, part fear.

"You have come," she said, and her voice trembled.

The hunter searched her face with his eyes but could not find what he was seeking. He walked past her to the cottage door. Hinda followed behind him, uncertain.

"I have come," he said. His back was to her. "I wish to God I had not."

"What do you mean?"

"I sought the deer today," he said.

Hinda's hand went to her mouth.

"I sought the deer today. And what I seek, I find." He did not turn. "We ran him long, my dogs and I. When he was at bay, he fought hard. I gave the beast's liver and heart to my dogs. But this I saved for you."

He held up his hands then, and a deerskin unrolled from it. With a swift, savage movement, he tacked it to the door with his knife. The hooves did not quite touch the ground.

Hinda could see two slashes in the hide, one on each side, under the heart. The slash on the left was an old wound, crusted but clean. The slash on the right was new, and from it blood still dripped.

She leaned forward and touched the wound with her hand, tears in her eyes. "Oh, my dear Brother Hart," she cried. "It was because of me you died. Now your enchantment *is* at an end."

The hunter whirled around to face her then. "He was your brother?" he asked.

She nodded. "He was my heart." Looking straight at him, she added, "We were one at birth. What was his is mine by right." Her chin was up, and her head held high. She reached past the hunter and pulled the knife from the door with an ease that surprised him. Gently she took down the skin. She shook it out once, and smoothed the nap with her hand. Then, as if putting on a cloak, she wrapped the skin around her shoulders and pulled the head over her own.

As the hunter watched, she began to change. It was as if he saw a rippled reflection in a pool coming slowly into focus: slim brown legs, brown haunch, brown body and head. The horns shriveled and fell to the ground. Only her eyes remained the same.

The doe looked at the hunter for a moment more. A single tear started in her eye, but before it had time to fall, she turned, sprang away into the fading light, and was gone.

SUN/FLIGHT

They call me the nameless one. My mother was the sea, and the sun itself fathered me. I was born fully clothed and on my boyish cheeks the beginnings of a beard. Whoever I was, wherever I came from, had been washed from me by the waves in which I was found.

And so I have made many pasts for myself. A honey-colored mother cradling me. A father with his beard short and shaped like a Minoan spade. Sisters and brothers have I gifted myself. And a home that smelled of fresh-strewn reeds and olives ripening on the trees. Sometimes I make myself a king's son, god-born, a javelin in my hand and a smear of honeycake on my lips. Other times I am a craftsman's child, with a length of golden string threaded around my thumbs. Or the son of a *dmos*, a serf, my back arched over the furrows where little birds search for seeds like farmers counting the crop. With no remembered pasts, I can pick a different one each day to suit my mood, to cater to my need.

But most of the time I think myself the child of the birds, for when the fishermen pulled me up from the sea, drowned of my past, I clutched a single feather in my hand. The feather was golden, sun-colored, and when it dried it was tufted with yellow rays. I carried it with me always, my talisman, my token back across the Styx. No one knew what bird had carried this feather in its wing or tail. The shaft is strong and white and the barbs soft. The little fingers of down are no-color at all; they change with the changing light.

So I am no-name, son of no-bird, pulled from the waters of the sea north and east of Delos, too far for swimming, my only sail the feather in my hand.

The head of the fishermen who rescued me was a morose man called Talos who would have spoken more had he no tongue at all. But he was a good man, for all that he was silent. He gave me advice but once, and had I listened then, I would not be here, now, in a cold and dark cavern listening to voices from my unremembered past and fearing the rising of the sun.

When Talos plucked me from the water, he wrung me out with hands that were horned from work. He made no comment at all about my own hands, whose softness the water-wrinkles could not disguise. He brought me home to his childless wife. She spread honey-balm on my burns, for my back and right side were seared as if I had been drawn from the flames instead of from the sea. The puckered scars along my side are still testimony to that fire. Talos was convinced I had come from the wreckage of a burning ship, though no sails or spars were ever found. But the only fire I could recall was red and round as the sun.

Of fire and water was I made, Talos's wife said. Her tongue ran before her thoughts always. She spoke twice, once for herself and once for her speechless husband. "Of sun and sea, my only child," she would say, fondly stroking my wine-dark hair, touching the feather I kept pinned to my chiton. "Bird child. A gift of the sky, a gift from the sea."

So I stayed with them. Indeed, where else could I, still a boy, go? And they were content. Except for the scar seaming my side, I was thought handsome. And my fingers were clever with memories of their own. They could make things of which I had no conscious knowledge: miniature buildings of strange design, with passages that turned back upon themselves; a mechanical bull-man that could move about and roar when wound with a hand-carved key.

"Fingers from the gods," Talos's wife said. "Such fingers. Your father must have been Hephaestus, though you have Apollo's face." And she added god after god to my string, a litany that comforted her until Talos's warning grunt stemmed the rising tide of her words.

At last my good looks and my clever fingers brought me to the attention of the local lord, I the nameless one, the child of sun and sea and sky. That lord was called Circinus. He had many slaves and many bondsmen, but only one daughter, Perdix.

She was an ox-eyed beauty, with a long neck. Her slim, boyish body, her straight, narrow nose, reminded me somehow of my time before the waves, though I could not quite say how. Her name was sighed from every man's lips, but no one dared speak it aloud.

Lord Circinus asked for my services and, reluctantly, Talos and his wife let me go. He merely nodded a slow acceptance. She wept all over my shoulder before I left, a second drowning. But I, eager to show the Lord Circinus my skills, paid them scant attention.

It was then that Talos unlocked his few words for me.

"Do not fly too high, my son," he said. And like his wife, he repeated himself. "Do not fly too high."

He meant Perdix, of course, for he had seen my eyes on her. But I was just newly conscious of my body's desires. I could not, did not listen.

That was how I came into Lord Circinus's household, bringing nothing but the clothes I wore, the feather of my past, and the strange talent that lived in my hands. In Lord Circinus's house I was given a sleeping room and a workroom and leave to set the pattern of my days.

Work was my joy and my excuse. I began simply, making clay-headed dolls, with wooden trunks and jointed limbs, testing out the tools that Circinus gave me. But soon I moved away from such childish things and constructed a dancing floor of such intricately mazed panels of wood, I was rewarded with a pocket of gold.

I never looked boldly upon the Lady Perdix. It was not my place. But I glanced longways, from the corners of my eyes. And somehow she must have known. For it was not long before she found my workroom and came to tease me with her boy's body and quick tongue. Like my stepfather Talos, I had no magic in my answers, only in my fingers, and Perdix always laughed at me twice: once for my slow speech and once for the quick flush that quickly burned my cheeks after each exchange.

I recall the first time she came upon me as I worked on a mechanical bird that could fly in short bursts toward the sun. She entered the workroom and stood by my side watching for a while. Then she put her right hand over mine. I could feel the heat from her hand burn me, all the way up my arm, though this burning left no visible scar.

"My Lady," I said. So I had been instructed to address her. She was a year younger than I. "It is said that a woman should wait upon a man's moves."

"If that were so," she answered swiftly, "all women would be called Penelope. But I would have woven a different ending to *that* particular tale." She laughed. "Too much waiting without an eye upon her, makes a maid mad."

Her wordy cleverness confounded me and I blushed. But she lifted her hand from mine and, still laughing, left the room.

It was a week before she returned. I did not even hear her enter, but when I turned around she was sitting on the floor with her skirts rolled halfway up her thighs. Her tanned legs flashed unmistakable signs at me that I dared not answer.

"Do you think it better to wait for a god or wait upon a man?" she asked, as if a week had not come between her last words and these.

I mumbled something about a man having but one form and a god many, and concluded lamely that perhaps, then, waiting for a god would be more interesting.

"Oh, yes," she said, "many girls have waited for a god to come. But not I. Men can be made gods, you know."

I did not know, and confessed it.

"My cousin Danae," she said, "said that great Zeus had come into her lap in a shower of gold. But I suspect it was a more mundane lover. After all, it has happened many times before that a man has showered gold into a girl's skirts and she opens her legs to him. That does not make *him* a god, or his coming gold." She laughed that familiar low laugh and added under her breath, "Cousin Danae always did have a quick answer for her mistakes."

"Like you, my Lady?" I asked.

She answered me with a smile and stood up slowly. As I watched, she walked toward me, stopping only inches away. I could scarcely breathe. She took the feather off the workbench where it lay among my tools and ran it down my chest. I was dressed only in a linen loincloth, my chiton set aside, for it was summer and very very hot.

I must have sighed. I know I bit my lip. And then she dropped the feather and it fluttered slowly to the floor. She used her fingers in the feather's place, and they were infinitely more knowing than my own. They found the pattern of my scar and traced it slowly as a blind child traces the raised fable on a vase.

I stepped through the last bit of space between us and put my arms around her as if I were fitting the last piece of my puzzle into a maze. For a moment we stood as still as any frieze; then she pushed me backwards and I tumbled down. But I held on to her, and she fell on top of me, fitting her mouth to mine.

Perdix came to my room that night, and the next I went to hers. And she made me a god. And so it continued night after night, a pattern as complicated as any I could devise, and as simple, too. I could not conceive of it ending.

But end it did.

One night she did not tap lightly at my door and slip in, a shadow in a night of shadows. I thought perhaps her moon time had come, until the next morning in the hallway near my workroom when I saw her whisper into the ear of a new slave. He had skin almost as dark as the wings of the bittern, and wild black hair. His nostrils flared like a beast's. Perdix placed her hand on his shoulder and turned him to face me. When I flushed with anger and with pain, they both laughed, he taking his cue from her, a scant beat behind.

Night could not come fast enough to hide my shame. I lay on my couch and thought I slept. A dream voice from the labyrinth that is my past cried out to me, in dark and brutish tones. I rose, not knowing I rose, and took my carving knife in hand. Wrapped only in night's cloak, the feather stuck in my hair, I crept down the corridors of the house.

I sniffed the still air. I listened for every sound. And then I heard it truly, the monster from my dream, agonizing over its meal. It screamed and moaned and panted and wept, but the tears that fell from its bullish head were as red as human blood.

I saw it, I tell you, in her room crouched over her, devouring my lady, my lost Perdix. My knife was ready, and I fell upon its back, black Minotaur of my devising. But it slid from the bed and melted away in the darkness, and my blade found her waiting heart instead.

She made no sound above a sigh.

My clever fingers, so nimble, so fast, could not hold the wound together, could not seam it closed. She seemed to be leaking away through my clumsy hands.

Then I heard a rush of wings, as if her soul had flown from the room. And I knew I had to fly after her and fetch her back before she left this world forever. So I took the feather from my hair and, dipping it into the red ocean of her life, printed great bloody wings, feathered tracings, along my shoulders and down my arms. And I flew high, high after her and fell into the bright searing light of dawn.

When they found me in the morning, by her bedside, crouched naked by her corpse, scarred with her blood, they took me, all unprotesting, to Lord Circinus. He had me thrown into this dark cave.

Tomorrow, before the sun comes again, I will be brought from this place and tied to a post sunk in the sand.

Oh, the cleverness of it, the cleverness. It might have been devised by my own little darling, my Perdix, for her father never had her wit. The post is at a place beyond the high water mark and I will be bound to it at the ebb. All morning my father, the sun, will burn me, and my father the rising tide will melt the red feathers of blood that decorate my chest and arms and side. And I will watch myself go back into the waters from which I was first pulled, nameless but alive.

Of fire and water I came, of fire and water I return. Talos was right. I flew too high. Truly there is no second fooling of the Fates.

SLIPPING SIDEWAYS THROUGH ETERNITY

Shanna opened the door slowly and peered out. The lake surface ruffled in the wind but there was no one on it. She shrugged, came back to the seder table. "No one there," she said. She was only five after all, ten years younger than me. She got to ask the questions, open the door. I got to drink watered wine. It was some sort of trade-off.

Everyone laughed.

"Elijah is there, only you can't see him," Nonny said.

But she was wrong. I could see him.

Elijah stood in the doorway, tall, gaunt, somewhere between a concentration camp victim and a Beat poet. I read a lot of poetry. Then I paint the poems, the words singing their colors onto the page. Sometimes I think I was born in the wrong century. Actually, I *know* I was born in the wrong century.

Elijah saw me see him and nodded. His eyes were black, his beard black and wavy, like a Labrador's coat. When he smiled, his eyes nearly closed shut. His tongue came out of his mouth tentatively, licked his upper lip. It was the pink of my toe shoes. Not that I dance anymore. Pink toe shoes and *The Nutcracker.* That's for babies. Now I'm into horses. But his tongue was so pink against his black beard, it made me tremble. I'm not sure why.

I motioned to the chair. No one but Elijah noticed.

He shook his head, his mouth formed the words: "Not yet." Then he turned and left, slipping sideways through eternity.

"He's gone," I said.

"No," Nonny contradicted, shaking her head, the blue hair a helmet that never moved. "Elijah is never gone. He is always here." But she looked at me strangely, her black-button eyes shining.

I took another sip of the watered wine.

The next time I saw Elijah was in shul. It's the only temple on the island so everyone Jewish goes there, even though it's a Reform temple. I was sitting snuggled up next to Shanna, more for the warmth than friendship. Shanna's okay, when she's quiet and cuddly. But little sisters can be a pain. Especially when they're ten years younger, an embarrassment, and a sign that your parents—your parents, for G-d's sake—are still having sex.

We were in the middle of one of Rabbi Shiller's long, rambling book reports. He rarely says anything religious. My mother likes that. Thinks it's important. "Keeps us in touch with the greater world," she says. Meaning non-Jews. I get enough book reports in school in my AP classes, where we call them essays but they are really only high school book reports, though with bigger words. Besides, the rabbi was talking about *Maus,* which I'd just done an AP report on, and got an A, and my insights were better than his. So I snuggled close to Shanna and closed my eyes.

Or I almost closed my eyes.

And there, standing on the bima, finger on his lips, was Elijah, same black eyes, same black wavy beard, same pink tongue. I was not sure if he was shushing me or the rabbi but he was definitely shushing someone.

I sat up, pushed Shanna off me, looked around to see if anyone else had noticed him.

But the congregation was intent on the rabbi, who had just announced that in *Maus*, "The commentary should disrupt the facile linear progression of the narration, introduce alternative interpretations, question any partial conclusion, withstand the need for closure . . ." which I recognized immediately as a quote from Friedlander. The rabbi had been doing his research online. And he was not giving credit where credit was due, as my AP English teacher, V. Louise, always reminds us. She would have had him gutted for breakfast.

I glanced back at Elijah, who was shaking his head, as if he, too, knew the rabbi was a plagiarist. But maybe if you had to give a sermon every Friday night for your entire life, plagiarism becomes a necessity.

To be certain I wasn't the only kid seeing things, I checked on my friends. Barry Goldblatt was picking boogers from his nose. Nothing new there. Marcia Damashek was whispering to her mother. They even dress alike. Carol Tropp had leaned forward, not to listen to the rabbi but to tap Gordon Berliner on the shoulder. She has a thing for him, though I can't imagine why. He may be funny—like a stand-up comic—but he's short and he smells.

I kept checking around. Every single one of the kids I knew was distracted. No one seemed to have seen Elijah but me. And this time I had no watered wine to blame.

Clearly, I thought, clearly I'm having a psychotic break. We studied psychotic breaks in our psychology class. They aren't pretty. Either that, or Elijah, that consummate time traveler, that tricky wizard of forever, was really standing behind the rabbi and snorting into a rather dirty handkerchief, the color of leaf mold. Couldn't he take some time out of his travels to go to a Laundromat? We've got several downtown I could tell him about.

I shook my head and Elijah looked up again, winked at me, and slipped sideways into some sort of time stream, and was gone. He didn't even disturb the motes of sunlight dusting the front of the ark.

Standing, I pushed past my sister and mother and father and walked out of the hall. I know they thought I had to pee, but that's not what I was doing. I went downstairs to wait in the religious center till the service was over. The door to the middle students' classroom was open and I went in. Turning on the light, I sighed, feeling safe. Here was where I'd studied Hebrew lessons with Mrs. Goldin for so many years. Where I'd learned about being Jewish. Where no one had ever said Elijah was real. I mean, we're Reform Jews, after all. We leave that sort of thing to the Chassids. Leaping in the air, having visions, wearing bad hats and worse wigs. Real nineteenth-century stuff.

I idled my way over to the kids' bookcase. Lots of books there. We Jews are big on books. The People of the Book and all. My father being a professor of literature at the university, we have a house filled with books. Even the bathrooms have bookshelves. We joke about the difference between litter-ature and literature. One to be used in the bathroom, the other to be read. Those sort of jokes.

My mom is a painter but even she reads. Not that I mind. I'm a big bookie myself, though I don't take bets on it. That's another family joke!

Finding a piece of gray poster paper, I began to doodle on it with a Magic Marker. Mom says that doodling concentrates the mind. I didn't draw my usual—horses. Instead I drew Elijah's head: the wavy hair, the dark beard, the tongue lolling out, like a dog's. A few more quick lines, and I turned him into a retriever.

"And what do you retrieve?" I asked my drawing. The drawing was silent. I guess the psychotic didn't break that far. Yeah—I have the family sense of humor.

I thought maybe there'd be a book or two in the classroom on Elijah. Squatting, I quickly scanned down the spines. I was right. Not one book but a whole bunch. A regular Jewish pop star.

Settling down to read the first one, I felt a tap on my shoulder that didn't make me jump as much as it set off a series of tremors running down my backbone

I turned slowly and looked up into Elijah's long face. Close, he was younger than I'd thought, the beard disguising the fact that he was probably in his twenties. A Jewish Captain Jack Sparrow with a yarmulke instead of a tricornered hat.

He crooked his finger at me; held out his hand.

Years of stranger-danger conversations flashed through my head. But who could be afraid of a figment of her imagination? Besides, he was cool-looking in a Goth beatnik kind of way.

I put my hand in his and stood. His hand seemed real enough.

We turned some sort of corner in the middle of the room, slid sideways, and found ourselves in a long gray corridor.

Was I afraid?

I was fascinated. It was like being in a sci-fi movie. The corridor flickered with flashes of starlight. Meteors rushed by. And a strange wandering sun seemed to be moving counterclockwise.

"Where are we go . . . ?" I began, the words floating out of my mouth like the balloons in a comic strip.

He put a finger of his free hand on his lips and I ate the rest of my question. What did it matter? We were science-fictional wanderers on a metaphysical road.

The sound of wind got wilder and wilder until it felt as if we were in a tunnel with trains racing by us on all sides. And then suddenly everything went quiet. The gray lifted, the flashes were gone, and we stepped out of the corridor into . . . into an even grayer world, full of mud.

I craned my neck trying to see where we were.

Elijah put his hands on both sides of my head and drew me around till we were facing.

"Do not look yet, Rebecca," he said to me, his voice made soft by his accent.

Was I surprised that he knew my name? I was beyond surprise.

"Is this place . . . bad?" I asked.

"Very bad."

"Am I dead and in Hell?"

"No, though this is a kind of hell." His face, always long, grew longer with sadness. Or anger. It was hard to tell.

"Why are we here?" I trembled as I spoke.

"Ah, Rebecca—that is always the most important question." His r's rattled like a teakettle left too long on the stove. "The question we all need to ask of the universe." He smiled at me. "You are here because I need you."

For a moment, the grayness around us seemed to lighten.

Then he added, "You are here because you saw me." He dropped his hands to my shoulders.

"I saw you?"

He smiled, and, for the first time, I realized there was a gap between his top front teeth. And that the teeth were very white. Okay, he might not hit the Laundromat often enough, but he knew a thing or three about brushing.

"I saw you? So why is that such a big deal?" I think I knew even before he told me.

Shrugging, he said, "Few see me, Rebecca. Fewer still can slip sideways through time with me."

"Through time?" Now I looked around. The place was a flat

treeless plain, not so much gray as hopeless. "Where are we?" I asked again.

He laughed into my hair. "'When are we?' is the question you should be asking."

I gulped, trying to swallow down something awful-tasting that seemed to have lodged in my throat. "Am I crazy?"

"No more than any great artist."

He knew I did art?

"You are a really fine artist. Remember, Rebecca, I travel through time. Past and future, they are all as one to me."

Even in that gray world, I felt a flutter in my breast. My cheeks grew hot with pleasure. A great artist. A fine artist. In the future. Then I shook my head. Now I knew I was dreaming. Too much watered wine at the seder. I was probably asleep with my cheek on Nonny's white tablecloth. Yet in my dream I painted a picture of Elijah brooding in that open door, dark and hungry, his lips slightly moist with secrets, his mouth framing an invitation in a language both dead and alive.

"You will paint that picture," he said, as if reading my mind. "And it will make the world notice you. It will make me notice you. But not now. Now we have work to do." He took my hand.

"What work?"

"Look closely."

This time when I looked I saw that the flat treeless plain was not empty. There were humans walking about, women, girls, all dressed in gray. Gray skirts, gray shirts, gray scarves on their heads, gray sandals or boots. Oh, I could see that the clothes they wore had not always been such a color, but had been worn thin and made old by terror and tragedy and hopelessness.

"You must bring them away," Elijah said. "Those who will go with you."

"You are the time traveler, the magician," I told him. "Why don't you do it?"

That long face looked down at me, his dark brown eyes softening. "They do not see me."

"Will they see me?" I asked. But I already knew. They were coming toward me, hands out.

"Elijah," I asked him, "how will I talk to them?"

He reached out a hand and touched my lips. "You will find a way, Rebecca. Now go. I can tell you no more." Then he disappeared, like the Cheshire cat, until there was only his mouth, and it wasn't smiling. Then he was gone entirely.

I turned to the women and let them gather me in.

They told me where we were, how they were there. I had read their stories in books so I had no reason to disbelieve them. We were in a camp.

Oh, not a summer camp with square dances and macramé projects and water sports. I'd been to those. Girl Scout camp, art camp, music camp. My parents, like all their friends, saw the summer as a time to ship-the-kids-off-to-camp. Some were like boot camp and some were like spas.

This was a Camp.

I asked the question that Elijah told me was the one I should be asking. "When are we?"

And when they told me—1943—I couldn't find the wherewithal to be surprised. I'd already seen a ghost out of time, traveled with him across a sci-fi landscape, been told about the future. Why not be landed in the past?

"Thanks for nothing, Elijah," I whispered.

Something—someone—whispered in my ear, the accent softening what he had to say. "Thanks for everything, Rebecca."

"I've done nothing," I whined.

"You will," he said.

And the women, hearing only me, answered, "None of us have done anything to put us in this place."

So my time in the Camp began. It was not Auschwitz or Dachau or Sobibor or Buchenwald or Treblinka, names I would have recognized at once.

"Where are we?"

"Near Lublin," one woman told me, her eyes a startling blue in that gray face.

I knew that name. Squinting my eyes, I tried to remember. And then I did. My great-grandmother had been born in Lublin.

"Do you know a . . ." I stopped. I only knew my great-grandmother's married name. Morewitz. What good would that do? Besides, she'd come over to America as a child anyway, and was dead long before I was born. I changed the sentence. "Do you know a good way to escape?"

They laughed, a gray kind of laugh. "And would we still be here if we did?" said the woman with the blue eyes. Her hand described a circle that took in the gray place.

I followed that circle with my eyes and saw a gray building, gray with settled ash. Ash. Something had been burned there. A lot of somethings. It was then I really understood what place Elijah had brought me to.

"So this a concentration camp?" I asked, though of course I already knew.

"There is nothing to concentrate on here, except putting one foot in front of the other," said the blue-eyed woman.

"And putting one bit of potato into your open mouth," said another.

"Not a concentration camp," said a third, "but a death camp."

"Hush," said the blue-eyed woman, looking over her shoulder.

I looked where she was looking but there was no one there to hear us.

"I have to get out of here," I said. Then bit my lip. "We all have to get out of here."

A gray child with eyes as black as buttons peeked from behind the skirts of the blue-eyed woman. She pointed to one of the buildings, which had an ominous metal door that was standing open. Like an open mouth waiting for those potatoes, I thought.

"That is the only way out," she said. Her face was a child's but her voice was old.

I took a deep breath, breathed in ash, and said, "We will not go that way. I promise."

The women moved away from me as one, leaving the child behind. One whispered hoarsely to me over her shoulder, "This is a place of broken promises. If you do not understand that, you will not live a moment longer." Then she said to the child, "Masha, it's time to go to bed. Morning comes too soon." But she was speaking to me as well.

The child slipped her cold gray hand in mine. "I believe your promise," she said. She looked at me with hope but did not smile, as if smiling was beyond hope, another country.

I smiled down at her and squeezed her hand. But I'd been a fool to promise her any such thing, and she was a fool to believe me.

"Elijah . . ." I began, "Elijah will help us." But he'd helped me into this mess, then disappeared. I realized with a sinking feeling that I was on my own here. Now. Whenever.

"Elijah the magician?" She scarcely seemed to breathe, staring at me with her black-button eyes.

I nodded, wondering what kind of magic could get us away from this terrible place and time.

Following the women, like a lamb after old ewes, the girl led me into a building that was filled with wide triple bunk beds. There were no sheets or pillows or blankets on the beds, only hard slats to lie upon. The only warmth at night came from the people who slept on either side. I had read about this, seen movies. What Jewish kid hadn't?

The cold was no worse than a bad camping trip. The slats

on the boards were like lying on the ground. But the smell—
there were three hundred or more women squeezed into that
building, with no bathing facilities but buckets of cold water.
No one had a change of clothing; some must have been living in
the same dresses for months. And those were the lucky ones, for
they were still alive.

Masha snuggled next to me, her body now a little furnace,
a warm spot against me. On the other side was the blue-eyed
woman who introduced herself as Eva. But that first night
my head raced with bizarre imaginings. Either I was crazy or
dreaming. Maybe I'd had some kind of psychotic break—like
my cousin Rachael, who one night after a rave party thought
she was in prison and tried to escape through a window, which
turned out to be on the third floor of their apartment building.
I just couldn't stop from wondering and I didn't sleep at all. A
mistake, it turned out. By morning I was exhausted. Besides,
sleep was the one real escape from that place. It was why the
women went to bed, side by side, as eagerly as if heading for a
party. After that there was the work.

Yes, there was work. That first morning they showed me. It
wasn't difficult work—not as difficult as the work the men
were doing, breaking stones on the other side of the barbed
wire—but still it broke the heart and spirit. We were to take
belongings from the suitcases inmates had brought with them,
separating out all the shoes in one pile, clothing in another on
long, wooden tables. Jewelry and money went into a third pile
that was given to the *blokova*—the head of the sorters—at day's
end. She had to give it to the soldiers who ran the camp. Then
there were family photographs and family Bibles and books of
commentary and books of poetry. Piles of women's wigs and a
huge pile of medicines, enough pills and potions for an army
of hypochondriacs. There were packets of letters and stacks of

documents, even official-looking contracts and certificates of graduation from law schools and medical schools. And then there was the pile of personal items: toothbrushes and hairbrushes and nail files and powder puffs. Everything that someone leaving home in a hurry and for the last time would carry.

I tried to think what I would have taken away with me had someone knocked on our door and said we had just minutes to pack up and leave for a resettlement camp, which is what all these people had been told. My diary and my iPod for sure, my underwear and several boxes of Tampax, toothbrush, hairbrush, blow-dryer, the book of poems my boyfriend had given me, a box of grease pencils and a sketchbook of course, and the latest Holly Black novel, which I hadn't had time to read yet. If that sounds pathetic, it's a whole lot less pathetic than the actual stuff we had to sort through.

And of course the entire time we were sorting, I alone knew what it all meant. That there were these same kinds of concentration camps throughout Poland and Germany. That six million Jews and six million other people were going to die in these awful places. And my having that knowledge was not going to help a single one of them.

Boy, it's going to be hard for me ever to go to a summer camp again, I thought. If I get out of here in one piece. That's when I began crying and calling out for Elijah.

"Who's Elijah?" a girl my age asked, putting an arm around me. "Your brother? Your boyfriend? Is he here? On the men's side?"

I turned, wiped my nose on my sleeve, and opened my mouth to tell her. When I realized how crazy it sounded, I said merely, "Something like that." And then I turned back to work.

The temptation to take a hairbrush or toothbrush or nail file back to the building was enormous.

But little Masha warned me that the guards searched everyone. "And if they find you with contraband," she said—without

117

stumbling on the big word, so I knew it was one everyone used—
"you go up in smoke."

The way she said that, so casually, but clearly understanding
what it meant, made my entire backbone go cold. I nodded. I
wasn't about to be cremated over a broken fingernail or messy
hair. I left everything on the long tables.

The days were long, the nights too short. I was a week at the
camp and fell into a kind of daze. I walked, I worked, I ate
when someone put a potato in my hand, but I had retreated
somewhere inside myself.

Masha often took my hand and led me about, telling me
what things to do. Saying, "Don't become a musselman." And
one day—a day as gray as the ash covering the buildings, gray
clouds scudding across the skies, I heard her.

"Musselman?" I asked.

She shrugged. A girl standing next to me in the work line
explained. "They are the shadows in the shadows. The ones who
give up. Who die before they are dead." She pointed out the
grimed window to a woman who looked like a walking skeleton
dressed in rags. "She is a musselman and will not need to go up
in smoke. She is already gone."

I shook my head vehemently. "I am not that."

Masha grabbed my hand and pulled. "Then wake up. You
promised."

And I remembered my promise. My foolish promise. I looked
out the window again and the woman was indeed gone. In her
place stood Elijah, staring at me. He put a finger to the side of
his nose and looked sad. The lines of his long face were repeated
in the length of his nose. There were shadows, dark blue with
streaks of brown, under his eyes. My hand sketched them.

"What are you doing?" Masha asked me.

"I need to paint something," I said.

"Foolishness," the girl next to me said.

"No—art is never foolish," I told her. "It is life-giving."

She laughed roughly and moved away from me as if I had something contagious.

I looked over the tables—the boxes of pills, the jewelry, the documents, the little baby shoes, the old women's handbags. And finally, I found a battered box of colored chalks some child must have carried with her. I picked the box up, grabbed up a marriage certificate, and went into a corner.

"What are you doing?" asked the *blokova*. "Get back here or I will have to report you."

But I paid no attention to her. I sat down on the filthy floor, turned the certificate over, and started to draw. With black chalk I outlined Elijah's body and the long oval of his face. I overlayered the outline with white till it was gray as ash. Having no gum eraser, I was careful with what I drew, yet not too careful, knowing that a good painting had to look effortless. At home I would have worked with Conté pastels. I had a box of twenty-four. But I used what I had, a box of twelve chalks, most of them in pieces. To keep my drawing from smudging, at home I would have coated the whole thing with a light misting of hairspray. But home was a long way—and a long time—from here. And hairspray was, I guessed, a thing of the future.

The *blokova* began to yell at me. "Get up! Get up!" And suddenly there was a flurry of legs around me, as some of the women were shouting the same.

Masha sneaked through the forest of legs and sat by me. "What are you doing?"

"I am making a picture of someone you need to see," I said. I sketched in the long nose, the black and wavy beard, and the closed-eye smile. I found a pink for his lips, then smudged them purposefully with fingers that still had black chalk on the tips.

The *blokova* had stopped yelling at me and was now yelling at the women who had formed a wall around Masha and me.

I kept drawing, using my fingers, the flat of my hand, my right thumb. I spit onto my left fingers and rubbed them down the line of his body. With the black chalk I filled in his long black coat. I used the white chalk for highlights, and to fill in around his black eyes. Brown chalk buffed in skin tones, which I then layered on top with the ashy gray.

"I see him. I see him," Masha said to me. "Is it Elijah?" She put her hand on the black coat, and her palm and small fingers became black at the tips.

Two of the women standing guard above us drew in a quick breath, and one said to the other, "I see him, too." It was Eva's voice. She knelt down and touched the paper.

Someone suddenly called my name. A man. I looked up. Elijah stood there, in the midst of all the women, though none of them seemed to notice him.

"Masha," I said urgently, "do you see him there?" I took her head in my hands and gently turned it so she was looking up as well.

"How did he get here?" she asked, pointing right at him. "In the women's side?"

Eva gasped at the sight of him.

But Elijah smiled, holding out his hands. I stood and took his right and Masha took his left. Eva grabbed hold of Masha's waist as if to drag her from me.

"There they are!" came the *blokova*'s shrill voice. "There!" The rest of the women had scattered back to the sorting tables, and Masha, Eva, and I were in her line of sight. Beside the *blokova* were two armed guards.

They pulled out their guns.

This time Elijah laughed. He dragged us toward him, and then we turned a corner in the middle of that room, sliding sideways into a familiar gray corridor.

Eva gasped again, then was silent, as if nothing more could surprise her. She held tight to Masha's waist.

120

And then we were flying through the flickering starlight and rushing meteors. A strange sun stood still overhead. As suddenly as they'd begun, the lights and sounds stopped when we came to the other side.

Masha dropped Elijah's hand and looked around, but Eva never let go of her waist.

This time I knew to ask the right question. "When are we?"

Elijah said, "We are still in the same year but five thousand miles away. We are in America now."

"We are in America then," I said.

He nodded. "Then," and he touched my shoulder. "Kiss the child, Rebecca. Assure her that she will be well taken care of here." His face seemed no longer gray, but blanched, as if the traveling had taken much of his energy.

"The woman, while not her own mother, will watch over her."

"Eva," I said. "First mother."

"Of course." We both nodded at the irony.

"But I can't just leave her," I said, though I saw the two of them had found a table of food and were happily filching stuff and hiding it in their pockets.

"You must. The child will have a fine life, a good family."

"Will I ever see her again?"

"No, Rebecca, she will be dead before you are born. Besides, you have pictures to paint. Of me." His smile was seductive, as if he were already posing for me.

I think my jaw dropped open. But not for long. "Why . . . you . . . you . . ." Suddenly I couldn't think of a word bad enough for him. Had this whole thing, this trip into the past, into that awful place, had it just been to satisfy his enormous ego? I stared at him. His face was positively gaunt, the eyes like a shark's, dead giving back no light. How could I ever have found him intriguing? My cheeks burned with shame. "I'll never paint that picture. Never."

He held up his hands as if to ward off the blow from my

words. "Hush, hush, Rebecca. The picture has to be painted. This is not about me but about you. Not about you but about your people. For the children of the great Jewish diaspora. To remind them of who they are. It will begin a renaissance in Judaism that will last well beyond your life and the lives of your great-great-grandchildren and to the twentieth generation."

I don't know what stunned me more—that a picture I was to paint someday would have that power, or that I would have great-great-grandchildren. I mean—I was only fifteen after all; who could think that far?

"But why me? And why Masha? Why Eva?"

He glanced over his shoulder at where Masha was sitting, now surrounded by a group of children her own age. She seemed to be playing, all that lost innocence returned to her in a single moment. Eva stood with her back to the wall, watching carefully, already Masha's guardian, her angel, her mother. Elijah turned back and cocked his head to one side. "Surely you have figured it out by now."

I looked at Masha again. She looked over at me and smiled. It was my sister's smile. How could I have not known—except Masha had never smiled before. Not in the camp, where there was nothing to smile at. Of course. My sister had been named after our great-grandmother, Mashanna.

"If she'd died in the camp, you would never have been born," Elijah said, even as he started to fade. "The picture never would have been painted. The great renaissance never to happen."

"But I was born . . ." I began.

"Born to paint," he said, before grabbing my hand and dragging us both sideways into the future and home.

THE FOXWIFE

It was the spring of the year. Blossoms sat like painted but-terflies on every tree. But the student Jiro did not enjoy the beauty. He was angry. It seemed he was always angry at some-thing. And he was especially angry because he had just been told by his teachers that the other students feared him and his rages.

"You must go to a far island," said the master of his school.

"Why?" asked Jiro angrily.

"I will tell you if you listen," said his master with great patience.

Jiro shut his mouth and ground his teeth but was otherwise silent.

"You must go to the furthest island you can find. An island where no other person lives. There you must study by yourself. And in the silence of your own heart you may yet find the peace you need."

Raging, Jiro packed his tatami mat, his book, and his brushes. He put them in a basket and tied the basket to his back. Though he was angry—with his master and with all the teachers and students in his school—he really *did* want to learn how to remain calm. And so he set out.

Sometimes he crossed bridges. Sometimes he waded rivers. Sometimes he took boats across the wild water. But at last he came to a small island where, the boatman assured him, no other person lived.

"Come once a week and bring me supplies," said Jiro, handing the boatman a coin. Then Jiro went inland and walked through the sparse woods until he came to a clearing in which he found a deserted temple.

"Odd," thought Jiro. "The boatman did not mention such a thing." He walked up the temple steps and was surprised to find the temple clean. He set his basket down in one corner, pulled out his mat, and spread it on the floor.

"This will be my home," he said. He said it out loud and there was an edge still to his voice.

For many days Jiro stayed on the island, working from first light till last. And though once in a while he became angry—because his brush would not write properly or because a dark cloud dared to hide the sun—for the most part he was content.

One day, when Jiro was in the middle of a particularly complicated text and having much trouble with it, he looked up and saw a girl walking across the clearing toward him.

Every few steps she paused and glanced around. She was not frightened but rather seemed alert, as if ready for flight.

Jiro stood up. "Go away," he called out, waving his arm.

The girl stopped. She put her head to one side as if considering him. Then she continued walking as before.

Jiro did not know what to do. He wondered if she were the boatman's daughter. Perhaps she had not heard him. Perhaps she was stupid. Perhaps she was deaf. She certainly did not belong on *his* island. He called out louder this time, "Go away. I am a student and must not be disturbed." He followed each statement with a movement of his arms.

But the girl did not go away and she did not stop. In fact, at his voice, she picked up her skirts and came toward him at a run.

Jiro was amazed. She ran faster than anyone he had ever seen, her dark russet hair streaming out behind her like a tail. In a moment she was at the steps of the temple.

"Go away!" cried Jiro for the third time.

The girl stopped, stared, and bowed.

Politeness demanded that Jiro return her bow. When he looked up again, she was gone.

Satisfied, Jiro smiled and turned back to his work. But there was the girl standing stone-still by his scrolls and brushes, her hands folded before her.

"I am Kitsune," she said. "I care for the temple."

Jiro could contain his anger no longer. "Go away," he screamed. "I must work alone. I came to this island because I was assured no other person lived here."

She stood as still as a stone in a river and let the waves of his rage break against her. Then she spoke. "No other person lives here. I am Kitsune. I care for the temple."

After that, storm as he might, there was nothing Jiro could do. The girl simply would not go away.

She did care for the temple—and Jiro as well. Once a week she appeared and swept the floors. She kept a bowl filled with fresh camellias by his bed. And once, when he had gone to get his supplies and tripped and hurt his legs, Kitsune found him and carried him to the temple on her back. After that, she came every day, as if aware Jiro needed constant attention. Yet she never spoke unless he spoke first, and even then her words were few.

Jiro wondered at her. She was little, lithe, and light. She moved with a peculiar grace. Every once in a while, he would see her stop and put her head to one side in that attitude of listening. He never heard what it was she heard, and he never dared ask.

At night she disappeared. One moment she would be there and the next moment gone. But in the morning Jiro would wake to find her curled in sleep at this feet. She would not say where she had been.

So spring passed, and summer too. Jiro worked well in the quiet world Kitsune helped him maintain, and he found a kind of peace beginning to bud in his heart.

On the first day of fall, with leaves being shaken from the trees by the wind, Jiro looked up from his books. He saw that Kitsune sat on the steps trembling.

"What is it?" he asked.

"The leaves. Aieee, the leaves," she cried. Then she jumped up and ran down to the trees. She leaped and played with the leaves as they fell about her. They caught in her hair. She blew them off her face. She rolled in them. She put her face to the ground and sniffed the dirt. Then, as if a fever had suddenly left her, she was still. She stood up, brushed off her clothing, smoothed her hair, and came back to sit quietly on the steps again.

Jiro was enchanted. He had never seen any woman like this before. He left his work and sat down on the steps beside her. Taking her hand in his, he stroked it thoughtfully, then brought it slowly to his cheek. Her hand was warm and dry.

"We must be married," he said at last. "I would have you with me always."

"Always? What is always?" asked Kitsune. She tried to pull away.

Jiro held her hand tightly and would not let her go. And after a while she agreed.

The boatman took them across to the mainland, where they found a priest who married them at once, though he smiled behind his hand at their haste. Jiro was supremely happy and he knew that Kitsune must be, too, though all the way in the boat going there and back again, she shuddered and would not look out across the waves.

That night Kitsune shared the tatami mat with Jiro. When the moon was full and the night whispered softly about the temple, Jiro awoke. He turned to look at Kitsune, his bride. She was not there.

"Kitsune," he called out fearfully. He sat up and looked about. He could not see her anywhere. He got up and searched around the temple, but she was not to be found. At last he fell asleep, sitting on the temple steps. When he awoke again at dawn, Kitsune was curled in sleep on the mat.

"Where were you last night?" he demanded.

"Where I should be," she said and would say no more.

Jiro felt anger flowering inside, so he turned sharply from her and went to his books. But he did not try to calm himself. He fed his rage silently. All day he refused to speak. At night, exhausted by his own anger, he fell asleep before dark. He woke at midnight to find Kitsune gone.

Jiro knew he had to stay awake until she returned. A little before dawn he saw her running across the clearing. She ran up the temple steps and did not seem to be out of breath. She came right to the mat, surprised to see Jiro awake.

Jiro waited for her explanation, but instead of speaking she began her morning chores. She had fresh camellias in her hands, which she put in a bowl as if nothing were wrong.

Jiro sat up. "Where do you go at night?" he asked. "What do you do?"

Kitsune did not answer.

Jiro leaped up and came over to her. He took her by the shoulders and began to shake her. "Where? Where do you go?" he cried.

Kitsune dropped the bowl of flowers and it shattered. The water spread out in little islands of puddles on the floor. She looked down and her hair fell around her shoulders, hiding her face.

Jiro could not look at the trembling figure so obviously terrified of him. Instead, he bent to pick up the pieces of the bowl.

127

He saw his own face mirrored a hundred times in the spilled drops. Then he saw something else. Instead of Kitsune's face or her russet hair, he saw the sharp-featured head of a fox reflected there. The fox's little pointed ears were twitching. Out of its dark eyes tears began to fall.

Jiro looked up but there was no fox. Only Kitsune, beginning to weep, trembling at the sight of him, unable to move. And then he knew. She was a *nogitsone*, a were-fox, who could take the shape of a beautiful woman. But the *nogitsone's* reflection in the water was always that of a beast.

Suddenly Jiro's anger, fueled by his terror, knew no bounds. "You are not human," he cried. "Monster, wild thing, demon, beast. You will rip me or tear me if I let you stay. Some night you will gnaw upon my bones. Go away."

As he spoke, Kitsune fell to her hands and knees. She shook herself once, then twice. Her hair seemed to flow over her body, covering her completely. Then twitching her ears once, the vixen raced down the temple steps, across the meadow, and out of sight.

Jiro stood and watched for a long, long time. He thought he could see the red flag of her tail many hours after she had gone.

The snows came early that year, but the season was no colder than Jiro's heart. Every day he thought he heard the barking of a fox in the woods beyond the meadow, but he would not call it in. Instead he stood on the steps and cried out, "Away. Go away." At night he dreamed of a woman weeping close by his mat. In his sleep he called out, "Away. Go away."

Then when winter was full and the nights bitter cold, the sounds ceased. The island was deadly still. In his heart Jiro knew the fox was gone for good. Even his anger was gone, guttered in the cold like a candle. What had seemed so certain to him, in the heat of his rage, was certain no more.

He wondered over and over which had been human and which had been beast. He even composed a haiku on it.

Pointed ears, red tail.
Wife covered in fox's skin,
The beast hides within.

He said it over many times to himself but was never satisfied with it.

Spring came suddenly, a tiny green blade pushing through the snow. And with it came a strange new sound. Jiro woke to it, out of a dream of snow. He followed the sound to the temple steps and saw prints in the dust of white. Sometimes they were fox, sometimes girl, as if the creature who made them could not make up its mind.

"Kitsune," Jiro called out impulsively. Perhaps she had not died after all.

He looked out across the meadow and thought he saw again that flag of red. But the sound that had wakened him came once more, from behind. He turned, hoping to see Kitsune standing again by the mat with the bowl of camellias in her hands. Instead, by his books, he saw a tiny bundle of russet fur. He went over and knelt by it. Huddled together for warmth were two tiny kit foxes.

For a moment Jiro could feel the anger starting inside him. He did not want these two helpless, mewling things. He wanted Kitsune. Then he remembered that he had driven her away. Away. And the memory of that long, cold winter without her put out the budding flames of his new rage.

He reached out and put his hands on the foxlings. At his touch, they sprang apart on wobbly legs, staring up at him with dark, discerning eyes. They trembled so, he was afraid they might fall.

"There, there," he crooned to them. "This big, rough beast will

129

not hurt you. Come. Come to me." He let them sniff both his hands, and when their trembling ceased, he picked them up and cradled them against his body, letting them share his warmth. First one, then the other, licked his fingers. This so moved Jiro that, without meaning to, he began to cry.

The tears dropped onto the muzzles of the foxlings and they looked as if they, too, were weeping. Then, as Jiro watched, the kits began to change. The features of a human child slowly superimposed themselves on each fox face. Sighing, they snuggled closer to Jiro, closed their eyes, put their thumbs in their mouths, and slept.

Jiro smiled. Walking very carefully, as if afraid each step might jar the babies awake, he went down the temple steps. He walked across the clearing leaving man-prints in the unmarked snow. Slowly, calmly, all anger gone from him, he moved toward the woods where he knew Kitsune waited. He would find her before evening came again.

THE FAERY FLAG

Long ago when the wind blew from one corner of Skye to another without ever encountering a house higher than a tree, the faery folk lived on the land and they were called the *Daoine Sithe*, the Men of Peace. They loved the land well and shepherded its flocks, and never a building did they build that could not be dismantled in a single night or put up again in a single day.

But then human folk set foot upon the isles and scoured them with their rough shoeing. And before long both rock and tree were in the employ of men; the land filled with forts and houses, byres and pens. Boats plowed the seas and netted the fish. Stones were piled up for fences between neighbors.

The *Daoine Sithe* were not pleased, not pleased at all. An edict went out from the faery chief: *Have nothing to do with this humankind.*

And for year upon year it was so.

Now one day, the young laird of the MacLeod clan—Jamie was his name—walked out beyond his manor seeking a brachet hound lost outside in the night. It was his favorite hound, as old as he, which—since he was just past fifteen years—was quite old indeed.

He called its name. "Leoid. Leeeeeeoid." The wind sent back the name against his face but the dog never answered.

The day was chill, the wind was cold, and a white mist swirled about the young laird. But many days on Skye are thus, and he thought no more about the chill and cold than that he must find his old hound lest it die.

Jamie paid no heed to where his feet led him, through the bogs and over the hummocks. This was his land, after all, and he knew it well. He could not see the towering crags of the Black Cuillins, though he knew they were there. He could not hear the seals calling from the bay. Leoid was all he cared about. A Macleod takes care of his own.

So without knowing it, he crossed over a strange, low, stone *drochit*, a bridge the likes of which he would never have found on a sunny day, for it was the bridge into Faerie.

No sooner had he crossed over than he heard his old dog barking. He would have known that sound were there a hundred howling hounds.

"Leoid!" he called. And the dog ran up to him, its hind end wagging, eager as a pup, so happy it was to see him. It had been made young again in the land of Faerie.

Jamie gathered the dog in his arms and was just turning to go home when he heard a girl calling from behind him.

"Leoid. Leoid." Her voice was as full of longing as his own had been just moments before.

He turned back, the dog still in his arms, and the fog lifted. Running toward him was the most beautiful girl he had ever seen. Her dark hair was wild with curls, her black eyes wide, her mouth generous and smiling.

"Boy, you have found my dog. Give it to me."

Now that was surely no way to speak to the young laird of the Macleods, he who would someday be the chief. But the girl did not seem to know him. And surely he did not know the girl, though he knew everyone under his father's rule.

"This is my dog," said Jamie.

The girl came closer and put out her hand. She touched him on his bare arm. Where her hand touched, he felt such a shock, he thought he would die, but of love not of fear. Yet he did not.

"It is my dog now, Jamie Macleod," she said. "It has crossed over the bridge. It has eaten the food of the *Daoine Sithe* and drunk our honey wine. If you bring it back to your world it will die at once and crumble into dust."

The young laird set the dog down and it frolicked about his feet. He put his hand into the girl's but was not shocked again.

"I will give it back to you for your name—and a kiss," he said.

"Be warned," answered the girl.

"I know about faery kisses," said Jamie, "but I am not afraid. And as you know my name, it is only fair that I should know yours."

"What we consider fair, you do not, young laird," she said. But she stood on tiptoe and kissed him on the brow. "Do not come back across the bridge, or you will break your parents' hearts."

He handed her the sprig of juniper from his bonnet.

She kissed the sprig as well and put it in her hair. "My name is Aizel and like the red hot cinder, I burn what I touch." Then she whistled for the dog and they disappeared at once into the mist.

Jamie put his hand to his brow where Aizel had kissed him, and indeed she had burned him, it was still warm and sweet to his touch.

Depite the faery girl's warning, Jamie MacLeod looked for the bridge not once but many times. He left off fishing to search for it, and interrupted his hunting to search for it; and often he left his bed when the mist was thick to seek it. But even in the mist and the rain and the fog he could not find it. Yet he never stopped longing for the bridge to the girl.

His mother and father grew worried. They guessed by the mark on his brow what had occurred. So they gave great parties and threw magnificent balls that in this way the young laird might meet a human girl and forget the girl of the *Daoine Sithe.*

But never was there a girl he danced with that he danced with again. Never a girl he held that he held for long. Never a girl he kissed that he did not remember Aizel at the bridge. As time went on, his mother and father grew so desperate for him to give the MacLeods an heir, that they would have let him marry any young woman at all, even a faery maid.

On the eve of Jamie's twenty-first birthday, there was a great gathering of the clan at Dunvegan Castle. All the lights were set out along the castle wall and they twinned themselves down in the bay below.

Jamie walked the ramparts and stared out across the bogs and drums. "Oh Aizel," he said with a great sigh, "if I could but see you one more time. One more time and I'd be content."

And then he thought he heard the barking of a dog.

Now there were hounds in the castle and hounds in the town and hounds who ran every day under his horse's hooves. But he knew that particular call.

"Leoid!" he whispered to himself. He raced down the stairs and out the great doors with a torch in his hand, following the barking across the bog.

It was a misty, moisty evening, but he seemed to know the way. And he came quite soon to the cobbled bridge that he had so long sought. For a moment he hesitated, then went on.

There, in the middle, not looking a day older than when he

had seen her six years before, stood Aizel in her green gown. Leoid was by her side.

"Into your majority, young laird," said Aizel. "I called to wish you the best."

"It is the best, now that I can see you," Jamie said. He smiled. "And my old dog."

Aizel smiled back. "No older than when last you saw us."

"I have thought of you every day since you kissed me," said Jamie. "And longed for you every night. Your brand still burns on my brow."

"I warned you of faery kisses," said Aizel.

He lifted his bonnet and pushed away his fair hair to show her the mark.

"I have thought of you, too, young laird," said Aizel. "And how the MacLeods have kept the peace in this unpeaceful land. My chief says I may bide with you for a while."

"How long a while?" asked Jamie.

"A faery while," replied Aizel "A year or an heir, whichever comes first."

"A year is such a short time," Jamie said.

"I can make it be forever," Aizel answered.

With that riddle Jamie was content. And they walked back to Dunvegan Castle hand in hand, though they left the dog behind.

If Aizel seemed less fey in the starlight, Jamie did not mind. If he was only human, she did not seem to care. Nothing really mattered but his hand in hers, her hand in his, all the way back to his home.

The chief of the MacLeods was not pleased and his wife was not happy with the match. But that Jamie smiled and was content made them hold their tongues. So the young laird and the faery maid were married that night and bedded before day.

And in the evening Aizel came to them and said, "The MacLeods shall have their heir."

The days went fast and slow, warm and cold, and longer than a human it took for the faery girl to bear a child. But on the last day of the year she had lived with them, Aizel was brought to labor till with a great happy sigh she birthed a beautiful babe.

"A boy!" the midwife cried out, standing on a chair and showing the child so that all the MacLeods might see.

A great cheer ran around the castle then. "An heir. An heir to the MacLeods."

Jamie was happy for that, but happier still that his faery wife was well. He bent to kiss her brow.

"A year or an heir, that was all I could promise. But I have given you forever," she said. "The MacLeods shall prosper and Dunvegan will never fall."

Before he could say a word in return, she had vanished and the bed was bare, though her outline could be seen on the linens for a moment more.

The cheer was still echoing along the stone passageways as the midwife carried the babe from room to room to show him to all the clan. But the young laird of the MacLeods put his head in his hands and wept.

Later that night, when the fires were high in every hearth and blackberry wine filled every cup; when the harp and fiddle rang throughout Dunvegan with their runes; when the bards' mouths swilled with whisky and swelled with the old songs; and even the nurse was dancing with her man, the young laird Jamie MacLeod walked the castle ramparts seven times round, mourning for his lost faery wife.

The youngest laird of the MacLeods lay in his cradle all alone.

So great was the celebration that no one was watching him.

And in the deepest part of the night, he kicked off his blankets as babies often do and he cried out with the cold.

But no one came to cover him. Not the nurse dancing with her man, nor his grandam listening to the runes, nor his grandfather drinking with his men, nor his father on the castle walk. No one heard the poor wee babe crying with the cold.

It was a tiny cry, a thin bit of sound threaded out into the dark. It went over hillock and hill, over barrow and bog, crossed the cobbled *drochit*, and wound its way into Faerie itself.

Now, they were celebrating in the faery world as well, not for the birth of the child but for the return of their own. There was feasting and dancing and the singing of runes. They drank honey wine, played on faery pipes, and all around was the high, sweet laughter of the *Daoine Sithe*.

But in all that fine company, Aizel alone did not sing and dance. She sat in her great chair with her arms around her brachet hound. If there were tears in her eyes, you would not have known it, for the *Daoine Sithe* do not cry, and besides the hound had licked away every one. But she heard that tiny sound as any mother would. Distracted, she stood.

"What is it, my daughter?" asked the great chief of the *Daoine Sithe* when he saw her stand, when he saw a single tear that Leoid had not had time to lick away. But before any of the fey could tell her no, Aizel ran from the faery hall, the dog at her heels. She raced across the bridge, herself as insubstantial as the mist.

And behind her came the faery troops. And the dog.

The company of fey stopped at the edge of the bridge and watched Aizel go. Leoid followed right after. But no sooner had the dog's legs touched the earth on the other side than it crumbled into dust.

Aizel hesitated not a moment, but followed that thread of sound, winding her back into the world of men. She walked over bog and barrow, over hill and hillock, through the great wooden doors and up the castle stairs.

When she entered the baby's room, he was between one breath and another.

"There, there," Aizel said, leaning over the cradle and covering him with her shawl, "thy mama's here." She rocked him till he fell back asleep, warm and content. Then she kissed him on the brow, leaving a tiny mark there for all to see, and vanished in the morning light.

The nurse found the babe sleeping soundly well into the day. He was wrapped in a cloth of stranger's weave. His thumb was in his mouth, along with a piece of the shawl. She did not know how the cloth got there, nor did his grandfather, the Great MacLeod. If his grandmother guessed, she did not say.

But the young laird Jamie knew. He knew that Aizel had been drawn back across the bridge by her son's crying, as surely as he had first been led to her by the barking of his hound.

"Love calls to love," he whispered softly to his infant son as he held him close. "And the fey, like the MacLeods, take care of their own."

The faery shawl still hangs on the wall at Dunvegan Castle on the Isle of Skye. Only now it is called a Faery Flag and the MacLeods carry it foremost into battle. I have seen it there. Like this story, it is a tattered remnant of stranger's weave and as true and warming as you let it be.

ONE OLD MAN, WITH SEALS

The day was clear and sharp and fresh when I first heard the seals. They were crying, a symphony of calls. The bulls coughed a low bass. The pups had a mewing whimper, not unlike the cry of a human child. I heard them as I ran around the lighthouse, the slippery sands making my ritual laps more exercise than I needed, more than the doctor said a seventy-five-year-old woman should indulge in. Of course he didn't say it quite like that. Doctors never do. He said: *"A woman of your age . . ."* and left it for me to fill in the blanks. It was a physician's pathetically inept attempt at tact. Any lie told then would be mine, not his.

However, as much as doctors know about blood and bones, they never do probe the secret recesses of the heart. And my heart told me that I was still twenty-five. Well, forty-five, anyway. And I had my own methods of gray liberation.

I had bought a lighthouse, abandoned as unsafe and no longer viable by the Coast Guard. (Much as I had been by the county library system. One abandoned and no longer viable children's librarian, greatly weathered and worth one gold watch, no more.)

I spent a good part of my savings renovating, building book-cases, and having a phone line brought in. And making sure the electricity would run my refrigerator, freezer, hi-fi, and TV set. I am a solitary, not a primitive, and my passion is the news. With in-town cable, I could have watched twenty-four hours a day. But in my lighthouse, news magazines and books of history took up the slack.

Used to a life of discipline and organization, I kept to a rigid schedule even though there was no one to impress with my dedication. But I always sang as I worked. As some obscure poet has written, "No faith can last that never sings." Up at daylight, a light breakfast while watching the morning news-casters, commercials a perfect time to scan *The New Yorker* or *Time*. Then off for my morning run. Three laps seemed just right to get lungs and heart working. Then back inside to read until my favorite nephew called; he is a classics scholar at the university and I have marked him down in the will to get all my books and subscriptions—and the lighthouse. The others will split the little bit of money I have left. Since I have been a collector of fine and rare history books for over fifty years, my nephew will be well off, though he doesn't know it yet.

The phone rings between ten and eleven every morning, and it is always Mike. He wants to be sure I'm still alive and kicking. The one time I had flu and was too sick to answer the phone, he was over like a shot in that funny lobster boat of his. I could hear him pounding up the stairs and shouting my name. He even had his friend, Dr. Lil Meyer, with him. A *real* doctor, he calls her, not his kind, "all letters and no learning."

They gave me plenty of juice and spent several nights, though it meant sleeping on the floor for both of them. But they didn't seem to mind. And when I was well again, they took off in the lobster boat, waving madly and leaving a wake as broad as a city sidewalk.

For a doctor, Lil Meyer wasn't too bad. She seemed to know

about the heart. She said to me, whispered so Mike wouldn't hear her, just before she left, "You're sounder than any seventy-five-year-old I've ever met, Aunt Lyssa. I don't know if it's the singing or the running or the news. But whatever it is, just keep doing it. And Mike and I will keep tabs on you."

The day I heard the seals singing, I left off my laps and went investigating. It never does to leave a mystery unsolved at my age. Curiosity alone would keep me awake, and I need my sleep. Besides, I knew that the only singing done on these shores recently was my own. Seals never came here, hadn't for at least as long as I had owned the lighthouse. And according to the records, which the Coast Guard had neglected to collect when they condemned the place, leaving me with a week-long feast of old news, there hadn't been any seals for the last one hundred years. Oh, there had been plenty else—wrecks and flotsam. Wrackweed wound around the detritus of civilization: Dixie cups, beer cans, pop bottles, and newsprint. And a small school of whales had beached themselves at the north tip of the beach in 1957 and had to be hauled off by an old whaling vessel, circa 1923, pressed into service. But no seals.

The lighthouse sits way out on a tip of land, some sixteen miles from town, and at high tide it is an island. There have been some minor skirmishes over calling it a wildlife preserve, but the closest the state has come to that has been to post some yellow signs that have weathered to the color of old mustard and are just as readable. The southeast shore is the milder shore, sheltered from the winds and battering tides. The little bay that runs between Lighthouse Point and the town of Tarryton-Across-the-Bay, as the early maps have it, is always filled with pleasure boats. By half May, the bigger yachts of the summer folk start to arrive, great white swans gliding serenely in while the smaller, colorful boats of the year-rounders squawk and gabble and gawk at them, darting about like so many squabbling mallards or grebes.

The singing of the seals came from the rougher northwest shore. So I headed that way, no longer jogging because it was a rocky run. If I slipped and fell, I might lie with a broken hip or arm for hours or days before Mike finally came out to find me. *If* he found me at all. So I picked my way carefully around the granite outcroppings.

I had only tried that northern route once or twice before. Even feeling twenty-five or forty-five, I found myself defeated by the amount of rock-climbing necessary to go the entire way. But I kept it up this time because after five minutes the seal song had become louder, more melodic, compelling. And, too, an incredible smell had found its way into my nose.

I say *found* because one of the sadder erosions of age has been a gradual loss of my sense of smell. Oh, really sharp odors eventually reach me, and I am still sensitive to the intense prickles of burned wood. But the subtle tracings of a good liqueur or the shadings of a wine's bouquet are beyond me. And recently, to my chagrin, I burned up my favorite teakettle because the whistle had failed and I didn't smell the metal melting until it was too late.

However, this must have been a powerful scent to have reached me out near the ocean, with the salt air blowing at ten miles an hour. Not a really strong wind, as coastal winds go, but strong enough.

And so I followed my ear—and my nose.

They led me around one last big rock, about the size of a small Minke whale. And it was then I saw the seals. They were bunched together and singing their snuffling hymns. Lying in their midst was an incredibly dirty bum, asleep and snoring.

I almost turned back then, but the old man let out a groan. Only then did it occur to me what a bizarre picture it was. Here was a bearded patriarch of the seals—for they were quite unafraid of him—obviously sleeping off a monumental drunk. In fact I had no idea where he had gotten and consumed his liquor or how he had ever made it to that place, sixteen miles from the nearest town by land, and a long swim by sea. There was no boat to be seen. He lay as if dropped from above, one arm flung over a large bull seal which acted like a pup, snuggling close to him and pushing at his armpit with its nose.

At that I laughed out loud and the seals, startled by the noise, fled down the shingle toward the sea, humping their way across the rocks and pebbly beach to safety in the waves. But the old man did not move.

It was then that I wondered if he were not drunk but rather injured, flung out of the sea by the tide, another bit of flotsam on my beach. So I walked closer.

The smell was stronger, and I realized it was not the seals I had been smelling. It was the old man. After years of dealing with children in libraries—from babies to young adults—I had learned to identify a variety of smells, from feces to vomit to pot. And though my sense of smell was almost defunct, my memory was not. But that old man smelled of none of the things I could easily recognize, or of anything the land had to offer. He smelled of seals and salt and water, like a wreck that had long lain on the bottom of the ocean suddenly uncovered by a freak storm. He smelled of age, incredible age. I could literally smell the centuries on him. If I was seventy-five, he had to be four, no forty times that. That was fanciful of me. Ridiculous. But it was my immediate and overwhelming thought.

I bent over him to see if I could spot an injury, something I might reasonably deal with. His gray-white, matted hair was thin and lay over his scalp like the scribbles of a mad artist. His beard was braided with seaweed, and shells lay entangled in the briery locks. His fingernails were encrusted with dirt. Even the lines of his face were deeply etched with a greenish grime. But I saw no wounds.

His clothes were an archeological dig. Around his neck were the collars of at least twenty shirts. Obviously he put on one shirt and wore it until there was nothing left but the ring, then simply donned another. His trousers were a similar ragbag of colors and weaves, and only the weakness of waistbands had kept him from having accumulated a lifetime supply. He was barefoot. The nails on his toes were as yellow as jingle shells, and so long they curled over each toe like a sheath.

He moaned again, and I touched him on the shoulder, hoping to shake him awake. But when I touched him, his shoulder burst into flames. Truly. Little fingers of fire spiked my palm. Spontaneous combustion was something I had only read about: a heap of oily rags in a hot closet leading to fire. But his rags were not oily, and the weather was a brisk 68 degrees, with a good wind blowing.

I leaped back and screamed and he opened one eye.

The flames subsided, went out. He began to snore again.

The bull seals came out of the water and began a large, irregular circle around us. So I stood up and turned to face them.

"Shoo!" I said, taking off my watch cap. I wear it to keep my ears warm when I run. "Shoo!" Flapping the cap at them and stepping briskly forward, I challenged the bulls.

They broke circle and scattered, moving about a hundred feet away in that awkward shuffling gait they have on land. Then they turned and stared at me. The younger seals and the females remained in the water, a watchful bobbing.

I went back to the old man. "Come on," I said. "I know you're awake now. Be sensible. Tell me if anything hurts or aches. I'll help you if you need help. And if not—I'll just go away."

He opened the one eye again and cleared his throat. It sounded just like a bull seal's cough. But he said nothing.

I took a step closer and he opened his other eye. They were as blue as the ocean over white sand. Clear and clean, the only clean part of him.

I bent over to touch his shoulder again, and this time the material of his shirt began to smolder under my hand.

"That's a trick," I said. "Or hypnotism. Enough of that."

He smiled. And the smoldering ceased. Instead, his shoulder seemed to tumble under my hand, like waves, like torrents, like a full high tide. My hand and sleeve were suddenly wet; sloppily, thoroughly wet.

I clenched my teeth. Mike always said that New England spinsters are so full of righteous fortitude they might be mistaken for mules. And my forebears go back seven generations in Maine. Maybe I didn't understand what was happening, but that was no excuse for lack of discipline and not holding on. I held on.

The old man sighed.

Under my hand, the shoulder changed again, the material and then the flesh wriggling and humping. A tail came from somewhere under his armpit and wrapped quickly around my wrist.

Now, as a librarian in a children's department I have had my share of snake programs, and reptiles as such do not frighten me. Spiders I am not so sanguine about. But snakes are not a phobia of mine. Except for a quick intake of breath, brought on by surprise, not fear, I did not lose my grip.

The old man gave a *humph*, a grudging sound of approval, closed his eyes, and roared like a lion. I have seen movies. I have watched documentaries. I know the difference. All of Africa was in that sound.

I laughed. "All right, whoever you are, enough games," I said. "What's going on?"

He sat up slowly, opened those clean blue eyes, and said, "Wrong question, my dear." He had a slight accent I could not identify. "You are supposed to ask, 'What *will* go on?'"

Angrily, I let go of his shoulder. "Obviously you need no help. I'm leaving."

"Yes," he said. "I know." Then, incredibly, he turned over on his side. A partial stuttering snore began at once. Then a whiff of that voice came at me again. "But of course you *will* be back."

"Of course I *will* not!" I said huffily. As an exit line it lacked both dignity and punch, but it was all I could manage as I walked off. Before I had reached the big rock, the seals had settled down around him again. I know because they were singing their lullabies over the roar of his snore—and I peeked. The smell followed me most of the way back home.

Once back in the lighthouse, a peculiar lethargy claimed me. I seemed to know something I did not want to know. A story suddenly recalled. I deliberately tried to think of everything but the old man. I stared out the great windows, a sight that always delighted me. Sky greeted me, a pallid slate of sky written on by guillemots and punctuated by gulls. A phalanx of herring gulls sailed by followed by a pale ghostly shadow that I guessed might be an Iceland gull. Then nothing but sky. I don't believe I even blinked.

The phone shrilled.

I picked it up and could not even manage a hello until Mike's voice recalled me to time and place.

"Aunt Lyssa. Are you there? Are you all right? I tried to call before and there was no answer."

I snapped myself into focus. "Yes, Mike. I'm fine. Tell me a story."

There was a moment of crackling silence at the other end. Then a throat clearing. "A story? Say, are you sure you're all right?"

"I'm sure."

"Well, what do you mean—a story?"

I held on to the phone with both hands as if to coax his answer. As if I had foresight. I knew his answer already. "About an old man, with seals," I said.

Silence.

"You're the classics scholar, Mike. Tell me about Proteus."

"Try Bulfinch." He said it for a laugh. He had long ago taught me that Bulfinch was not to be trusted, for he had allowed no one to edit him, had made mistakes. "Why do you need to know?"

"A poem," I said. "A reference." No answer, but answer enough.

The phone waited a heartbeat, then spoke in Mike's voice. "One old man, with seals, coming up. One smelly old god, with seals, Aunt Lyssa. He was a shape-changer with the ability to foretell the future, only you had to hold on to him through all his changes to make him talk. Ulysses was able . . ."

"I remember," I said. "I know."

I hung up. The old man had been right. Of course I would be back. In the morning.

In the morning I gathered up pad, pencils, a sweater, and the flask of Earl Grey tea I had prepared. I stuffed them all into my old backpack. Then I started out as soon as light had bleached a line across the rocks.

Overhead a pair of laughing gulls wrote along the wind's pages with their white-bordered wings. I could almost read their messages, so clear and forceful was the scripting. Even the rocks signed to me, the water murmured advice. It was as if the world was a storyteller, a singer of old songs. The seas along the coast, usually green-black, seemed wine-dark and full of a churning energy. I did not need to hurry. I knew he would be there. Sometimes foresight has as much to do with reason as with magic.

The whale rock signaled me, and the smell lured me on. When I saw the one, and the other found my nose, I smiled. I made the last turning, and there he was—asleep and snoring.

I climbed down carefully and watched the seals scatter before me, then I knelt by his side.

I shook my head. Here was the world's oldest, dirtiest, smelliest man. A bum vomited up by the ocean. The centuries layered on his skin. And here was I thinking he was a god.

Then I shrugged and reached out to grab his shoulder. Fire. Water. Snake. Lion. I would outwait them all.

Of course I knew the question I would *not* ask. No one my age needs to know the exact time of dying. But the other questions, the ones that deal with the days and months and years after I would surely be gone, I would ask them all. And he, being a god who cannot lie about the future, must tell me everything, everything that is going to happen in the world.

After all, I am a stubborn old woman. And a curious one. And I have always had a passion for the news.

SLEEPING UGLY

Princess Miserella was a beautiful princess if you counted her eyes and nose and mouth and all the way down to her toes. But inside, where it was hard to see, she was the meanest, wickedest, and most worthless princess around. She liked stepping on dogs. She kicked kittens. She threw pies in the cook's face. And she never—not even once—said thank you or please. And besides, she told lies.

In that very same kingdom, in the middle of the woods, lived a poor orphan named Plain Jane. She certainly was. Her hair was short and turned down. Her nose was long and turned up. And even if they had been the other way round, she would not have been a great beauty. But she loved animals, and she was always kind to strange old ladies.

One day Princess Miserella rode out of the palace in a huff. (A huff is not a kind of carriage. It is a kind of temper tantrum. Her usual kind.) She rode and rode and rode, looking beautiful as always, even with her hair in tangles. She rode right into the middle of the woods and was soon lost. She got off her horse and slapped it sharply for losing the way. The horse said

149

nothing, but ran right back home. It had known the way back all the time, but it was not about to tell Miserella.

So there was the princess, lost in a dark wood. It made her look even prettier.

Suddenly, Princess Miserella tripped over a little old lady asleep under a tree.

Now, little old ladies who sleep under trees deep in the dark wood are almost always fairies in disguise. Miserella guessed who the little old lady was, but she didn't care. She kicked the old lady on the bottoms of her feet. "*Get up and take* me *home,*" said the princess.

So the old lady got to her feet very slowly—for the bottoms now hurt. She took Miserella by the hand. (She used only her thumb and second finger to hold Miserella's hand. Fairies know quite a bit about *that* kind of princess.) They walked and walked even deeper into the wood. There they found a little house. It was Plain Jane's house. It was dreary. The floors sank. The walls stank. The roof leaked even on sunny days. But Jane made the best of it. She planted roses around the door. And little animals and birds made their home with her. (That may be why the floors sank and the walls stank, but no one complained.)

"This is not *my* home," said Miserella with a sniff.

"Nor mine," said the fairy.

They walked in without knocking, and there was Jane.

"It is mine," she said.

The princess looked at Jane, down and up, up and down.

"Take me home," said Miserella, "and as a reward I will make you my maid."

Plain Jane smiled a thin little smile. It did not improve her looks or the princess's mood.

"Some reward," said the fairy to herself. Out loud she said, "If you could take *both* of us home, I could probably squeeze out a wish or two."

"Make it three," said Miserella to the fairy, "and *I'll* get us home."

Plain Jane smiled again. The birds began to sing.

"My home is your home," said Jane.

"I like your manners," said the fairy. "And for that good thought, I'll give three wishes to you."

Princess Miserella was not pleased. She stamped her foot.

"Do that again," said the fairy, taking a pine wand from her pocket, "and I'll turn your foot to stone." Just to be mean, Miserella stamped her food again. It turned to stone.

Plain Jane sighed. "My first wish is that you change her foot back."

The fairy made a face. "I like your manners, but not your taste," she said to Jane.

"Still, a wish is a wish."

The fairy moved the wand. The princess shook her foot. It was no longer made of stone.

"Guess my foot fell asleep for a moment," said Miserella. She really liked to lie. "Besides," the princess said, "that was a stupid way to waste a wish."

The fairy was angry.

"Do not call someone stupid unless you have been properly introduced," she said, "or are a member of the family."

"*Stupid, stupid, stupid,*" said Miserella. She hated to be told what to do.

"Say stupid again," warned the fairy, holding up her wand, "and I will make toads come out of your mouth."

"*Stupid!*" shouted Miserella.

As she said it, a great big toad dropped out of her mouth.

"Cute," said Jane, picking up the toad, "and I *do* like toads, but . . ."

"But?" asked the fairy.

Miserella did not open her mouth. Toads were among her least favorite animals.

151

"But," said Plain Jane, "my second wish is that you get rid of the mouth toads."

"She's lucky it wasn't mouth elephants," mumbled the fairy.

She waved the pine wand. Miserella opened her mouth slowly. Nothing came out but her tongue. She pointed it at the fairy.

Princess Miserella looked miserable. That made her look beautiful, too.

"I definitely have had enough," she said. "I want to go home." She grabbed Plain Jane's arm.

"Gently, gently," said the old fairy, shaking her head. "If you aren't gentle with magic, none of us will go anywhere."

"You can go where you want," said Miserella, "but there is only one place I want to go."

"*To sleep!*" said the fairy, who was now much too mad to remember to be gentle. She waved her wand so hard she hit the wall of Jane's house.

The wall broke.

The wand broke.

And before Jane could make her third wish, all three of them were asleep.

It was one of those famous hundred-year naps that need a prince and a kiss to end them. So they slept and slept in the cottage in the wood. They slept through three and a half wars, one plague, six new kings, the invention of the sewing machine, and the discovery of a new continent.

The cottage was deep in the woods so very few princes passed by. And none of the ones who did even tried the door.

At the end of one hundred years a prince named Jojo (who was the youngest son of a youngest son and so had no gold or jewels or property to speak of) came into the woods. It began to rain, so he stepped into the cottage over the broken wall. He saw three women asleep with spiderwebs holding them to the floor. One of them was a beautiful princess. Being the kind of young man who read fairy tales, Jojo knew just what to do. But because he was the youngest son of a youngest son, with no gold or jewels or property to speak of, he had never kissed anyone before, except his mother, which doesn't count, and his father, who had a beard.

Jojo thought he should practice before he tried kissing the princess. (He also wondered if she would like marrying a prince with no property or gold or jewels to speak of. Jojo knew with princesses that sort of thing really matters.) So he puckered up his lips and kissed the old fairy on the nose. It was quite pleasant. She smelled slightly of cinnamon. He moved on to Jane.

He puckered up his lips and kissed her on the mouth. It was delightful. She smelled of wildflowers. He moved on to the beautiful princess. Just then the fairy and Plain Jane woke up.

Prince Jojo's kisses had worked. The fairy picked up the pieces of her wand. Jane looked at the prince and remembered the kiss as if it were a dream.

"I wish he loved me," she said softly to herself.

"Good wish!" said the fairy to herself.

She waved the two pieces of the wand gently.

The prince looked at Miserella, who was having a bad dream and enjoying it. Even frowning she was beautiful. But Jojo knew that kind of princess. He had three cousins just like her. Pretty on the outside. Ugly within. He remembered the smell of wildflowers and turned back to Jane.

"I love you," he said. "What's your name?"

So they lived happily ever after in Jane's cottage. The prince fixed the roof and the wall and built a house next door for the old fairy. They used the sleeping princess as a conversation piece when friends came to visit. Or sometimes they stood her up (still fast asleep) in the hallway and let her hold coats and hats. But they never let anyone kiss her awake, not even their children, who numbered three.

Moral: Let sleeping princesses lie or lying princesses sleep,
whichever seems wisest.

THE UNDINE

Aqua est mutabile. Water is changeable, female, mutable. The gods of the sea are male, but the sea herself female. Restless. Changing.

So the prince thought as he stared over the waves, the furrows becoming mountains, the mountains tumbling down into troughs. Female into male, male into female. Changing.

He pushed his scarlet hat to the back of his head because the feather tickled his cheek. Women were in his thoughts all the time, as bothersome as the feather on his skin. Flickering, always flickering, on the edge of thought. He could not leave women alone. He was to be married within a week.

He had never met his bride; that was not the courtship of royalty. But he had seen a portrait of her, a miniature done by a painter whose pockets were even now lined with gold from the girl's father. Such paintings told nothing truly, not even the color of hair. His own portrait, sent in return, showed a handsome youth with yellow curls, though in fact his hair was more the color of a sparrow's belly, buffy and streaked. The lies of kings are lightly told.

"I will not mind," he thought to himself. "I will not mind if she is less than beautiful, as long as she is not *too* changeable. As long as she is not under the water sign." He longed for stability even as he sought change, a king's wish.

But a messenger arrived that night who was one of his own. Under the cover of darkness the messenger confessed, "It is worse than we thought, my lord. She has a face the very map of disease, with the pox having carved out the central cities. Her nose is mountainous, her chin the gift of ancestors. A castle could be built on that promontory."

The prince sighed and dismissed the news-bringer. Then he began to pace the castle battlements, staring out across the crenellations to the sea beyond. His father's father had built wisely; one face of the castle was always turned toward the ocean. It was a palace for sailors and every room was full of the sound of waves.

The prince leaned out over the wall and breathed in the salt spray. A wife whose face put a mountain range to shame. How could he—who loved the seascape, who loved beauty in women above all things—abide it? He longed suddenly for an ending, a sea-change from his situation, but he had neither the heart for it nor the imagination. Princes are not bred to it. He sighed again.

It was the sigh that did it. It reeled out as eagerly as a fisherman's line and cast itself into the sea. What woman can resist the sound of a man's sigh? He had caught many maidens on it, many matrons as well. But this time it was the daughter of a sea-king who was caught on *that* hook.

She rose to his bait and sang him back his sigh.

Now, it must be remembered that the songs of mermaids have a charm compounded of water and air, the signs of impermanence. That is both their beauty and their danger. Many men have been caught, gaffed, reeled under, and drowned by the lure of that song.

Rising only to the edge of her waist—for she knew full well how the sight of a tail affects mortal men—the mermaid showed the prince her shell-like breasts, her pearly skin, the phosphorescence of her hair. She held a webbed hand over her mouth, her fingers as slim as the ribs of a fan. Then she pulled her hand away, displaying her smile. She was well trained in the arts of seduction, as was he. Royalty abounds in it.

The prince leaned out over the castle wall, his legs on land but his arms and head over water. As amphibious as she, he gave himself to her, though he was not his own to give. It was a promise as mutable as water, for the lies of kings are lightly told.

We have all been warned of such bargains. That promise worked its own kind of magic, and the undine rose from the waves on legs, her scales washed away by the prince's rote of love. But magic has consequences, as any magic-maker knows. The undine half expected the worst—and got it. Her new legs bit like knifepoints into her waist. Still, it was no worse than the pain of menses; even seamaids are slaves to the tides. She smiled again and walked gingerly ashore.

The prince ran down to greet her, leaving bootmarks in the sand. If he had asked, she would have even danced before him and never felt the pain. Some women believe lies—even the ones they tell themselves. Especially those.

The undine put her hand in his, and he shivered at her touch. Her hand was cold and slippery as a fish; the webbing between her fingers pulsed strangely against his skin. There was a strong sea scent about her, like tuna or crab. But her chin and nose were small, her eyes as blue as lagoons, and fathomless. He smiled his watery promise at her and gestured toward his room. He did not speak, knowing that mermaids have no tongues, forgetting in his human way that they had ears. Still, in love, gesture can be enough.

She followed him, knife upon knife, smiling. The prince took her to his room by a hidden route, the steps up to it smoothed by the passage of many dainty feet. Each step up was another gash in her side. She gasped and he asked her why.

"It is nothing," she signed, holding her waist. Her mouth was open, gasping in the air, and she was momentarily as ugly as any fish. But the moment passed.

He did not ask again. Some men believe lies—especially if it is to their convenience.

His room was like a ship's cabin, the waves always knocking at the walls. He locked the door behind them and turned toward her. She did not ask for ceremony. His touch was enough, rougher on her skin than the ocean. She enjoyed the novelty of it. She enjoyed his bed, heavy with humanity. Lying on it, her knife legs no longer ached.

Her touch on him was water-smooth and soothing. He forgot his marriage. He was always able to forget the demands of royalty in this manner. It was why he forgot so often—and so well.

But those demands are as constant as clockwork. The week ticked away as inexorably as a gold watch and the monstrous bride was shipped across the waves.

She resembled an armada, rough-hewn and wooden, with a mighty prow and guardsmen in her wake. Noisy as seagulls, her attendants knocked on his door. He was forced by tradition to attend her. The undine he left behind.

"I love you. My love is an ocean," he whispered into her seashell ear before he left.

But she knew that such water was changeable. It was subject to tides. Hers was at an ebb. She no longer trusted his sighs. As soon as the door shut, she left the bed. The knifepoints were as sharp as if newly honed. The mirror on the wall did not reflect her beauty. It showed only a watery shadow, changing and shifting, as she passed.

The salt smell of the ocean, sharp and steady, called to her from the window. Looking out, she saw her sisters, the waves, beckoning her with their white arms. She could even hear the rough neighing of the horses of the sea. She left two mermaid tears, crystals with a bit of salt embedded in them, on his pillow. Then painfully she climbed up onto the corbeled windowsill and flung herself back at the sea.

It opened to her, gathered her in, washed her clean.

The prince found the crystals and made them into earbobs for his ugly wife. They did not improve her looks. But she proved a strong, stable queen for him, and ruled the kingdom on her own. She gave him much line, she played him like a fish. She swore to him that she did not mind his many affairs or that he spoke in his sleep of undines.

She swore, and he believed her. But the lies of kings are not always lightly told.

GREAT-GRANDFATHER DRAGON'S TALE

1.

"**L**ong, long ago," said the old dragon, and the gray smoke curled around his whiskers in thin, tired wisps, "in the time of the Great-Grandfather of All Dragons, there was no Thanksgiving."

The five little dragons looked at one another in alarm. The boldest of them, Sskar, said, "No Thanksgiving? No feasting? No chestnuts on the fire? Hasn't there always been a Thanksgiving?"

The old dragon wheezed. The smoke came out in huge, alarming puffs. Then he started speaking, and the smoke resumed its wispy rounds. "For other animals, perhaps. For rabbits or lions or deer. Perhaps for them there has always been a Thanksgiving."

"Rabbits and lions and deer!" The little dragons said the names with disdain. And Sskar added, "Who cares about rabbits and lions and deer. We want to know about dragons!"

"Then listen well, young saurs. For what was once could come again. What was then could be now. And once there was no dragons' Thanksgiving."

The little dragons drew closer, testing their claws against the stone floor of the cave, and listened.

Long, long ago *began the old dragon* the world was ice and fire, fire and ice. In the south, great mountains rained smoke and spat flame.

In the north, glaciers like beasts crept down upon the land and devoured it.

It was then that the Great-Grandfather of All Dragons lived.

He was five hundred slithes from tip to tail. His scales shimmered like the moon on waves. His eyes were black shrouds. He breathed firestorms, which he could fan to flame with his mighty wings. And his feet were broad enough to carry him over the thundering miles. All who saw him were afraid.

And the Great-Grandfather of All Dragons ate up the shaking fear of the little animals. He lived on it and thrived. He would roar and claw and snatch and hit about with his tail just to watch fear leap into the eyes of the watchers. He was mighty, yet he was just one of many, for in those days dragons ruled the earth.

One day, up from the south, from the grassy lands, from the sweet lands, where the red sun pulls new life from the abundant soil, a new creature came. He was smaller than the least of the dragons, not even a slithe and a half high. He had no claws. His teeth were puny and blunt. He could breathe neither fire nor smoke, and he had neither armor to protect himself nor fur to keep himself warm. His legs could only carry him from here—to there. *And the old dragon drew a small line on the rock face with his littlest toenail.*

But when he opened his mouth, the sounds of all beasts, both large and small, of the air and the sea and the sky, came out. It was this gift of sound that would make him the new king.

"Fah!" said little Sskar. "How could something that puny be a king? The only sound worth making more than once or twice is this." And he put his head back and roared. It was a small roar, for he was still a small dragon, but little as it was, it echoed for miles and caused three trees to wither on the mountain's face. True, they were stunted trees that had weathered too many storms and were above the main tree line. But they shivered at the sound, dropped all their remaining leaves, and died where they stood.

The other little dragons applauded the roar, their claws clack-etting together. And one of them, Sskitter, laughed. Her laugh was delicate and high-pitched, but she could roar as loudly as Sskar.

"Do not laugh at what you do not understand," said the old dragon. "Look around. What do you see? We are few, yet this new creature is many. We live only in this hidden mountain wilderness while he and his children roam the rest of the world. We glide on shrunken wings over our shrunken kingdom while he flies in great silver birds all over the earth."

"Was it not always so?" asked the smallest dragon, Sskarma. She was shaken by the old one's words.

"No, it was not always so," said the old dragon.

"Bedtime," came a soft voice from the corner. Out from behind a large rock slithered Mother Dragon. "Settle down, my little fire-tongues. And you, Grandfather, no more of that story for this night."

"Tomorrow?" begged Sskarma, looking at the old one.

He nodded his mighty head, and the smoke made familiar patterns around his horns.

As they settled down, the little dragons listened while their mother and the old one sang them a lullaby:

> *Firelight and firebright,*
> *Bank your dragon flames tonight.*
> *Close your eyes and still your roar,*
> *Sleep is here, my little saur*
> *Hiss, hiss, hush.*

By the time the song was over, all but little Sskar had dropped off. He turned around and around on the cave floor, trying to get settled. "Fah!" he muttered to himself. "What kind of king is that?" But at last he, too, was asleep, dreaming of bones and fire.

"Do not fill their heads with nonsense," said Mother Dragon when the hatchlings were quiet.

"It is not nonsense," said the old dragon. "It is history."

"It is dreams," she retorted. In her anger, fire shot out of her nostrils and singed the old one's nose. "If it cannot feed their bellies, it is worthless. Good night, Grandfather." She circled her body around the five little dragons and, covering them, slept.

The old dragon looked at the six of them long after the cave was silent. Then he lay down with his mouth open, facing the cave entrance as he had done ever since he had taken a mate. He hardly slept at all.

2.

In the morning, the five little dragons were up first, yawning and hissing and stretching. They sharpened their claws on the stone walls, and Sskar practiced breathing smoke. None of the others was even close to smoke yet. Most were barely trickling straggles through their nose slits.

It was midmorning before Grandfather Dragon moved. He had been up most of the night thinking, checking the wind currents for scents, keeping alert for dangerous sounds carried on the air. When morning had come, he had moved away from the cave mouth and fallen asleep. When Grandfather awoke it was in sections. First his right foreleg moved, in short hesitations as if testing its flexibility. Then his left. Then his massive head moved from side to side. At last he thumped his tail against the far rocks of the cave. It was a signal the little dragons loved.

Sskarma was first to shout it out. "The story! He is going to tell us the story!" She ran quickly to her grandfather and curled around his front leg, sticking her tail into her mouth. The others took up their own special positions and waited for him to begin.

"And what good was this gift of sound?" asked the old dragon at last, picking up the tale as if a night and half a day had not come between tellings.

"What good?" asked the little dragons. Sskar muttered, "What good indeed?" over and over until Sskitter hit him on the tip of the nose with a claw.

This gift of sound *said Grandfather Dragon* which made the creature king, could be used in many ways. He could coax the birds and beasts into his nets by making the sound of a hen calling the cock or a lioness seeking the lion or a bull elk spoiling for a fight. And so cock and lion and bull elk came. They came at this mighty hunter's calling, and they died at his hand.

Then the hunter learned the sounds that a dragon makes when he is hungry. He learned the sounds that a dragon makes when he is sleepy, when he looks for shelter, calls out warning, seeks a mate. All these great sounds of power the hunter learned—and more. And so one by one the lesser dragons came at his calling; one by one they came—and were killed.

The little dragons stirred uneasily at this. Sskarma shivered and put her tail into her mouth once more.

So we dragons named him Ssgefah, which, in the old tongue, means "enemy." But he called himself Man.

"Man," they all said to one another. "Ssgefah. Man."

At last one day the Great-Grandfather of All Dragons looked around and saw that there were only two dragons left in the whole world—he and his mate. The two of them had been very cunning and had hidden themselves away in a mountain fastness, never answering any call but a special signal that they had planned between themselves.

"I know that signal," interrupted Sskitter. She gave a shuddering, hissing fall of sound.

The old dragon smiled at her, showing 147 of his secondary teeth. "You have learned it well, child. But do not use it in fun. It is the most powerful sound of all."

The little dragons all practiced the sound under their breaths while the old dragon stretched and rubbed an itchy place under his wing.

"Supper!" hissed Mother Dragon, landing on the stone outcropping by the cave mouth. She carried a mountain goat in her teeth. But the little dragons ignored her.

"Tell the rest," pleaded Sskarma.

"Not the rest," said the old dragon, "but I will tell you the next part."

3.

"We must find a young Man who is unarmed," said the Great-Grandfather of All Dragons. "One who has neither net nor spear."

"And *eat* him!" said his mate. "It has been such a long time since we have had any red meat. Only such grasses and small birds as populate tops of mountains It is dry, rib-y fare at best." She yawned prettily and showed her sharp primary teeth.

"No," said the Great-Grandfather of All Dragons. "We shall capture him and learn his tongue. And then we will seal a bargain between us."

His mate looked shocked. Her wings arched up, great ribbed

wings they were, too, with the skin between the ribbings as bright as blood. "A bargain? With such a puny thing as Man?"

The Great-Grandfather of All Dragons laughed sadly then. It was a dry, deep, sorrowful chuckle. "Puny!" he said, as quietly as smoke. "And what are we?"

"Great!" she replied, staring black eye into black eye. "Magnificent. Tremendous. Awe-inspiring." She stood and stretched to her fullest, which was 450 slithes in length. The mountaintop trembled underneath her magnificently ponderous legs.

"You and I," said the Great-Grandfather of All Dragons, "and who else?"

She looked around, saw no other dragons, and was still.

"Why, that's just what you said last night, Grandfather," said little Sskitter.

Grandfather Dragon patted her on the head. "Good girl. Bright girl. Perceptive girl."

Sskar drew his claws lazily over the floor of the cave, making awful squeaks and leaving scratches in the stone. "I knew that," he said. Then he blew smoke rings to show he did not care that his sister had been praised.

But the other dragons were not afraid to show they cared. "I remember," said Ssgrum.

"Me, too," said Sstok.

They both came in for their share of praises.

Sskarma was quiet and stared. Then she said, "But more story, Grandfather."

"First comes supper," said Mother Dragon. "Growing bodies need to eat."

This time they all listened.

But when there was not even a smidgen of meat left, and only the bones to gnaw and crack, Mother Dragon relented.

"Go ahead now," she said. "Tell them a story. But no nonsense."

"This is true history," said Sskitter.

"It's dumb!" said Sskar. He roared his roar again. "How could there be us if they were the last of the dragons!"

"It's a story," said Sskarma. "And a story should be its own reward. I want to hear the rest."

The others agreed. They settled down again around Grandfather Dragon's legs, except for Sskar, who put his back against the old dragon's tail. That way he could listen to the story but pretend not to be interested.

4.

So the Great-Grandfather of All Dragons *the story began once more* flew that very night on silent wings, setting them so that he could glide and catch the currents of air. And he was careful not to roar or to breathe fire or to singe a single tree.

He quartered town after town, village after village, farm after farm, all fitted together as carefully as puzzles. And at last he came to a young shepherd boy asleep beside his flock out in a lonely field.

The Great-Grandfather of All Dragons dropped silently down at the edge of the field, holding his smoke so that the sheep—silly creatures—would not catch the scent of him. For dragons, as you know, have no odor other than the brimstone smell of their breath. The black-and-white sheepdog with the long hair twitched once, as if the sound of the Great-Grandfather's alighting had jarred his sleep, but he did not awaken.

Then the Great-Grandfather of All Dragons crept forward slowly, trying to sort out the sight and sound and smell of the youngling. He seemed to be about twelve Man years old and unarmed except for his shepherd's staff. He was fair-haired and had a sprinkling of spots over the bridge of his nose that

Men call freckles. He wore no shoes and smelled of cheese and bread, slightly moldy. There was also a green smell coming from his clothes, a tree and grass and rain and sun smell, which the Great-Grandfather of All Dragons liked.

The boy slept a very deep sleep. He slept so deeply because he thought that the world was rid of dragons, that all he had to worry about were wolves and bears and the sharp knife of hunger. Yes, he believed that dragons were no more until he dreamed them and screamed—and woke up, still screaming, in a dragon's claw.

Sskar applauded. "I like the part about the dragon's claw," he said, looking down at his own golden nails.

Sskitter poked him with her tail, and he lashed back. They rolled over and over until the old dragon separated them with his own great claws. Only then did they settle down to listen.

But when he saw that screaming would not help, the young Man stopped screaming, for he was very brave for all that he was very young.

And when he was set down in the lair and saw he could not run off because the dragon's mate had blocked the door, the young Man made a sign against his body with his hand and said, "Be gone, Worm." For that is how Man speaks.

"Be gone, Worm," Sskitter whispered under her breath.

And Sskarma made the Man sign against her own body, head to heart, shoulder to shoulder. It did not make sense to her, but she tried it anyway.

Sskar managed to look amused, and the two younger dragons shuddered.

"Be gone, Worm," the Manling said again. Then he sat down on his haunches and cried, for he was a very young Man after all. And the sound of his weeping was not unlike the sound of a baby dragon calling for its food.

At that, the Great-Grandmother of All Dragons moved away from the cave mouth and curled herself around the Man and tried to comfort him, for she had no hatchlings of her own yet, though she had wished many years for them. But the Man buffeted her with his fist on the tender part of her nose, and she cried out in surprise—and in pain. Her roar filled the cave. Even the Great-Grandfather closed his earflaps. And the young Man held his hands up over the sides of his face and screamed back. It was not a good beginning.

But at last they both quieted down, and the Manling stretched out his hand toward the tender spot and touched it lightly. And the Great-Grandmother of All Dragons opened her second eyelid—another surprise—and the great fires within her eyes flickered.

It was then that the Great-Grandfather of All Dragons said quietly in dragon words, "Let us begin."

The wonder of it was that the young Man understood.

"My name," he replied in Man talk, in a loud, sensible voice, "is Georgi." He pointed to himself and said "Georgi" again.

The Great-Grandfather of All Dragons tried. He said "Ssgggi," which we have to admit was not even close.

The Great-Grandmother of All Dragons did not even try.

So the youngling stood and walked over, being careful not to make any sudden gestures, and pointed straight at the Great-Grandfather's neck.

"Sskraken," roared the Great-Grandfather, for as you know a dragon always roars out his own name.

"Sskar!" roared Sskar, shattering a nearby tree. A small, above-the-frost-line tree. The others were silent, caught up in the story's spell.

And when the echo had died away, the youngling said in a voice as soft as the down on the underwing of an owl, "Sskraken." He did not need to shout it to be heard, but every syllable was there. It made the Great-Grandfather shiver. It made the Great-Grandmother put her head on the floor and think.

"Sskraken," the youngling said again, nodding as if telling himself to remember. Then he turned to Sskraken's mate and pointed at her. And the pointing finger never trembled.

"Sskrema," she said, as gently as a lullaby. It was the first time in her life that she had not roared out her name.

The youngling walked over to her, rubbed the spot on her nose that had lately been made sore. "Sskrema," he crooned. And to both their astonishments, she thrummed under his hand.

"She thrummed!" said Skitter. "But you have told us . . ."

"Never to thrumm except to show the greatest happiness with your closest companions," the youngest two recited dutifully.

"So I did," said Grandfather Dragon. With the tip of his tail, he brushed away a fire-red tear that was caught in his eye. But he did it cleverly, so cleverly the little dragons did not notice. "So I did."

"Fah!" said Sskar. "It was a mistake. All a mistake. She never would have thrummed knowingly at a Man."

"That's what makes it so important," answered Sskarma. She reached up with her tail and flicked another tear from the old dragon's eye, but so cleverly the others never noticed. Then she thrummed at him. "Tell us more."

5.

The youngling Georgi lived with the two saurs for a year and a day. He learned many words in the old tongue: *sstek* for red meat and *sstik* for the dry, white meat of birds; *ssova*, which means "egg," and *ssouva*, which means "soul." Learning the old tongue was his pleasure, his task, and his gift.

In return, the Great-Grandfather of All Dragons and his mate learned but one word. It was the name of the Man—Georgi. Or as they said it, "Ssgggi."

At the end of the year and a day, the Great-Grandfather called the boy to him, and they walked away from the sweet-smelling nest of grasses and pine needles and attar of wild rose that Georgi had built for them. They walked to the edge of the jagged mountainside where they could look down on the rough waste below.

"Ssgggi," said the Great-Grandfather of All Dragons, speaking the one word of Man's tongue he had learned, though he had never learned it right. "It is time for you to go home. For though you have learned much about us and much from us, you are not a dragon but a Man. Now you must take your learning to them, the Men, and talk to them in your own Man's tongue. Give them a message from us. A message of peace. For if you fail, we who are but two will be none." And he gave a message to the Man.

Georgi nodded and then quietly walked back to the cave. At his footsteps, the Great-Grandmother of All Dragons appeared. She looked out and stared at the boy. They regarded one another solemnly, without speaking. In her dark eyes the candle flame flickered.

"I swear that I will not let that light go out," said Georgi, and he rubbed her nose. And then they all three thrummed at one another, though the Man did it badly.

Then he turned from the saurs without a further good-bye. And this was something else he had learned from the Great-Grandfather, for Men tend to prolong their good-byes, saying meaningless things instead of leaping swiftly into the air.

"It is their lack of wings," said Sskarma thoughtfully.

Georgi started down the mountain, the wind in his face and a great roar at his back. The mountains shook at his leaving, and great boulders shrugged down the cliff sides. And high above him, the two saurs circled endlessly in the sky, guarding him though he knew it not.

And so the Manling went home and the dragons waited.

"Dragons have a long patience," the two youngest saurs recited dutifully. "That is their genius." And when no one applauded their memories, they clattered their own claws together and smiled at one another, toothy smiles, and slapped their tails on the stone floor.

6.

In dragon years *continued Grandfather Dragon* it was but an eyelid's flicker, though in Man years it was a good long while.

And then one day, when the bright eye of the sun was for a moment shuttered by the moon's dark lid, a great army of Men appeared at the mouth of the canyon and rode their horses almost to the foot of the mountain.

The Great-Grandmother of All Dragons let her rough tongue lick around her jaws at the sight of so much red meat.

"*Sstek*," she said thoughtfully.

But the Great-Grandfather cautioned her, remembering how many dragons had died in fights with Men, remembering the message he had sent with the Manling. "We wait," he said.

"I would not have waited," hissed Sskar, lashing his tail.

His sister Sskitter buffeted him on the nose. He cried out once and was still.

At the head of the Men was one Man in white armor with a red figure emblazoned on his white shield.

It was when he saw this that the Great-Grandfather sighed. "Ssgggi," he said.

"How can you tell?" asked the Great-Grandmother. "He is too big and too wide and too old for our Ssgggi. Our Ssgggi was this tall," and she drew a line into the pine tree that stood by the cave door.

"Men do not grow as dragons grow," reminded the Great-Grandfather gently. "They have no egg to protect their early days. Their skin is soft. They die young."

The Great-Grandmother put her paw on a certain spot on her nose and sighed. "It is not *our* Ssgggi," she said again. "He would not lead so many Men to our cave. He would not have to wear false scales on his body. He would come to the mountain by himself. I am going to scorch that counterfeit Ssgggi. I will roast him before his friends and crack his bones and suck out the marrow."

Then the Great-Grandfather of All Dragons knew that she spoke out of sorrow and anger and fear. He flicked a red tear from his own eye with his tail and held it to her. "See, my eyes cry for our grown-up and grown-away Manling," he said. "But though he is bigger and older, he is our Ssgggi nonetheless. I told him to identify himself when he returned so that we might know him. He has done so. What do you see on his shield?"

The Great-Grandmother rose to her feet and peered closely at the Man so many slithes below them. And those dragon eyes, which can see even the movement of a rabbit cowering in its burrow, saw the figure of a red dragon crouched on the white shield.

"I can see a mole in its den," said Sskar. *"I can see a shrew in its tunnel. I can see . . ."*

"You will see very little when I get finished with you if you do not shut up," said Sskitter and hit him once again.

"I see a red dragon," said the Great-Grandmother, her tail switching back and forth with anger.

"And what is the dragon doing?" asked the Great-Grandfather even more gently.

She looked again. Then she smiled, showing every one of her primary teeth. "It is covering a certain spot on its nose," she said.

7.

Just then the army stopped at a signal from the white knight. They dismounted from their horses and waited. The white knight raised his shield toward the mountain and shouted. It took a little while for his voice to reach the dragons, but when it did, they both smiled, for the white knight greeted them in the old tongue.

He said: "I send greetings. I am Ssgggi, the dragon who looks like a Man. I am taller now, but nowhere near as tall as a dragon. I am wiser now, but nowhere near as wise as a dragon. And I have brought a message from Men."

"Of course they did not trust him. Not a Man. Did they?" Sskar hissed.

"They trusted this Man," said Sskitter. "Oh, I know they did. I know I do."

Sskarma closed her eyes in thought. The other two little dragons were half-asleep.

Grandfather Dragon did not answer their questions, but let the story answer the questions for him.

The Great-Grandfather of All Dragons stretched and rose.

He unfurled his wings to their farthest point and opened his mouth and roared out gout after gout of flames. All the knights save the white knight knelt in fear. And then the Great-Grandfather pumped his wings twice and leaped into the air. Boulders buffeted by the winds rolled down the mountainside toward the Men.

The Great-Grandmother followed him, roaring as she flew. And they circled around and around in a great, widening gyre that was much too high for the puny Man arrows to reach.

Then the white knight called on all his archers to put down their bows, and the others to put aside their weapons. Reluctantly they obeyed, though a few grumbled angrily and they were all secretly very much afraid.

When the white knight saw that all his knights had disarmed themselves, he held his shield up once more and called out "Come, Worm" in his own tongue. He made the Man sign again, head to heart, shoulder to shoulder. At that signal, the Great-Grandfather of All Dragons and his mate came down. They crested a current of air and rode it down to the knight's feet.

When they landed, they jarred nearly fifty slithes of earth, causing several of the Men to fall over in amazement or fear or from the small quaking of the ground. Then the dragons lowered their heads to Ssgggi.

And the Man walked over to them, and first to the Great-Grandmother and then to the Great-Grandfather he lifted his fist and placed it ever so gently on a certain spot on the nose.

The Great-Grandmother thrummed at this. And then the Great-Grandfather thrummed as well. And the white knight joined them. The two dragons' bodies shook loud and long with their thrumming. And the army of Men stared and then laughed and finally cheered, for they thought that the great-grandparents were afraid.

"Afraid? Afraid of puny Men? They were shaking because they

were thrumming. Only lower *animals like rabbits and lion and deer—and Men—shake when they are afraid. I'll show them afraid!" cried Sskar.* He leaped into the air and roared so hard that this time real flames came out of his nose slits, which so surprised him that he turned a flip in the air and came back to earth on his tailbone, which hurt enormously.

Grandfather Dragon ignored him, and so did the other little dragons. Only Mother Dragon, from her corner in the cave, chuckled. It was a sound that broke boulders.

Sskar limped back proudly to his grandfather's side, eager to hear the rest of the story. "I showed them, didn't I?" he said.

8.

"Hear this," said the white knight Georgi, first in Man talk and then in the old tongue so that the dragons could understand as well. "From now on dragons shall raid no Man lands, and Men shall leave dragons alone. We will not even recognize you should we see you. You are no longer real to us.

"In turn, dragons will remain here, in this vast mountain wilderness untouched by Men. You will not see us or prey on us. You will not even recognize us. We are no longer real to dragons."

The Great-Grandfather roared out his agreement, as did the Great-Grandmother. Their roaring shattered a small mountain, which, to this day, Men called Dragon's Fall. Then they sprang up and were gone out of the sight of the army of Men, out of the lives of Men.

"Good," said Sskar. "I am glad they are out of our sight and out of our lives. Men are ugly and unappetizing. We are much better off without them." He stretched and curled and tried to fall asleep. Stories made him feel uncomfortable and sleepy at the same time.

175

But Sskitter was not happy with the ending. "What of Ssgggi?" *she said. "Did they ever see him again? Of all Men, he was my* *favorite."*

"And what of the dragons' Thanksgiving?" said the littlest two, *wide awake now.*

Sskarma was silent, looking far out across the plains, across to *Dragon's Fall, where the boulders lay all in a jumble.*

Grandfather touched Sskarma's shoulder gently. "There is more," *he said.*

She turned her head to look at him, her black eyes glistening. "I *know," she said. "Ssgggi came back. He would have to. He loved* *them so. And they loved him."*

Grandfather shook his head. "No," he said. "He never came *back. He could not. Dragons no longer existed for him, except* *in his heart. Did not exist for him—or for any Men. Of course,"* *Grandfather added, "Men still exist for us. We do not have Man's* *gift of tongue or of the imagination. What is—for dragons—is. We* *cannot wish it away. We cannot make the real unreal, or the unreal* *real. I envy Man this other gift."*

Sskarma closed her eyes and tried not to cry. "Never?" she asked *softly. "He never came back? Then how could there have been a* *Thanksgiving?"*

Dragons keep promises *Grandfather continued* for they do not have the imagination to lie. And so the Great-Grandfather and the Great-Grandmother and all their children, for they finally had many, and their children's children never bothered Men again. And, since Men did not believe dragons existed, Men did not bother dragons. That is what dragons give thanks for. In fact, Men believed that Saint George—as they called him in later years—had rid them forever of dragons.

And so things have stood to this very day.

9.

Mother Dragon rose at the story's end. "You have a Man's imagination, old one, though you deny it. You have a gift for making up stories, which is another way of saying you lie. Sometimes I think you are more Man than dragon."

"I tell the truth," growled the old dragon. "This is dragon history." Huffily, he cleaned his front claws.

"It is true that the word history *contains the word* story," *said Mother Dragon. "But that is the only thing I will admit."*

Grandfather Dragon houghed, and the smoke straggled out of his nose slits.

"And now if we are to have a real old-fashioned dragons' Thanksgiving, to celebrate the end of stories and the beginning of food, I will have to go hunting again," said Mother Dragon. "A deer, I think. I saw a fat herd by Dragon's Fall, grazing on the sweet spring grass."

"May I come?" asked Sskar.

Mother Dragon smiled and groomed his tail for him. "Now that you have real flames you may."

"The others and I will gather chestnuts," said Grandfather. "For the celebration. For Thanksgiving."

Sskarma shook her head. "I would like to stay behind and clean the cave."

The others left without an argument. No one liked to clean the cave, sweeping the bones over the side of the cliff. Mother Dragon and Sskar rose into the air, banked to the left, and winged out of sight so that they could approach the Fall from downwind. Grandfather Dragon and the three young dragons moved slowly along the deeply rutted mountain path.

Sskarma waited until they had all left; then she went out and looked at the great old pine tree that grew near the cave mouth. About five slithes up was a slash of white, the mark left by a dragon nail, a slash they all called Ssgggi's Mark. *She looked at it for a long time and calculated how quickly trees grow. Then she stood up alongside the tree. The mark came up to her shoulder.*

"Ssgggi," *she said. Then she said it three more times. The fourth time she said it, it came out* "Georgi."

"Georgi," *she said a fifth time. This time it sounded right. Smiling quietly to herself, Sskarma glanced around the wilderness and then once into the sky. Far away she could see one of the great silver birds Grandfather always warned them about.* "Georgi," *she said, and went back in to clean the cave.*

GREEN PLAGUE

It was only a small village high up in the mountains, but the tourists loved it. The water was clean, the air fresh, and the native population wore quaint costumes, not unlike the ones their great-great-grandparents had worn, only made more comfortable with zippers and Velcro fastenings.

The village's fortunes were based on the legend of a piper and a plague of rats some five centuries earlier, and they had carefully cultivated it for tourist trade.

Not that anyone believed the legend. As the mayor said, "A lie, but our own."

And a very profitable lie it was. There were dioramas of the alleged incident in the town hall. Schoolchildren, in their adorable costumes, sang songs about the rats in the amphitheater for visitors, in German, Spanish, Italian, French, English, and Japanese. Trips to the town's cheese factories were the highlight of every tour, with twiddly oompapa music piped in to the factory elevators. In fact, all of the brochures about holidays in the little town were decorated with pictures of rats, though they bore little resemblance to the rodents of old, but were as

179

cuddly as the plush toy mice that were sold in the village gift shop, along with plastic piccolos that could flute half an octave at best.

Very profitable indeed.

Still the townsfolk were more than a little surprised when they awoke one morning, less than a month till high season, to another kind of plague.

"Frogs!" thundered the village mayor to the hastily convened council. His fleshy jowls trembled with the word. He held one of the offending green invaders by a leg and waved it above his head.

"They're everywhere," complained a thin-faced man who was the mayor's chief rival. He shuddered with distaste.

"In the bathtub," said one councilor.

"And the buttery," said another.

"Under the beds," said a third.

"And doing the breaststroke in the toilet bowl," thundered the mayor. He was popular for saying things plainly and because of it had been elected seven years in a row, a village record. "These frogs will ruin business. And we have just been named Attraction of the Year by the National Board of Tourism." They all knew that this was an important citation. It meant that booklets about the village would be in every guide and information shop in the country free of charge. It meant they could expect an increase in visitors of almost 300 percent in the upcoming year. "We must do something to rid ourselves of this green invasion," the mayor concluded.

The council wrestled for about an hour with the problem while green peepers, leopard frogs, and bullfrogs hopped about their feet.

At last the mayor thundered, "This is a plague of biblical proportions!"

"In proportion to what?" asked the thin man.

That started them on one of their epic arguments. No one expected to get out of council chambers until noon.

But just then a very large and hairy frog climbed onto the council table. Its eyes bulged in a horrible manner, as if any minute they were going to fall right out of its head.

"*Trichobatrachus robustus*," the thin man said, shuddering again as he did so, "from West Africa. I, at least, have been doing my homework."

The big frog stared right at the mayor, who, in a sudden panic, hastily adjourned the meeting until the early afternoon.

Gratefully, the councilors all fled the room, leaving the frogs in charge.

In the center of the village, the full extent of the green plague could now be seen. What had been a trickle of family Ranidae at breakfast had, by lunch, become a tidal wave.

Put simply: There were frogs everywhere.

Some were small green blobs and some were enormous ten-inch-round boulders. They seemed to stretch from the foot of Grossmutter to the foot of Harlingberg, the two mountains that made up the sides of the village's valley.

The children were the only ones who were enjoying the spectacle. They had abandoned their own games of tag and hide-and-seek to start frog-racing and frog-jumping contests with the more agreeable frogs.

But as frogs continued to flood into the town, even the children lost interest. A frog or two or seven in the street is one thing. But a frog floating languidly in your milk glass or curled up on your pillow or draped across your toothbrush is another.

By evening the frogs outnumbered the citizens by a thousand-fold. And still the green plague continued.

"We need a piper!" the mayor whispered. A day of thundering had reduced his vocal chords to single notes. The councilors had to strain to hear him in a room now crowded with frogs who were peeping and thrumming and harrumphing with spring pleasure.

At that point, everyone on the council—and the mayor himself—trooped down to the village gift shop and tried tootling on the plastic piccolos. They hoped, one and all, that the legend might actually have some base in reality. But tootle as they might, it was soon quite clear that there was not a real piper among them.

A second day of frogs went by and the roadways were thronged with green. Beds were slimed. Kitchen floors uncrossable. The school yard was a mass of undulating froggery.

The locals began to pack up and move—slowly, because the one highway into the village was covered with both frogs and persons from the media trying to get in. The news organizations, at least, were delighted with the green plague.

"Maybe that will get us a piper," the mayor said to the council after one particularly grueling interview with CNN. And even the thin man had to agree.

And then down the side of Harlingberg Mountain, which being quite steep was relatively frogless, came a drummer. He was a tall, skinny, scruffy man with legs like a stork's. His clothes resembled a personal rummage sale: a green jacket that had once had some sort of emblem on the sleeve; dark pants that were neither black nor blue but somewhere in between; and a white shirt that had certainly seen better days, and probably a better night or two, for it was the tattered remnant of a fancy dress outfit. The drummer had been only partially successful in tucking his shirttails into the pants and one side hung down, obscuring the right-hand pocket, which was just as well as the pocket was no longer there. A pair of granny glasses were perched on his rather prominent nose and made his eyes seem to bulge, rather like those of *Trichobatrachus robustus*. He had a green swatch of cloth tied around his forehead, which did not succeed in keeping his scraggly yellow hair out of his mouth.

A pair of bongo drums were strapped to the tattered man's back and he was carrying a bodhran, a Gaelic hand drum that is played in the best Irish bands.

Once he made his way down the mountainside and found himself right at the town gates, the tattered man marched on his long stork legs through the green swale of frogs, banging all the while on his bodhran. Unaccountably, the frogs opened a path for him, then fell in line behind, hopping feverishly in 4/4 time to keep up with his long strides.

He marched right up the stairs and into the town hall, marking time with the drum. Pushing aside the green invaders, clerks and secretaries opened their doors to stare at him.

"The mayor?" he cried, over the sound of his drum.

Two secretaries and the assistant in charge of weddings, funerals, and bank holidays pointed to the council room door.

Without losing a beat, the drummer stork-legged into the room with his hopping parade behind.

The mayor and council were once again hard at work arguing, but when they saw the drummer and what followed him in two precise lines, they stopped.

"Welcome indeed," said the mayor. "A drummer will do. Name your price." He really knew how to get to the point.

"A bag of gold bullion and a twice yearly gig at the amphitheater," said the tattered drummer. "For me and my band."

The mayor pulled out a piece of paper, swatting away a large guppyi frog from the pen drawer as he did so.

"It's from the Solomon Islands," remarked the thin councilor, pointing to the large frog. The mayor ignored him.

Pen in hand, the mayor asked the drummer, "What is the name of your band?"

"Frog," said the drummer. "Formerly known as Prince."

"Figures," said the mayor. He began to write.

"We'll want guarantees and merchandise rights as well," said the drummer. "And the ability to do a video of the concert intercut with frames from the frog parade."

"Done," said the mayor. He knew better than to argue. Or to go back on his promise. The town legend had taught him that much.

They both signed the paper and then the mayor had one of his secretaries run off copies in triplicate. The councilors put their own signatures in the margins and the mayor handed the drummer a bag of gold. He had, in his own way, done his homework.

The drummer carefully lifted his shirttail, tucked his copy of the agreement in his right pocket, and turned. Smiling, he began drumming in earnest on the bodhran; it was a rhythm in 5/8 time.

The frogs hopped about, forming two straight lines behind him.

Then they all marched out the door, down the steps, along the road, through the village gates, up over Grossmutter Mountain, and were gone, followed by the eager media.

Every last frog left behind the drummer.

For good.

Or for bad.

It depends on how you feel about frogs.

Back at the council room only the thin councilor had noticed that the signed contract the drummer put in his missing pocket had floated down onto the floor. Surreptitiously he picked it up and stuck it in his own pants, under the belt, for safekeeping. He knew how short memories were—for plagues and for promises. He ran against the mayor at the next election.

"We will not go from one plague to another!" was his rallying cry. The villagers knew what he meant. Frogs were one thing. A little bit of slime here, a pond full of tadpoles there. Rock-and-roll fests, however, were another: farmyards destroyed; garbage everywhere; and any number of hippies staying on in the village forever. It had happened to a dozen towns on the other side of the mountain.

The thin man won the election overwhelmingly. No one seemed to remember the tale of the piper and the rats when in the voting booth, except for the loud mayor.

"We must not break our promise," he warned.

"What promise?" retorted the thin man, patting the paper under his belt surreptitiously.

The mayor could not convince the voters that history and story have more in common than five letters. He lost in a landslide.

In the fall all the children in the village over the age of fourteen left in a school bus for a rock concert in the next town over the mountain. There was a group called Forever Green that was currently popular. The drummer was known to be toadally awesome.

Only the youngest three children ever returned. They said the others had found their little mountain village stifling. They said the others complained that there were no jobs for them except as tour guides. They said the others wanted to see the world.

The three who came back mentioned that the band had needed roadies.

"You mean toadies," thundered the ex-mayor. It was the line that would carry him back into politics. Into the winner's circle.

And into story.

If not into history.

THE UNICORN
AND THE POOL

It was evening at the pool, and the animals gathered to drink. It was the only time of day when they did not fight or feed on one another.

This dusk there was a strange oily substance floating on the water.

"What is this befouling our pool?" growled Lion. "Monkey, did you put that there?"

"Not I," said Monkey. He crept closer and touched the water tentatively. The substance moved away from his finger, then slid back, fouling his hand.

"Venom," Monkey said. He knew this sort of thing. "Monkeys do not have venom."

"Nor do buffalo," said Buffalo.

"Or giraffes," said Giraffe.

Hyena only giggled, but they knew he was not capable of any deceit, being open about his cravenness.

"Snake has done it," Lion said at last. And the others knew this was true, not because Lion said it, but because Snake had done the same thing many times before.

"We dare not drink now," Monkey added. And this, too, the animals knew.

Just then, as the last light of the sun sank behind the mountains, Unicorn came stepping across the veldt. Monkey, Buffalo, Giraffe, and Hyena gave way to him. Even Lion bowed his head, though just a little, one king to another.

Unicorn's eyes were cloudy, his skin was yellow with age. Still he moved with grace. He stopped at the water's age and stared, then bent his head toward the pond.

At the last moment, Monkey cried out, "O, King of Kings, do not drink or you will die."

Unicorn hesitated but a moment, then dipped his horn into the pool.

Where the horn touched, the poison turned a bright blue, as if reflecting a pure cloudless sky. Then in a moment, the poison darkened as if night had fallen, and was gone.

"Now you may drink, my children," the unicorn said. His eyes were cloudier than before. He turned and left the pool slowly, as if his bones ached, and where he stepped, flowers sprang up in his hoofprints.

All the animals thought they would see him again—all that is, but Monkey. Gathering flowers—the red with the gold—Monkey made a crown of them.

Days later, when the flowers had wilted, Monkey wept. He wept not for the crown of flowers, or the unicorn, but for all of them who would soon have no proof against Snake's poison or their own bitter hearts.

THE GOLDEN BALLS

Not all princesses are selfish. No. But it is an occupational hazard. Perhaps it is even in the genes, inbred along with fine, thin noses and high arches, along with slender fingers and a swanlike neck.

There was a princess once endowed with all those graces at birth. Her father—a robust sort, given to hunting and sharing bones with his dogs—had married well. That meant his wife came with property and looks, and was gracious enough to expire after producing an heir. The heir was a boy who looked a lot like his father and screamed in similar lusty tones from one wet nurse to another until he found an ample breast that pleased him.

The heir was not the firstborn, however. He came second, after a sister. But primogeniture ruled him first. First at school, first at play, first in the hearts of his countrymen.

His sister turned her attention to golden balls.

She dallied with these golden balls in all manner of places: behind the cookstove, in the palace garden, under privet hedges, and once—just once—on the edge of a well deep in the forest. That was a mistake.

The splash could be heard for no more than a meter, but her cries could be heard for a mile.

No doubt she might have remained hours weeping by the well, unheard, unsung in song or story, had not an ambitious, amphibious hero climbed flipper after flipper to the rim of his world.

He gave her back what she most desired. He took from her what she did not wish to give.

"And will we meet again?" he whispered at last, his voice as slippery as kitchen grease, as bubbly as beer.

"By the wellspring," she gasped, putting him off, pushing his knobby body from hers.

"In your bed," he said. It was not a frog's demand.

To escape him, to keep him, she agreed. Then, raising her skirts to show her slim ankles and high arches, she made a charming moue with her mouth and fled.

He leaped after her but was left behind. By the hop, it was many miles to the palace door. He made it in time for dinner.

By then the princess had changed her dress. The dampness had left a rash on her swanlike neck. The front of the skirt had been spotted with more than tears. She smiled meaningfully at the table, blandly at her brother who was now the king. He recognized the implications of that smile.

"Answer the door," said the king before there was a knock. He knew it would come, had come, would come again. "Answer the door," he said to his sister, ignoring the entire servant class.

She went to the door and lifted the latch, but the frog had already slipped in.

Three hops, seven hops, nine hops, thirteen; he was at the table. He dragged one frogleg, but he was on time.

The princess would have fed him tidbits under the table. She

189

would have put her foot against his. She would have touched him where no one could see. But the king leaned down and spoke to the frog. "You are well suited," he said lifting the creature to her plate.

"Eat," commanded the king.

It was a royal performance. The frog's quick tongue darted around the princess's plate. Occasionally it flicked her hand, between her fingers, under her rings.

"After dinner comes bed," said the king, laughing at his sister's white face. He guessed at hidden promises. She had never shared her golden balls with him.

"I am not tired," she said to her plate. "I have a headache," she said to her bowl. "Not tonight," she said to her cup.

The frog led the way up the stairs. It was very slow going.

Her bed was too high for a hop. She lay upon it, trembling, moist as a well.

The frog stood at the foot of the bed. He measured the draperies for flipper-holds. He eyed the bellpull for a rope ladder. He would have been all night on the floor but for the king, who picked him up between thumb and finger and flung him onto the bed.

The bedclothes showed no signs in the morning, but a child grew in her like a wart.

Marriage transformed the frog but not the princess. He became a prince, Prince Grenouille. She became colder than a shower to him. She gave the child her golden balls. And she gave herself to cooks and choirboys, to farriers and foresters, but never again to a frog.

And Prince Grenouille suffers from her love for others. He wanders from his desk down to the wellspring in the forest. He dips his hand into the water and drinks a drop or two. The air is full of moist memories, and his burdens, like an ill-fitting skin, drop from him while he is there.

Frogs lust, but they do not love. Human beings have a choice.

And, oh, a princess is a very large and troublesome golden ball indeed.

SISTER DEATH

You have to understand, it is not the blood. It was never the blood. I swear that on my own child's heart, though I came at last to bear the taste of it, sweetly salted, as warm as milk from the breast.

The first blood I had was from a young man named Abel, but I did not kill him. His own brother had already done that, striking him down in the middle of a quarrel over sheep and me. The brother preferred the sheep. How like a man.

Then the brother called me a whore. His vocabulary was remarkably basic, though it might have been the shock of his own brutality. The name itself did not offend me. It was my profession, after all. He threw me down on my face in the bloody dirt and treated me like one of his beloved ewes. I thought it was the dirt I was eating.

It was blood.

Then he beat me on the head and back with the same stick he had used on his brother, till I knew only night. *Belilah*. Like my name.

How long I lay there, unmoving, I was never to know. But

when I came to, the bastard was standing over me with the authorities, descrying my crime, and I was taken as a murderess. The only witnesses to my innocence—though how can one call a whore innocent—were a murderer and a flock of sheep. Was it any wonder I was condemned to die?

Oh how I ranted in that prison. I cursed the name of G-d, saying: "Let the day be darkness wherein I was born and let G-d not inquire about it for little does He care. A woman is nothing in His sight and a man is all, be he a murderer or a thief." Then I vowed not to die at all but to live to destroy the man who would destroy me. I cried and I vowed and then I called on the demonkin to save me. I remembered the taste of blood in my mouth and offered that up to any who would have me.

One must be careful of such prayers.

The night before I was to be executed, Lord Beelzebub himself entered my prison. How did I know him? He insinuated himself through the keyhole as mist, re-forming at the foot of my pallet. There were two stubby black horns on his forehead. His feet were like pigs' trotters. He carried around a tail as sinuous as a serpent. His tongue, like an adder's, was black and forked.

"You do not want a man, Lillake," he said, using the pretty pet name my mother called me. "A demon can satisfy you in ways even you cannot imagine."

"I am done with lovemaking," I answered, wondering that he could think me desirable. After a month in the prison I was covered with sores. "Except for giving one a moment's pleasure, it brings me nothing but grief."

The mist shaped itself grandly. "This," he said pointing, "is more than a moment's worth. You will be well repaid."

"You can put that," I gestured back, "into another keyhole. Mine is locked forever."

One does not lightly ignore a great lord's proposal, nor make light of his offerings. It was one of the first things I had learned. But I was already expecting to die in the morning. And horribly. So, where would I spend his coin?

"Lillake, hear me," Lord Beelzebub said, his voice no longer cozening but black as a burnt cauldron. *Shema* was the word he used. I had not known that demons could speak the Lord G-d's holy tongue.

I looked up, then, amazed, and saw through the disguise. This was no demon at all but the Lord G-d Himself testing me, though why He should desire a woman—and a whore at that—I could not guess.

"I know you, *Adonai*," I said. "But God or demon, my answer is the same. Women and children are nothing in your sight. You are a bringer of death, a maker of carrion."

His black aspect melted then, the trotters disappeared, the horns became tendrils of white hair. He looked chastened and sad and held out His hand.

I disdained it, turning over on my straw bed and putting my face to the wall.

"It is no easy thing being at the Beginning and at the End," He said. "And so you shall see, my daughter. I shall let you live, and forever. You will see the man, Cain, die. Not once but often. It will bring you no pleasure. You will be Death's sister, chaste till the finish of all time, your mouth filled with the blood of the living."

So saying, He was gone, fading like the last star of night fading into dawn.

Of course I was still in prison. So much for the promises of G-d.

At length I rose from the mattress. I could not sleep. Believing I had but hours before dying, I did not wish to waste a moment of the time left, though each moment was painful. I walked to the single window, where only a sliver of moon was visible. I put my hands between the bars and clutched at the air as though I could hold it in my hands. And then, as if the air itself had fallen in love with me, it gathered me up through the bars, lifted me through the prison wall, and deposited me onto the bosom of the dawn and I was somehow, inexplicably, free.

Free.

As I have been these five thousand years.

Oh, the years have been kind to me. I have not aged. I have neither gained nor lost weight nor grayed nor felt the pain of advancing years. The blood has been kind to me, the blood I nightly take from the dying children, the true innocents, the Lord G-d's own. Yet for all the children I have sucked rather than suckled, there has been only one I have taken for mine.

I go to them all, you understand. There is no distinction. I take the ones who breathe haltingly, the ones who are misused, the ones whose bodies are ill shaped in the womb, the ones whom fire or famine or war cut down. I take them and suck them dry and send them, dessicated little souls, to the Lord G-d's realm. But as clear-eyed as I had been when I cast out *Adonai* in my prison, so clear-eyed would a child need to be to accept me as I am and thus become my own. So for these five thousand years there has been no one for me in my lonely occupation but my mute companion, the Angel of Death.

If I could still love, he is the one I would desire. His wings are the color of sun and air as mine are fog and fire. Each of the vanes in those wings are hymnals of ivory. He carries the keys to Heaven in his pocket of light. Yet he is neither man nor woman, neither demon nor god. I call the Angel "he" for as I am Sister Death, he is surely my brother.

We travel far on our daily hunt.

We are not always kind.

But the child, my child, I will tell you of her now. It is not a pretty tale.

As always we travel, the Angel and I, wingtips apart over a landscape of doom. War is our backyard, famine our feast. Most fear the wind of our wings and even, in their hurt, pray for life. Only a few, a very few, truly pray for death. But we answer all their prayers with the same coin.

This particular time we were tracking across the landscape of the Pale, where grass grew green and strong right up to the iron railings that bore the boxcars along. In the fields along the way, the peasants swung their silver scythes in rhythm to the trains. They did not hear the counterpoint of cries from the cars or, if they did, they showed their contempt by stopping and waving gaily as the death trains rolled past.

They did not see my brother Death and me riding the screams but inches overhead. But they would see us in their own time.

In the cars below, jammed together like cattle, the people vomited and pissed on themselves, on their neighbors, and prayed. Their prayers were like vomit, too, being raw and stinking and unstoppable.

My companion looked at me, tears in his eyes. I loved him for his pity. Still crying, he plucked the dead to him like faded flowers, looking like a bridegroom waiting at the feast.

And I, no bride, flew through the slats, to suck dry a child held overhead for air. He needed none. A girl crushed by the door. I took her as well. A teenager, his head split open by a soldier's gun, died unnoticed against a wall. He was on the cusp of change but would never now be a man. His blood was bitter in my mouth but I drank it all.

What are Jews that nations swat them like flies? That the Angel of Death picks their faded blooms? That I drink the blood, now bitter, now sweet, of their children?

The train came at last to a railway yard that was ringed about with barbs. BIRKENAU, read the station sign. It creaked back and forth in the wind. BIRKENAU.

When the train slowed, then stopped, and the doors pushed open from the outside, the living got out. The dead were already gathered up to their G-d.

My companion followed the men and boys, but I—I flew right above the weeping women and their weeping children, as I have done all these years.

There was another Angel of Death that day, standing in the midst of the madness. He hardly moved, only his finger seemed alive, an organism in itself, choosing the dead, choosing the living.

"Please, Herr General," a boy cried out. "I am strong enough to work."

But the finger moved, and having writ, moved on. To the right, boy. To the arms of Lilith, Belilah, Lillake.

"Will we get out?" a child whispered to its mother.

"We will get out," she whispered back.

But I had been here many times before. "You will only get out of here through the chimney," I said.

Neither mother nor child nor General himself heard.

There were warning signs at the camp. BEWARE, they said. TENSION WIRE, they said.

There were other signs, too. Pits filled with charred bones. Prisoners whose faces were imprinted with the bony mask death.

JEDEM DAS SEINE. Each one gets what he deserves.

In the showers, the naked mothers held their naked children to them. They were too tired to scream, too tired to cry. They had no tears left.

Only one child, a seven-year-old, stood alone. Her face was angry. She was not resigned. She raised her fist and looked at the heavens and then, a little lower, at me.

Surprised, I looked back.

The showers began their rain of poison. Coughing, praying, calling on G-d to save them, the women died with their children in their arms.

The child alone did not cough, did not pray, did not call on G-d. She held out her two little hands to me. *To me.*

"Imma," she said. "Mother."

I trembled, flew down, and took her in my arms. Then we flew through the walls as if they were air.

So I beg you, as you love life, as you master Death, let my brother be the sole harvester. I have served my five thousand years; not once did I complain. But give me a mother's span with my child, and I will serve you again till the end of time. The child alone chose me in all those years. You could not be so cruel a god as to part us now.

SULE SKERRY

Mairi rowed the coracle with quick, angry strokes, watching the rocky shoreline and the little town of Caith perched on its edge recede. She wished she could make her anger disappear as easily. She was sixteen, after all, and no longer a child. The soldiers whistled at her, even in her school uniform, when she walked to and from the Academy. And wasn't Harry Stones, who was five years older than she and a lieutenant in the RAF, a tail gunner, mad about her? Given a little time, he might have asked her dad for her hand, though she was too young yet, a schoolgirl. Whenever he came to visit, he brought her something. Once even a box of chocolates, though they were very dear.

But to be sent away from London for safekeeping like a baby, to her gran's house, to this desolate, isolated Scottish sea town because of a few German raids—it was demeaning. She could have helped, could have at least cooked and taken care of the flat for her father now that the help had all gone off to war jobs. She had wanted to be there in case a bomb *did* fall, so she could race out and help evacuate all the poor unfortunates, maybe even win a medal, and wouldn't Jenny Eivensley look green then. But he had sent her off, her dad, and Harry had agreed, even though it meant they couldn't see each other very often. It was not in the least fair.

She pulled again on the oars. The little skin boat tended to wallow and needed extra bullying. It wasn't built like a proper British rowboat. It was roundish, shaped more like a turtle shell than a ship. Mairi hated it, hated all of the things in Caith. She knew she should have been in London helping rather than fooling about in a coracle. She pulled on the oars and the boat shot ahead.

The thing about rowing, she reminded herself, was that you watched where you had been, not where you were heading. She could see the town, with its crown of mewing seabirds, disappear from sight. Her destination did not matter. It was all ocean anyway—cold, uninviting, opaque; a dark-green mirror that reflected nothing. And now there was ocean behind as well as ahead, for the shore had thinned out to an invisible line.

Suddenly, without warning, the coracle fetched up against a series of water-smoothed amphibious mounds that loomed up out of the sea. Only at the bump did Mairi turn and look. Out of the corner of her eye she saw a quick scurry of something large and gray and furry on the far side of the rocks. She heard a splash.

"Oh," she said out loud. "A seal!"

The prospect of having come upon a seal rookery was enough to make her leap incautiously from the coracle onto the rock, almost losing the boat in her eagerness. But her anger was forgotten. She leaned over and pulled the little boat out of the water, scraping its hull along the gray granite. Then she upended the coracle and left it to dry, looking for all the world like a great dozing tortoise drying in the hazy sun.

Mairi shrugged out of her mackintosh and draped it on the rock, next to the boat. Then, snugging the watch cap down over her curls and pulling the bulky fisherman's sweater over her slim hips, she began her ascent.

The rocks were covered with a strange purple-gray lichen that was both soft and slippery. Mairi fell once, bruising her right knee without ripping her trousers. She cursed softly, trying out swear words that she had never been allowed to use at home or in Gran's great house back on shore. Then she started up again, on her hands and knees, more carefully now, and at last gained the high point on the rocks after a furious minute of climbing that went backwards and sideways almost as often as it went up. The top of the gray rocks was free of the lichen and she was able to stand up, feeling safe, and look around.

She could not see Caith, with its little, watchful, wind-scored houses lined up like a homefront army to face the oncoming tides in the firth, with Gran's grand house standing on one side, the sergeant major. She could not even see the hills behind, where cliffs hunched like the bleached fossils of some enormous prehistoric ocean beast washed ashore. All that she could see was the unbroken sea, blue and black and green and gray, with patterns of color that shifted as quickly as the pieces in a child's kaleidoscope. Gray-white foam skipped across wave tops, then tumbled down and fractured into bubbles that popped erratically, leaving nothing but a grayish scum that soon became shiny water again. She thought she saw one or two dark seal heads in the troughs of the waves, but they never came close enough for her to count. And overhead the sky was lowering, a color so dirty that it would have made even the bravest sailor long for shore. There was a storm coming, and Mairi guessed she should leave.

She shivered, and suddenly knew where she was. These rocks were the infamous Sule Skerry rocks that Gran's cook had told her about.

"Some may call it a rookery," Cook had said one morning

when Mairi had visited with her in the dark kitchen. Cook's cooking was awful—dry, bland, and unvaried. But at least she knew stories and always imparted them with an intensity that made even the strangest of them seem real. "Aye, some may call it a rookery. But us from Caith, we know. It be the home of the selchies, who are men on land and seals in the sea. And the Great Selchie himself lives on that rock. Tall he is. And covered with a seal skin when he tumbles in the waves. But he is a man for all that. And no maiden who goes to Sule Skerry returns the same."

She had hummed a bit of an old song, then, with a haunting melody that Mairi, for all her music training at school, could not repeat. But the words of the song, some of them, had stuck with her:

> *An earthly nourrice sits and sings,*
> *And aye she sings, "Ba, lily wean!*
> *Little ken I my bairn's father,*
> *Far less the land that he staps in."*
>
> *Then ane arose at her bed-fit,*
> *An a grumly guest I'm sure was he:*
> *"Here am I, thy bairn's father,*
> *Although I be not comelie.*
>
> *I am a man upon the land,*
> *I am a selchie in the sea*
> *And when I'm far frae ev'ry strand*
> *My dwelling is in Sule Skerry."*

A warning tale, Mairi thought. A bogeyman story to keep foolish girls safe at home. She smiled. She was a Londoner, after all, not a silly Scots girl who'd never been out of her own town.

And then she heard a strange sound, almost like an echo

of the music of Cook's song, from the backside of the rocks. At first she thought it was the sound of wind against water, the sound she heard continuously at Gran's home where every room rustled with the music of the sea. But this was different somehow, a sweet, low throbbing, part moan and part chant. Without knowing the why of it, only feeling a longing brought on by the wordless song, and excusing it as seeking to solve a mystery, she went looking for the source of the song. The rock face was smooth on this side, dry, without the slippery, somber lichen; and the water was calmer so it did not splash up spray. Mairi continued down the side, the tune reeling her in effortlessly.

Near the waterline was a cave opening into the west face of the rock, a man-sized opening as black and uninviting as a colliers' pit. But she took a deep, quick breath, and went in.

Much to her surprise, the inside of the cave glowed with an incandescent blue-green light that seemed to come from the cave walls themselves. Darker pockets of light illuminated the concave sections of the wall. Pieces of seaweed caught in these niches gave the appearance of household gods.

Mairi could scarcely breathe. Any loud sound seemed sacrilegious. Her breath itself was a violation.

And then she heard the moan-song again, so loud that it seemed to fill the entire cave. It swelled upward like a wave, then broke off in a bubbling sigh.

Mairi walked in slowly, not daring to touch the cave walls in case she should mar the perfection of the color, yet fearing that she might fall, for the floor of the cave was slippery with scattered puddles of water. Slowly, one foot in front of the other, she explored the cave. In the blue-green light, her sweater and skin seemed to take on an underwater tinge as if she had been transformed into a mermaid.

And then the cave ended, tapering off to a rounded apse with a kind of stone altar the height of a bed. There was something dark lying on the rock slab. Fearfully, Mairi inched toward it, and when she got close, the dark thing heaved up slightly and spoke to her in a strange guttural tongue. At first Mairi thought it was a seal, a wounded seal, but then she saw it was a man huddled under a sealskin coat. He suddenly lay back, feverish and shuddering, and she saw the beads of dried blood that circled his head like a crown.

Without thinking, Mairi moved closer and put her hand on his forehead, expecting it to burn with temperature, but he was cold and damp and slippery to the touch. Then he opened his eyes and they were the same blue-green color as the walls, as the underside of a wave. She wondered for a moment if he were blind, for there seemed to be no pupil in those eyes. Then he closed the lids and smiled at her, whispering in that same unknown tongue.

"Never mind, never mind, I'll get help," whispered Mairi. He might be a fisherman from the town or an RAF man shot down on a mission. She looked at his closed-down face. Here, at last, was her way to aid the war effort. "Lie still. First I'll see to your wounds. They taught us first aid at school."

She examined his forehead under the slate-gray hair, and saw that the terrible wound that had been there was now closed and appeared to be healing, though bloody and seamed with scabs. But when she started to slip the sealskin coat down to examine him for other wounds, she was shocked to discover he had no clothes on under it. No clothes at all.

She hesitated then. Except for the statues in the museum, Mairi had never seen a man naked. Not even in the first aid books. But what if he were hurt unto death? The fearsome poetry of the old phrase decided her. She inched back the sealskin covering as gently as she could.

He did not move except for the rise and fall of his chest. His body was covered with fine hairs, gray as the hair on his head. He had broad, powerful shoulders and slim, tapering hips. The skin on his hands was strangely wrinkled as if he had been under water too long. She realized with a start that he was quite, quite beautiful—but alien. As her grandmother often said, "Men are queer creatures, so different from us, child. And someday you will know it."

Then his eyes opened again and she could not look away from them. He smiled, opened his mouth, and began to speak, to chant, really. Mairi bent down over him and he opened his arms to her, the gray webbing between his fingers pulsing strongly. And without willing it, she covered his mouth with hers. All the sea was in that kiss, cold and vast and perilous. It drew her in till she thought she would faint with it, with his tongue darting around hers as quick as a minnow. And then his arms encircled her and he was as strong as the tide. She felt only the briefest of pain, and a kind of drowning, and she let the land go.

When Mairi awoke, she was sitting on the stone floor of the cavern, and cold, bone-chilling cold. She shivered and pushed her hand across her cheeks. They were wet, though whether with tears or from the damp air she could not say.

Above her, on the stone bed, the wounded man breathed raggedly. Occasionally he let out a moan. Mairi stood and looked down at him. His flesh was pale, wan, almost translucent. She put her hand on his shoulder but he did not move. She wondered if she had fallen and hit her head, if she had dreamed what had happened.

Help. I must get help for him, she thought. She covered him again with the coat and made her way back to the cave mouth. Her entire body ached and she decided she must have fallen and blacked out.

The threatening storm had not yet struck, but the dark slant of rain against the horizon was closer still. Mairi scrambled along the rocks to where the coracle waited. She put on her mac, then heaved the boat over and into the water and slipped in, getting only her boots wet.

It was more difficult rowing back, rowing against the tide. Waves broke over the bow of the little boat, and by the time she was within sight of the town, she was soaked to the skin. The stones of Sule Skerry were little more than gray wave tops then, and with one pull on the oars, they disappeared from sight. The port enfolded her, drew her in. She felt safe and lonely at once.

When Mairi reached the shore there was a knot of fishermen tending their boats. A few were still at work on the bright orange nets, folding them carefully in that quick, intricate pattern that only they seemed to know.

One man, in a blue watch cap, held up a large piece of tattered white cloth, an awning of silk. It seemed to draw the other men to him. He gestured with the silk and it billowed out as if capturing the coming storm.

Suddenly Mairi was horribly afraid. She broke into the circle of men. "Oh, please, please," she cried out, hearing the growing wail of wind in her voice. "There's a man on the rocks. He's hurt."

"The rocks?" The man with the silk stuffed it into his pocket, but a large fold of it hung down his side. "Which rocks?"

"Out there. Beyond the sight line. Where the seals stay," Mairi said.

"Whose child is she?" asked a man who still carried an orange net. He spoke as if she were too young to understand him or as if she were a foreigner.

"Old Mrs. Goodleigh's grandchild. The one with the English father," came an answer.

"Mavis's daughter, the one who became a nurse in London."

"Too good for Caith, then?"

Mairi was swirled about in their conversation.

"Please," she tried again.

"Suppose'n she means the Rocks?"

"Yes," begged Mairi. "The rocks out there. Sule Skerry."

"Hush, child. Must na say the name in sight of the sea," said the blue cap man.

"Toss it a coin, Jock," said the white silk man.

The man called Jock reached into his pocket and flung a coin out to the ocean. It skipped across the waves twice, then sank.

"That should quiet en. Now then, the Rocks you say?"

Mairi turned to the questioner. He had a face like a map, wrinkles marking the boundaries of nose and cheek. "Yes, sir," she said breathily.

"Aye, he might have fetched up there," said the white silk man, drawing it out of his pocket again for the others to see.

Did they know him, then? Mairi wondered.

"Should we leave him to the storm?" asked Jock.

"He might be one of ours," the map-faced man said.

They all nodded at that.

"He's sheltered," Mairi said suddenly. "In a cave. A grotto, like. It's all cast over with a blue and green light."

"Teched, she is. There's no grotto there," said blue cap.

"No blue and green light either," said the map-faced man, turning from her and speaking earnestly with his companions.

"Even if he's one of them, he might tell us summat we need. Our boys could use the knowledge. From that bit of parachute silk, it's hard to say which side he's on." He reached out and touched the white cloth with a gnarled finger.

"Aye, we'd best look for him."

"He won't be hard to find," Mairi began. "He's sick. Hurt. I touched him."

"What was he wearing then?" asked blue cap.

The wind had picked up and Mairi couldn't hear the question. "What?" she shouted.

"Wearing. What was the fellow wearing?"

Suddenly remembering that the man had been naked under the coat, she was silent.

"She doesn't know. Probably too scared to go close. Come on," said Jock.

The men pushed past her and dragged along two of the large six-man boats that fished the haaf banks. The waves were slapping angrily at the shore, gobbling up pieces of the sand and churning out pebbles at each retreat. Twelve men scrambled into the boats and headed out to sea, their oars flashing together.

Three men were left on shore, including the one holding the remnant of white silk. They stood staring out over the cold waters, their eyes squinted almost shut against the strange bright light that was running before the storm.

Mairi stood near them, but apart.

No one spoke.

It was a long half hour before the first of the boats leaped back toward them, across a wave, seconds ahead of the rain.

The second boat beached just as the storm broke, the men jumping out onto the sand and drawing the boat up behind them. A dark form was huddled against the stern.

Mairi tried to push through to get a close glimpse of the man, but blue cap spoke softly to her.

"Nay, nay girl, don't look. He's not what you would call a pretty sight. He pulled a gun on Jock and Jock took a rock to him."

But Mairi had seen enough. The man was dressed in a flier's suit, and a leather jacket with zippers. His blond hair was matted with blood.

"That's not the one I saw," she murmured. "Not the one I . . ."

"Found him lying on the rocks, just as the girl said. Down by the west side of the rocks," said Jock. "We threw his coins to the sea and bought our way home. Though I don't know that German coins buy much around here. Bloody Huns."

"What's a German flier doing this far west, I'd like to know," said map-face.

"Maybe he was trying for America," Jock answered, laughing sourly.

"Ask him. When he's fit to talk," said blue cap.

The man with the white silk wrapped it around the German's neck. The parachute shroud lines hung down the man's back. Head down, the German was marched between Jock and blue cap up the strand and onto the main street. The other men trailed behind.

With the rain soaking through her cap and running down her cheeks, Mairi took a step toward them. Then she turned away. She kicked slowly along the water's edge till she found the stone steps that led up to her gran's house. The sea pounded a steady reminder on her left, a basso continuo to the song that ran around in her head. The last three verses came to her slowly.

> Now he has ta'en a purse of goud
> And he has put it upon her knee
> Sayin' "Gie to me my little young son
> An tak ye up thy nourrice-fee."

She shivered and put her hands in her pockets to keep them warm. In one of the mac's deep pockets, her fingers felt something cold and rough to the touch. Reluctantly she drew it out. It was a coin, green and gold, slightly crusted, as if it had lain on the ocean bottom for some time. She had never seen it before and could only guess how it had gotten into her coat pocket. She closed her hand around the coin, so tightly a second coin was imprinted on her palm.

An it shall pass on a summer's day
When the sun shines het on every stane
That I will tak my little young son
An teach him for to swim his lane.

An thu sall marry a proud gunner
An a right proud gunner I'm sure he'll be.
An the very first shot that ere he shoots
He'll kill baith my young son and me.

Had it truly happened, or was it just some dream brought on by a fall? She felt again those cold, compelling hands on her, the movement of the webbings pulsing on her breasts; smelled again the briny odor of his breath. And if she *did* have that bairn, that child? Why, Harry Stones would *have* to marry her, then. Her father could not deny them that.

And laughing and crying at the same time, Mairi began to run up the stone steps. The sound of the sea followed her all the way home, part melody and part unending moan.

ONCE A GOOD MAN

Once a good man lived at the foot of a mountain. He helped those who needed it and those who did not.

And he never asked for a thing in return.

Now it happened that one day the Lord was looking over his records with his Chief Angel and came upon the Good Man's name.

"*That* is a good man," said the Lord. "What can we do to reward him? Go down and find out."

The Chief Angel, who was nibbling on a thin cracker, swallowed hastily and wiped her mouth with the edge of her robe.

"Done," she said.

So the Chief Angel flew down, the wind feathering her wings, and landed at the foot of the mountain.

"Come in," said the man, who was not surprised to see her. For in those days angels often walked on Earth. "Come in and drink some tea. You must be aweary of flying."

And indeed the angel was. So she went into the Good Man's house, folded her wings carefully so as not to knock the furniture about, and sat down for a cup of tea.

While they were drinking their tea, the angel said, "You have led such an exemplary life, the Lord of Hosts has decided to reward you. Is there anything in the world that you wish?"

The Good Man thought a bit. "Now that you mention it," he said, "there is one thing."

"Name it," said the angel. "To name it is to make it yours."

The Good Man looked slightly embarrassed. He leaned over the table and said quietly to the angel, "If only I could see both Heaven and Hell I would be completely happy."

The Chief Angel choked a bit, but she managed to smile nonetheless. "Done," she said, and finished her tea. Then she stood up and held out her hand.

"Hold fast," she said. "And never lack courage."

So the Good Man held fast. But he kept his eyes closed all the way. And before he could open them again, the man and the angel had flown down, down, down, past moles and mole hills, past buried treasure, past coal in seams, past layer upon layer of the world, till they came at last to the entrance to Hell.

The Good Man felt a cool breeze upon his lids and opened his eyes.

"Welcome to Hell," said the Chief Angel.

The Good Man stood amazed. Instead of flames and fire, instead of mud and mire, he saw long sweeping green meadows edged around with trees. He saw long wooden tables piled high with food. He saw chickens and roasts, fruits and salads, sweetmeats and sweet breads, and goblets of wine.

Yet the people who sat at the table were thin and pale. They devoured the food only with their eyes.

"Angel, oh angel," cried the Good Man, "why are they hungry? Why do they not eat?"

And at his voice, the people all set up a loud wail.

The Chief Angel signaled him closer.

And this is what he saw: The people of Hell were bound fast to their chairs with bands of steel. There were sleeves of steel from their wrists to their shoulders. And though the tables were piled high with food, the people were starving. There was no way they could bend their arms to lift the food to their mouths.

The Good Man wept and hid his face. "Enough!" he cried.

So the Chief Angel held out her hand. "Hold fast," she said. "And never lack courage."

So the Good Man held fast. But he kept his eyes closed all the way. And before he could open them again, the man and the angel had flown up, up, up, past eagles in their eyries, past the plump clouds, past the streams of the sun, past layer upon layer of sky, till they came at last to the entrance to Heaven.

The Good Man felt a warm breeze upon his lids and opened his eyes.

"Welcome to Heaven," said the Chief Angel.

The Good Man stood amazed. Instead of clouds and choirs, instead of robes and rainbows, he saw long sweeping green meadows edged around with trees. He saw long wooden tables piled high with food. He saw chickens and roasts, fruits and salads, sweetmeats and sweet breads, and goblets of wine.

But the people of Heaven were bound fast to their chairs with bands of steel. There were sleeves of steel from their wrists to their shoulders. There seemed no way they could bend their arms to lift the food to their mouths.

Yet these people were well fed. They laughed and talked and sang praises to their host, the Lord of Hosts.

"I do not understand," said the Good Man. "It is the same as Hell, yet it is not the same. What is the difference?"

The Chief Angel signaled him closer.

And this is what he saw: Each person reached out with his steel-banded arm to take a piece of food from the plate. Then he reached over—and fed his neighbor.

When he saw this, the Good Man was completely happy.

ALLERLEIRAUH

Her earliest memory was of rain on a thatched roof, and surely it was a true one, for she had been born in a country cottage two months before time, to her father's sorrow and her mother's death. They had sheltered there, out of the storm, and her father had never forgiven himself or the child who looked so like her mother. *So* like her, it was said, that portraits of the two as girls might have been exchanged and not even Nanny the wiser.

So great had been her father's grief at the moment of his wife's death, he might even have left the infant there, still bright with birth blood and squalling. Surely the crofters would have been willing, for they were childless themselves. His first thought was to throw the babe away, his wife's Undoing as he called her ever after, though her official name was Allerleirauh. And he might have done so had she not been the child of a queen. A royal child, whatever the crime, is not to be tossed aside so lightly, a feather in the wind.

But he had made two promises to the blanched figure that lay on the rude bed, the woolen blankets rough against her long, fair legs. White and red and black she had been then. White of skin, like the color of milk after the whey is skimmed out. Red as the toweling that carried her blood, the blood they could not staunch, the life leaching out of her. And black, the color of her eyes, the black seas he used to swim in, the black tendrils of her hair.

"Promise me." Her voice had stumbled between those lips, once red, now white.

He clasped her hands so tightly he feared he might break them, though it was not her bones that were brittle, but his heart. "I promise," he said. He would have promised her anything, even his own life, to stop the words bleeding out of that white mouth. "I promise."

"Promise me you will love the child," she said, for even in her dying she knew his mind, knew his heart, knew his dark soul. "Promise."

And what could he do but give her that coin, the first of two to close her dead eyes?

"And promise me you will not marry again, lest she be . . ." and her voice trembled, sighed, died.

"Lest she be as beautiful as thee," he promised wildly in the high tongue, giving added strength to his vow. "Lest she have thy heart, thy mind, thy breasts, thy eyes . . ." and his rota continued long past her life. He was speaking to a dead woman many minutes and would not let himself acknowledge it, as if by naming the parts of her he loved, he might keep her alive, the words bleeding out of him as quickly as her lost blood.

"She is gone, my lord," said the crofter's wife, not even sure of his rank except that he was clearly above her. She touched his shoulder for comfort, a touch she would never have ventured in other circumstances, but tragedy made them kin.

The king's litany continued as if he did not hear, and indeed he did not. For all he heard was the breath of death, that absence made all the louder by his own sobs.

"She is dead, sire," the crofter said. He had known the king all along, but had not mentioned it till that one moment. Blunter than his wife, he was less sure of the efficacy of touch. "Dead."

And this one final word the king heard.

"*She is not dead!*" he roared, bringing the back of his hand around to swat the crofter's face as if he were not a giant of a man but an insect. The crofter shuddered and was silent, for majesty does make gnats of such men, even in their own homes. Even there.

The infant, recognizing no authority but hunger and cold, began to cry at her father's voice. On and on she bawled, a high, unmusical strand of sound till the king dropped his dead wife's hand, put his own hands over his ears, and ran from the cottage screaming, "I shall go mad!"

He did not, of course. He ranged from distracted to distraught for days, weeks, months, and then the considerations of kingship recalled him to himself. It was his old self recalled: the distant, cold, considering king he had been before his marriage. For marriage to a young, beautiful, foreign-born queen had changed him. He had been for those short months a better man, but not a better ruler. So the councilors breathed easier, certainly. The barons and nobles breathed easier, surely. And the peasants—well, the peasants knew a hard hand either way, for the dalliance of kings has no effect on the measure of rain or the seasons in the sun, no matter what the poets write or the minstrels pluck upon their strings.

Only two in the kingdom felt the brunt of his neglect. Allerleirauh, of course, who would have loved to please him; but she scarcely knew him. And her nanny, who had been her mother's nanny, and was brought across the seas to a strange land. Where Allerleirauh knew hunger, the nurse knew hate. She blamed the king as he blamed the child, for the young queen's death, and she swore in her own dark way to bring sorrow to him and his line.

The king was mindful in his own way of his promises. Kingship demands attention to be paid. He loved his daughter with the kindness of kings, which is to say he ordered her clothed and fed and educated to her station. But he did not love her with his heart. How could he, having seen her first cloaked in his wife's blood? How could he, having named her Undoing?

He had her brought to him but once a year, on the anniversary of his wife's death, that he might remind himself of her crime. That it was also the anniversary of Allerleirauh's birth, he did not remark. She thought he remembered, but he did not.

So the girl grew unremarked and unloved, more at home in the crofter's cottage where she had been born. And remembering each time she sat there in the rain—learning the homey crafts from the crofter's stout wife—that first rain.

The king did not marry again, though his counselors advised it. Memory refines what is real. Gold smelted in the mind's cauldron is the purer. No woman could be as beautiful to him as the dead queen. He built monuments and statues, commissioned poems and songs. The palace walls were hung with portraits that resembled her, all in color—the skin white as snow, the lips red as blood, the hair black as raven's wings. He lived in a mausoleum and did not notice the live beauty for the dead one.

Years went by, and though each spring messengers went through the kingdom seeking a maiden "white and black and red," the king's own specifications, they came home each summer's end to stare disconsolately at the dead queen's portraits.

"Not one?" the king would ask.

"Not one," the messengers replied. For the kingdom's maidens had been blond or brown or redheaded. They had been pale or rosy or tan. And even those sent abroad found not a maid who looked like the statues or spoke like the poems or resembled in the slightest what they had all come to believe the late queen had been.

So the king went through spring and summer and into snow, still unmarried and without a male heir.

In desperation, his advisers planned a great three-day ball, hoping that—dressed in finery—one of the rejected maidens of the kingdom might take on a queenly air. Notice was sent that all were to wear black the first night, red the second, and white the third.

Allerleirauh was invited, too, though not by the king's own wishes. She was told of the ball by her nurse.

"I will make you three dresses," the old woman said. "The first dress will be as gold as the sun, the second as silver as the moon, and the third one will shine like the stars." She hoped that in this way, the princess would stand out. She hoped in this way to ruin the king.

Now if this were truly a fairy tale (and what story today with a king and queen and crofter's cottage is not?) the princess would go outside to her mother's grave. And there, on her knees, she would learn a magic greater than any craft, a woman's magic compounded of moonlight, elopement, and deceit. The neighboring kingdom would harbor her, the neighboring prince would marry her, her father would be brought to his senses, and the moment of complete happiness would be the moment of story's end. Ever after is but a way of saying: "There is nothing more to tell." It is but a dissembling. There is always more to tell. There is no happy *ever* after. There is happy *on occasion* and happy *every once in a while.* There is happy *when the memories do not overcome the now.*

But this is not a fairy tale. The princess is married to her father and, always having wanted his love, does not question the manner of it. Except at night, late at night, when he is away from her bed and she is alone in the vastness of it.

The marriage is sanctioned and made pure by the priests,

despite the grumblings of the nobles. One priest who dissents is murdered in his sleep. Another is burned at the stake. There is no third. The nobles who grumble lose their lands. Silence becomes the conspiracy; silence becomes the conspirators.

Like her mother, the princess is weak-wombed. She dies in childbirth surrounded by that silence, cocooned in it. The child she bears is a girl, as lovely as her mother. The king knows he will not have to wait another thirteen years.

It is an old story.

Perhaps the oldest.

THE GWYNHFAR

The *gwynhfar*—*the* white one, the pure one, the anointed one—waited. She had waited every day since her birth, it seemed, for this appointed time. Attended by her voiceless women in her underground rooms, the *gwynhfar*'s limbs had been kept oiled, her bone-white hair had been cleaned and combed. No color was allowed to stain her dead-white cheeks, no *maurish* black to line her eyes. White as the day she had been born, white as the foam on a troubled sea, white as the lilybell grown in the wood, she waited.

Most of her life had been spent on her straw bed in that half-sleep nature spent on her. She moved from small dream to small dream, moment to moment, hour to hour, day to day, without any real knowledge of what awaited her. Nor did she care. The *gwynhfar* did not have even creature sense, nor had she been taught to think. All she had been taught was waiting. It was her duty, it was her life.

She had been the firstborn of a dour landholder and his wife. Pulled silently from between her mother's thighs, bleached as bone, her tiny eyes closed tight against the agonizing light, the *gwynhfar* cried only in the day—a high, thin, mewling call. At night, without the sun to torment her, she seemed content; she waited.

They say now that the old mage attended her birth, but that is not true. He did not come for weeks, even months, till word of the white one's birth had traveled mouth to ear, mouth to ear, over and over the intervening miles. He did not come at first, but his messengers came, as they did to every report of a marvel. They had visited two-headed calves, fish-scaled infants, and twins joined at the hip and heart. When they heard of the white one, they came to her, too.

She waited for them as she waited for everything else.

And when the messengers saw that the stories were true enough, they reported back to the stone hall. So the Old One himself came, wrapped in his dignity and the sour trappings of state.

He had to bend down to enter the cottage, for age had not robbed him of the marvelous height that had first brought him to the attention of the Oldest Ones, those who dwell in the shadows of the Circle of Stones. He bent and bent till it seemed he would bend quite in two, and still he broke his head on the lintel.

"A marvel," it was said. "The blood anointed the door." That was no marvel, but a failing of judgment and the blood a mere trickle where the skin broke apart. But that is what was said. What the Old One himself said was in a language far older than he and twice as filled with power. But no one reported it, for who but the followers of the oldest way even know that tongue?

As the Old One stood there, gazing at the mewling white babe in her half sleep before the flickering fire, he nodded and stroked his thin beard. This, too, they say, and I have seen him often enough musing in just that way, so it could have been so.

Then he stretched forth his hand, that parchment-colored,

five-fingered magician's wand that could make balls and cards and silken banners disappear. He stretched forth his hand and touched the child. She shivered and woke fully for the first time, gazing at a point somewhere beyond his hand but not as far as his face with her watery pink eyes.

"So," he said in that nasal excuse for a voice. "So." He was never profligate with words. But it was enough.

The landholder gladly gave up the child, grateful to have the monster from his hearth. Sons could help till the lands. Only the royals crave girls. They make good counters in the bargaining games played across the castle boundary lines. But this girl was not even human enough to cook and clean and wipe the bottoms of her sisters and brothers to come. The landholder would have killed the moon-misbegotten thing on its emergence from his child-bride's womb had not the midwife stayed him. He sold the child for a single gold piece and thought himself clever in the bargain.

And did the Old One clear his throat then and consecrate their trade with words? Did he speak of prophesy or pronounce upon omens? If the landholder's wife had hoped for such to ease her guilt, she got short shrift of him. He had paid with a coin and a single syllable.

"So," he had said. And so it was.

The Old One carried the *gwynhfar* back over the miles with his own hands. "With his own hands," run the wonder tales, as if this were an awesome thing, carrying a tiny, witless babe. But think on it. Would he have trusted her to another, having come so far, across the years and miles, to find her? Would he have given her into clumsier hands when his own could still pull uncooked eggs from his sleeves without a crack or a drop?

Behind him, they say, came his people: the priests and the seers, a grand processional. But I guess rather he came by himself and at night. She would have been a noisy burden to carry through the bright, scalding light; squalling and squealing

at the sun. The moon always quieted her. Besides, he wanted to
surprise them with her, to keep her to himself till the end. For
was it not written that the *gwynhfar* would arise and bind the
kingdom:

> *Gwynhfar,* white as bone,
> Shall make the kingdom one.

Just as it had been written in the entrails of deer and the bloody
leavings of carrion crow that the Tall One, blessed be, would
travel the length of the kingdom to find her. Miracles are made
by hands such as his, and prophesies can be invented.

And then, too, he would want to be sure. He would want
time to think about what he carried, that small, white-haired
marvel, that unnature. For if the Old One was anything, he
was a planner. If he had been born better, he would have been a
mighty king. So, wrapped in the cloak of night, keeping the babe
from her enemy light, which drained even the small strength she
had, and scheming—always scheming—the Old One moved
through the land.

By day, of course, there would have been no mistaking him.
His height ever proclaimed him. Clothes were no disguise. A
mask but pointed the finger. At night, though, he was only a
long shadow in a world of long shadows.

I never saw him then, but I know it all. I can sort through
stories as a crow pecks through grain. And though it is said he
rode a whirlwind home, it was a time of year for storms. They
were no worse than other years. It is just that legend has a poor
memory, and hope an even worse.

The Old One returned with a cough that wracked his long,
thin body and an eye scratched out by a tree limb. The black
patch he wore thereafter gave rise to new tales. They say he had
been blinded in one eye at his first sight of her, the *gwynhfar.*
But I have it from the physician who attended him that there

was a great scar on his cheek and splinters still in the flesh around the eye.

And what did the Old One say of the wound?

"Clean it," he said. And then, "So!" There is no story there. That is why words of power have been invented for him.

The Old One had a great warren built for the child under the ground so the light would not disturb her rest. Room upon room was filled with things for a growing princess, but nothing there to speak to a child. How could he know what would interest a young one? It was said he had never been a babe. This was only partly a lie. He had been raised by the Oldest Ones himself. He had been young but he had never had a youth. So he waited impatiently for her to grow. He wanted to watch the unfolding of this white, alien flower, his only child.

But the *gwynhfar* was slow. Slow to sit, slow to crawl, slow to eat. Like a great white slug, she never did learn speech or to hold her bowels. She had to be kept wrapped in swaddling under her dresses to keep her clean, but who could see through the silk to know? She grew bigger but not much older, both a natural and unnatural thing. So she was never left alone.

It meant that the Old One had to change his plan. And so his plan became this. He had her beaten every day, but never badly. And on a signal, he would enter her underground chambers and put an end to her punishment. Again and again he arrived just as blood was about to be drawn. Then he would send away her tormentors, calling down horrid punishments upon them. It was not long before the *gwynhfar* looked only to him. She would turn that birch-white face toward the door waiting for him to enter, her watery eyes glistening. The overbig head on the weak neck seemed to strain for his words, though it was clear soon enough that she was deaf as well.

If he could have found another as white as she, he would likely have gotten rid of her. Perhaps. But there have been stranger loves. And only he could speak to her, a language of simple hand signs and finger plays. As she grew into womanhood, the two would converse in a limited fashion. It was some relief from statecraft and magecraft and the tortuous imaginings of history.

On those days and weeks when he did not come to see her, the *gwynhfar* often fell into a half sleep. She ate when fed, roused to go out into the night only when pulled from her couch. The women around her kept her exercised as if she were some exotic, half-wild beast, but they did take good care of her. They guessed what would happen if they did not.

What they did not guess was that they were doomed anyway. Her raising was to be the Old One's secret. Only one woman, who escaped with a lover, told what really happened. No one ever believed her, not even her lover, and he was soon dead in a brawl and she with him.

But I believed. I am bound to believe what cannot be true, to take fact from fancy, fashion fancy from fact.

The plan was changed, but not the promise.

> *Gwynhfar*, white as bone,
> Shall make the kingdom one.

The rhyme was known, sung through the halls of power and along the muddy country lanes. Not a man or woman or child but wished it to be so: for the kingdom to be bound up, its wounds cleansed. Justice is like a round banquet table—it comes full circle, and none should be higher or lower than the next. So the mage waited, for the *gwynhfar*'s first signs of womanhood. And the white one waited for the dark prince she had been promised, light and dark, two sides of the same coin. She of the old tribes, he of the new. She of the old faith and he of the new. He listened to new advisers, men of action, new gods. She had but one adviser, knew no action, had one god.

That was the promise: old and new wedded together. How else can a kingdom be made one?

How did the mage tell her this, finger upon finger? Did she understand? I only know she waited for the day with the patience of the dreamer, with the solidity of a stone. For that was what she was, a white pebble in a rushing stream, which does not move but changes the direction of the water that passes over it.

I know the beginning of the tale, but not yet the end. Perhaps this time the wisdom of the Oldest Ones will miscarry. Naught may come of naught. Such miracles are often barren. There have been rumors of white ones before. Beasts sometimes bear them. But they are weak, they die young, they cannot conceive. A queen without issue is a dreadful thing. Unnatural.

And the mage has planned it all except for the dark prince. He is a young bear of a king and I think will not be bought so easily with hand-wrought miracles. His hunger for land and for women, his need for heirs, will not be checked by the mage's blanched and barren offering. He is, I fear, of a lustier mind.

And I? I am no one, a singer of songs, a teller of tales. But I am the one to be wary of, for I remake the past and call it truth. I leave others to the rote of history, which is dry, dull, and unbelievable. Who is to say which mouth's outpourings will lift the soul higher—that which *is* or that which could be? Did it really flood, or did Noah have a fine story-maker living in his house? I care not either way. It is enough for me to sing.

But stay. It is my turn on the boards. Watch. I stride to the room's center, where the song's echo will linger longest. I lift my hands toward the young king, toward the old mage, toward the *gwynhfar* swaddled in silk who waits, as she waits for everything else. I bow my head and raise my voice.

"Listen," I say, my voice low and cozening.

"Listen, lords and ladies, as I sing of the coming days. I sing of the time when the kingdom will be one. And I call my song, the lay of the dark King Artos and of Guinevere the Fair."

CINDER ELEPHANT

There was once a lovely big girl who lived with her father in a large house near the king's park.

Her mother had been called *Pleasingly Plump*. Her grandmother had been called *Round and Rosy*. Her great-grandmother had been called *Sunny and Solid*. And her great-great-grandmother had been called *Fat!*

But though she was bigger than most, the girl had a sweet face, a loving heart, a kind disposition, and big feet.

Her name was Eleanor.

Her father called her Elly.

Now, Elly and her father did everything together. They rambled and scrambled over the rolling hills. They bird-watched and dish-washed and trout-fished and star-wished together.

In fact they were happy for a long long time.

But one day Elly's father grew lonely for someone his own age; someone who laughed at the same jokes; someone who'd memorized the words to the same songs; someone who knew the steps to dances like the turkey trot and the mashed potato and didn't think those were just food groups.

So he married again, a woman so thin, it took her three tries to throw a shadow. She had two skinny daughters. One was as skinny as a straw, one was as skinny as a reed. They had thin smiles, too. And thin names: Reen and Rhee. And hearts so thin you could read a magazine through them.

Reen and Rhee smiled their thin smiles all through the wedding, and the very next morning they made Elly their maid.

They made her do the dishes. They made her make the beds. They even made her sit in the fireplace, where she got covered with soot and cinders.

To make matters worse, they called her names:

> *"Elly, Elly,*
> *Big fat belly,*
> *Cinder Elephant."*

So Elly cried.

But crying only made things worse. It made the soot into mud pies and the cinders into bogs. So Elly stopped crying.

Elly may have been big, but she wasn't stupid. She did the sisters' work without complaining and she did it very well. And in her spare time—which meant long after her stepmother and the skinnies were asleep—she read books. Books about football and baseball, books about tennis and golf. It was how she preferred to get her exercise.

One day as Elly worked in the kitchen, two little bluebirds peeked in the window.

Elly guessed they were hungry, so she gave them each a crumb of bread.

Just then, in came the skinnies, Reen and Rhee, one thin as a reed, one thin as a straw. "Mama, Mama," they screamed in their thin little voices. "Look what Cinder Elephant has done!"

Their skinny mother came quickly in her best running shoes, size five-and-a-half narrow. (Very narrow.)

She took the bread crumbs away, saying, "Cinder Elephant, this is all you will get for *your* dinner. Dieting will do you a world of good, and you will thank me for it later."

Then she turned to her skinny daughters. "I have great news. Prince Junior is home from school."

"The PRINCE!" Reen and Rhee squealed, for of course they had heard of him. He wore great clothes. He had straight teeth, which in the days before dentists took a lot of doing. And he was sure to inherit the kingdom.

Then, they smiled their thin smiles at one another, and ran to their bedrooms to pick out their prettiest dresses to wear just in case they should bump into him.

Elly stayed on in the kitchen pretending to cry. But as soon as the skinnies were gone, and her stepmother, too, she gave her bread-crumb dinner to the bluebirds, anyway.

They ate it in one gulp each, singing:

> *"The bigger the heart,*
> *The greater the prize.*
> *You will be perfect*
> *In somebody's eyes."*

Fairy-tale birds always sing like this. It's annoying to everyone except the heroine.

Meanwhile, in the palace Prince Junior had just had a serious talk with his father the king.

"Time to get married," said the king. "Time to grow up. Time to run the kingdom." The king always spoke that way to his son: short and to the point. Pointed remarks were his specialty.

"I'm not in love," said Prince Junior.

"Doesn't matter," said the king.

"I'm not even in like," said Prince Junior.

"Doesn't matter," said the king.

"I don't even know any girls," said Prince Junior.

"*That* matters," said the king. "Time to think about it." So the king began to think.

It took hours.

It took days.

It took help. The queen was his helpmeet.

At last they came up with a plan.

"Time for a ball," the king said.

Prince Junior was pleased. "Oh good," he said. "I like balls." He meant he liked footballs and baseballs and tennis balls. (Though he wasn't terribly fond of mothballs. They stank something fierce.)

"Your father means a fancy-dress, drinking champagne from slippers ball," said his mother, the queen.

Prince Junior groaned. He really preferred watching birds to that kind of ball.

"Invite everyone in the kingdom," said the king, priming his prime minister. "As long as they are girls. Send invitations to every shop girl, cop girl, mop girl, prop girl, and champagne-in-the-slipper girl in the kingdom."

"And," added the queen, "remind everyone—no invitation, no admittance."

So invitations went out on creamy invitation paper, and every girl in the kingdom was invited except for Elly because her stepsisters tore up her invitation. Then they made Elly pick up the creamy pieces.

On the night of the royal ball, the stepsisters swept out of the house in yellow gowns, skinny as straws and looking like brooms. They rode to the castle and their skinny mother went with them.

And to the castle as well went every shop girl, cop girl, prop girl, and champagne-in-the-slipper girl in the kingdom.

But Elly stayed at home staring into the cinders. She had no invitation to the ball. Even worse—she had nothing to wear. To make sure Elly didn't try to go to the castle, the stepsisters had hidden her clothes except for the slip she had on, and didn't tell her where.

At ten o'clock, there came a noise at the kitchen window. It was the bluebirds.

> *"You gave us something*
> *Yummy to eat.*
> *Now we are back*
> *With a marvelous treat."*

Elly threw open the window.

In flew the bluebirds with all their bird friends carrying a large gown made of feathers. Blue feathers from the bluebirds, gold feathers from the goldfinches, green feathers from the greenfinches, and brown feathers from the owls.

They slipped the gown over Elly's head before she could say a word. The birds sang:

> *"You look beautiful,*
> *As trees in the fall.*
> *And now you can set off*
> *For Prince Junior's ball."*

Actually, with all those feathers, Elly looked more like a big fat hen. And as much as she wanted to go to the royal dance, Elly knew a thing or two about such balls herself. *No* one could get in without a proper invitation. But she didn't want to hurt the birds' feelings.

So she said, "I have no dancing slippers. Size nine-and-a-half wide. (Very wide.)"

The birds flew away all atwitter and did not return until eleven o'clock, when they pecked excitedly at the kitchen window.

"Let us in, let us in,
We've come with a treat:
A pair of new shoes
To put on your feet."

(Please remember that the expression "birdbrain" had been invented by someone who knew quite a bit about birds. Possibly John J. Audubon, who may have said it first in French.)

Elly opened the window and in flew the bluebirds with all their bird friends carrying two big slippers made of twigs and grass which they slipped onto Elly's feet.

"How do I look?" Elly asked.

Actually now she looked like a big fat hen sitting on a nest. But the birds all thought she looked beautiful and said so.

Elly didn't want to hurt their feelings. But she still had no invitation. So instead she said, "I have no carriage to ride in. And if I walk to the palace, I will be too late for the ball."

The birds convened a quick parliament, took a vote, and a minute later came back with an answer:

"Here we are,
birds of a feather,
and so we must all
flock together."

And before Elly could ask them what they meant, they'd lifted her up and up and up. The wind blew under the arms of the feather gown. And away Elly flew with the flock to Prince Junior's fancy-dress ball.

By now, of course, it was nearly midnight.

Prince Junior was tired of talking about things he didn't enjoy—the weather, the price of fancy dresses, and the name of every single dance that had been played by the very busy orchestra. He was slightly sick from the shoe champagne. So he slipped away out onto the terrace by himself for a breath of fresh air and a bit of bird-watching. There were usually owls outside in the trees.

He had just put his field glasses up to his eyes, when what should drop from the skies but a giant hen on a nest.

Prince Junior was amazed. He stared at the lovely round face through his glasses. He checked his field guide.

There was no such hen listed among the chickens.

It was Elly, of course, come to the royal ball but without an invitation.

"Sorry to make an end run around the guards at the door," she said.

"You know football!" cried the prince.

"And baseball," Elly said.

"What about tennis?" asked the prince.

"Adore it," she said. "Golf, too."

Prince Junior wasn't too sure about golf. So he asked slyly, "Mothballs?"

"They stink something fierce," she answered.

"I think I love you," said the prince, smiling at Elly with his perfect teeth.

Just then, a big wind blew across the terrace, lifting Elly and her feather dress back into the air.

One of her slippers fell off, landing in the undergrowth.

Then she was gone, blown back home, before answering Prince Junior's modified declaration of love.

By the time she was dropped onto her own front porch, the

feather gown was a ruin. She put the remaining slipper on the windowsill over the kitchen sink and filled it with ferns.

Poor Elly.

Poor Prince.

The skinny sisters came home in a twit. That's not a carriage. It's a snit, a boil, a caterwaul of discontent. They were so mad, they could barely talk. So they yelled.

"PRINCE JUNIOR IS A LOON!"
"WHICH IS A KIND OF BIRD!"
"HE'S IN LOVE WITH A BIG FAT HEN!"
(They said this last together.)

Elly smiled into the cinders. It was a happy smile and a sad smile, too. But she didn't tell them anything. A secret only works in silence. That much she knew.

Prince Junior found the slipper under a tree the very next day when he was out bird-watching, which some people do when they have broken hearts or just a free afternoon. He picked up the slipper, first thinking it was a nest, and was about to set it in the tree when he took a second look.

"I know what this is," he whispered, not even glancing at a flock of bluebirds which suddenly rose up from the grass. He was pretty smart for a prince.

He ran inside with the slipper in hand. He found his parents in the drawing room having tea. "I want to marry the hen who fits this grass slipper," he announced.

"*Glass* slippers are more usual," his mother said.

"Princes marry swans—not hens," added his father, looking at the queen.

Then they both sighed.

But Prince Junior was adamant.

So he searched high. (Very high.)

And low. (Very low.)

In fact he searched the entire kingdom. But all the eligible girls (and even their mothers) had small feet, tiny feet, five- to seven-and-a-half narrow feet. (Very narrow.) The grass slipper fell off everyone.

At last Prince Junior arrived at Elly's house, the very last house on the very last block in the kingdom. And there Elly sat among the cinders, staring at the soot.

The skinny sisters tried on the grass slipper. They each wadded paper in the toe-end and cotton at the heel. They each put Super Glue on their instep and duct tape around the ankle.

But still the grass slipper fell off. (It was, after all, a slipper and was slippery with the sweat of dozens and dozens of previous girls who had tried desperately to keep the slipper on.)

Reen threw the slipper on the floor and Rhee stomped on it. "If it doesn't fit us," they said together, "it won't be tried on anyone else."

"Oh no!" cried Prince Junior. "Now how will I ever find my own true love?" Well, maybe he wasn't much smarter than the average prince. But he'd tried. Indeed, as the king and queen could attest to, there were times he was very trying.

Furious, the skinnies called out, "Elly, come clean up this mess."

Then they swept out of the room with Prince Junior in tow, while Elly swept the room up by herself.

When she was done, Elly got the other slipper from the windowsill. She was about to take out the fern to show Prince Junior who she really was, when she noticed the bluebirds had used the slipper as a nest. There amongst the curling ferns were three little eggs. So she put the slipper-nest back on the sill and sat down again in the cinders.

Poor Elly.

Poor Prince.

And that would have been the end of that, except the blue-birds flew back to the nest, and upset that it had been moved, began to squawk and scold in bluebird, a dialect that Ella had just about mastered.

"I am truly sorry. . ." she began.

Prince Junior heard the sounds, knew a bit of bluebird himself, plus sparrow, swallow, and—from a January term in the African desert—a few words of ostrich as well. He ran back into the kitchen, leaving the skinnies behind.

"Bluebirds!" he cried, and said to them in the High Tongue, "Do not distress yourselves on my account."

"*Sialia sialis*," said Elly, "if you insist on being formal." It was the scientific name which only bird-watchers seem to know or care about.

Prince Junior turned his field glasses from the birds on the nest to Elly. Close up he recognized her face. "My dear hen!" he cried. "I love you. Every inch of you."

"My dear prince," she cooed.

Then they kissed, and all that nonsense about slippers— glass, grass, or good sturdy leather—was forgotten.

Elly and Prince Junior were married, of course. Her father and the king took turns dancing with the queen.

Elly and the prince named their children Blue, Green, Goldie, and Owl, starting a fad in bird names for new babies throughout the kingdom, which left a few children with unfortunate monikers like Titmouse, Turkey, Booby, and Loon.

As for Rhee and Reen and their skinny mother, they were often invited to the palace for tea, but they never went. Their lips were too thin to ask forgiveness and their minds too mean to understand love.

Moral: If you love a waist, you waste a love.
Second Moral: Not everyone who loves balls has them.
Third Moral: Be kind to birds. You may need them someday.

MAMA GONE

Mama died four nights ago, giving birth to my baby sister, Ann. Bubba cried and cried, "Mama gone," in his little-boy voice, but I never let out a single tear.

There was blood red as any sunset all over the bed from that birthing, and when Papa saw it he rubbed his head against the cabin wall over and over and over and made little animal sounds. Sukey washed Mama down and placed the baby on her breast for a moment. "Remember," she whispered.

"Mama gone," Bubba wailed again.

But I never cried.

By all rights we should have buried her with garlic in her mouth and her hands and feet cut off, what with her being vampire kin and all. But Papa absolutely refused.

"Your Mama couldn't stand garlic," he said when the sounds had stopped rushing out of his mouth and his eyes had cleared. "It made her come all over with rashes. She had the sweetest mouth and hands."

And that was that. Not a one of us could make him change his mind, not even Grandad Stokes or Pop Wilber or any of

239

the men who came to pay their last respects. And as Papa is a preacher, and a brimstone man, they let it be. The onliest thing he would allow was for us to tie red ribbons 'round her ankles and wrist, a kind of sign like a line of blood. Everybody hoped that would do.

But on the next day she rose from out her grave and commenced to prey upon the good folk of Taunton.

Of course she came to our house first, that being the dearest place she knew. I saw her outside my window, gray as a gravestone, her dark eyes like the holes in a shroud. When she stared in she didn't know me, though I had always been her favorite.

"Mama be gone," I said, and waved my little cross at her, the one she had given me the very day I'd been born. "Avaunt." The old Bible word sat heavy in my mouth.

She put her hand up on the window frame, and as I watched, the gray fingers turned splotchy pink from all the garlic I had rubbed into the wood.

Black tears dropped from her black eyes, then. But I never cried.

She tried each window in turn, and not a person awake in the house but me. But I had done my work well and the garlic held her out. She even tried the door, but it was no use. By the time she left, I was so sleepy I dropped down right by the door. Papa found me there at cockcrow. He never did ask what I was doing, and if he guessed, he never said.

Little Joshua Greenough was found dead in his crib. The doctor took two days to come over the mountains to pronounce it. By then the garlic around his little bed—to keep him from walking, too—had mixed with death smells. Everybody knew. Even the doctor, and him a city man. It hurt Joshua's mama and papa sore to do the cutting. But it had to be done.

The men came to our house that very noon to talk about what had to be. Papa kept shaking his head all through their talking. But even his being preacher didn't stop them. Once a vampire walks these mountain hollers, there's nary a house or barn that's safe. Nighttime is lost time. And no one can afford to lose much stock.

So they made their sharp sticks out of green wood, the curling shavings littering our cabin floor. Bubba played in them, not understanding. Sukey was busy with the baby, nursing it with a bottle and a sugar teat. It was my job to sweep up the wood curls. They felt slick on one side, bumpy on the other. Like my heart.

Papa said, "I was the one let her turn into a nightwalker. It's my business to stake her out."

No one argued. Specially not the Greenoughs, their eyes still red from weeping.

"Just take my children," Papa said. "And if anything goes wrong, cut off my hands and feet and bury me at Mill's Cross, under the stone. There's garlic hanging in the pantry. Mandy Jane will string me some."

So Sukey took the baby and Bubba off to the Greenoughs' house, that seeming the right thing to do, and I stayed the rest of the afternoon with Papa, stringing garlic and pressing more into the windows. But the strand over the door he took down.

"I have to let her in somewhere," he said. "And this is where I'll make my stand." He touched me on the cheek, the first time ever. Papa never has been much for show.

"Now you run along to the Greenoughs', Mandy Jane," he said. "And remember how much your mama loved you. This isn't her, child. Mama's gone. Something else has come to take her place. I should have remembered that the Good Book says, 'The living know that they shall die; but the dead know not anything.'"

I wanted to ask him how the vampire knew to come first to our house, then; but I was silent, for Papa had been asleep and hadn't seen her.

I left without giving him a daughter's kiss, for his mind was well set on the night's doing. But I didn't go down the lane to the Greenoughs' at all. Wearing my triple strand of garlic, with my cross about my neck, I went to the burying ground, to Mama's grave.

It looked so raw against the greening hillside. The dirt was red clay, but all it looked like to me was blood. There was no cross on it yet, no stone. That would come in a year. Just a humping, a heaping of red dirt over her coffin, the plain pinewood box hastily made.

I lay facedown in that dirt, my arms opened wide. "Oh, Mama," I said, "the Good Book says you are not dead but sleepeth. Sleep quietly, Mama, sleep well." And I sang to her the lullaby she had always sung to me and then to Bubba and would have sung to Baby Ann had she lived to hold her.

> *"Blacks and bays,*
> *Dapples and grays,*
> *All the pretty little horses."*

And as I sang I remembered Papa thundering at prayer meeting once, "Behold, a pale horse: and his name that sat on him was Death." The rest of the song just stuck in my throat then, so I turned over on the grave and stared up at the setting sun.

It had been a long and wearying day, and I fell asleep right there in the burying ground. Any other time fear might have overcome sleep. But I just closed my eyes and slept.

When I woke, it was dead night. The moon was full and sitting between the horns of two hills. There was a sprinkling of stars overhead. And Mama began to move the ground beneath me, trying to rise.

The garlic strands must have worried her, for she did not come out of the earth all at once. It was the scrabbling of her long nails at my back that woke me. I leaped off that grave and was wide awake.

Standing aside the grave, I watched as first her long gray arms reached out of the earth. Then her head emerged with its hair that was once so gold now gray and streaked with black, and its shroud eyes. And then her body in its winding sheet, stained with dirt and torn from walking to and fro upon the land. Then her bare feet with blackened nails, though alive Mama used to paint those nails, her one vanity and Papa allowed it seeing she was so pretty and otherwise not vain.

She turned toward me as a hummingbird toward a flower, and she raised her face up and it was gray and bony. Her mouth peeled back from her teeth and I saw that they were pointed and her tongue was barbed.

"Mama gone," I whispered in Bubba's voice, but so low I could hardly hear it myself.

She stepped toward me off that grave, lurching down the hump of dirt. But when she got close, the garlic strands and the cross stayed her.

"Mama."

She turned her head back and forth. It was clear she could not see with those black shroud eyes. She only sensed me there, something warm, something alive, something with blood running like satisfying streams through blue veins.

"Mama," I said again. "Try and remember."

That searching awful face turned toward me again, and the pointy teeth were bared once more. Her hands reached out to grab me, then pulled back.

"Remember how Bubba always sucks his thumb with that funny little noise you always said was like a little chuck in its hole. And how Sukey hums through her nose when she's baking bread. And how I listened to your belly to hear the baby. And how Papa always starts each meal with the blessing on things that grow fresh in the field."

The gray face turned for a moment toward the hills, and I wasn't even sure she could hear me. But I had to keep trying.

"And remember when we picked the blueberries and Bubba fell down the hill, tumbling head-end over. And we laughed until we heard him, and he was saying the same six things over and over till long past bed."

The gray face turned back toward me and I thought I saw a bit of light in the eyes. But it was just reflected moonlight.

"And the day Papa came home with the new ewe lamb and we fed her on a sugar teat. You stayed up all the night and I slept in the straw by your side."

It was as if stars were twinkling in those dead eyes. I couldn't stop staring, but I didn't dare stop talking, either.

"And remember the day the bluebird stunned itself on the kitchen window and you held it in your hands. You warmed it to life, you said. To life, Mama."

Those stars began to run down the gray cheeks.

"There's living, Mama, and there's dead. You've given so much life. Don't be bringing death to these hills now." I could see that the stars were gone from the sky over her head; the moon was setting.

"Papa loved you too much to cut your hands and feet. You gotta return that love, Mama. You gotta."

Veins of red ran along the hills, outlining the rocks. As the sun began to rise, I took off one strand of garlic. Then the second. Then the last. I opened my arms. "Have you come back, Mama, or are you gone?"

The gray woman leaned over and clasped me tight in her arms. Her head bent down toward mine, her mouth on my forehead, my neck, the outline of my little gold cross burning across her lips.

She whispered, "Here and gone, child, here and gone," in a voice like wind in the coppice, like the shaking of willow leaves. I felt her kiss on my cheek, a brand.

Then the sun came between the hills and hit her full in the face, burning her as red as earth. She smiled at me and then there were only dust motes in the air, dancing. When I looked down at my feet, the grave dirt was hardly disturbed but Mama's gold wedding band gleamed atop it.

I knelt down and picked it up, and unhooked the chain holding my cross. I slid the ring onto the chain, and the two nestled together right in the hollow of my throat. I sang:

> *"Blacks and bays,*
> *Dapples and grays . . ."*

and from the earth itself, the final words sang out,

> *"All the pretty little horses."*

That was when I cried, long and loud, a sound I hope never to make again as long as I live.

THE WOMAN WHO
LOVED A BEAR

It was early in the autumn, the leaves turning over yellow in the puzzling wind, that a woman of the Cheyennes and her father went to collect meat he had killed. They each rode a horse and led a pack horse behind, for the father had killed two fine antelopes and had left them, skinned and cut up and covered well with hide.

They didn't know that a party of Crows had found the cache and knew it for a Cheyenne kill by the hide covering it.

"We will wait for the hunter to come and collect his meat," they said. "We will get both a Cheyenne and his meat." It made them laugh at the thought.

And so it happened. The Cheyenne man and his daughter came innocently to the meat and the Crows charged down on them. The man was killed and his daughter was taken away as a prisoner, well to the north, to a village on the Sheep River which is now called the Big Horn.

Is that the end of the story, grandfather?
It is only the beginning. This is called

"The Woman Who Loved A Bear." I have not
even come to the bear yet.

The man who carried the pipe of the Crow war party was named
Fifth Man Over and he had two wives. But when he looked at
the Cheyenne girl he thought that she was very fine looking
and wanted her for his wife. Of course his two wives were both
Crow women, which means they were ugly and hard. They were
not pleased about the Cheyenne woman becoming his third
wife. When they asked her name, she told them she was called
"Walks with the Sun," so they called her "Flat Foot Walker."
But they could call her what they wanted, it did not change the
fact that she was beautiful and they were not.

So whenever Fifth Man Over was away from the lodge, they
abused the Cheyenne girl. They hit her with quirts and sticks
and stones till her arms and legs were bruised. But they were
careful not to hit her in the face, where even Fifth Man Over
would see and ask questions.

The days and weeks went by and the beautiful Cheyenne
wife had to do all the hard work. She had to pack the wood and
dress the hides; she had to make moccasins, not only for her
Crow husband, but for his ugly wives as well.

Grandfather, I have heard this story before. I
have seen a movie of it. It is called "Cinderella."

Is there a bear in "Cinderella"?

No, of course not.

Then you do not know this story. This is a
true story, from the time when children played
games suited to their years and spoke with
respect to their grandfathers. You will listen
carefully so that you may tell the story just as I
tell it to you.

Now, in Fifth Man Over's lodge there also lived a young man, about a year older than the Cheyenne woman, who was an Arapaho and had been taken as a slave in a raid when he was a small child. He had the keeping and herding of Fifth Man Over's horses. He was not straight and tall like a Cheyenne, but limped because his left foot had been burned in the raid that made him a slave. But he had a strong nose and straight black hair and he spoke softly to the Cheyenne woman.

"These women abuse you," he said. "You must not let them do so."

"I cannot do otherwise," Walks with the Sun answered. "They are my husband's elder wives." It was the proper answer, but she was a Cheyenne woman and they were only Crows, and so she said it through set teeth.

"Make many moccasins," the Arapaho told her. "Many more than are needed. Hide some away for yourself."

"Why should I do this?" she asked.

"Because you will need them on the trail back to your people."

She looked straight in his face and saw that there was no deceit there. She did not look at his crooked leg.

"You will wear out many moccasins on the trail," he said.

> When does the bear come in, grandfather?
> Soon.
> How soon?
> Soon enough. It is not time to cut this story off. Listen. You will have to tell it back to me, you know.

Walks with the Sun made many moccasins, and for every three she made, she hid one away. This took her through winter and into the spring when the snow melted and the first flowers appeared down by the river bank.

"We will go in the morning for the buffalo," said Fifth Man

Over to his wives. By this he meant he would ride a horse and they would come behind with the pack horse pulling the travois sled.

"She should not come with us," said his first wife, pointing to Walks with the Sun. "She is a Cheyenne and has no stamina and will not be able to keep up and will want more than her share of the meat."

"And she is ugly," said the second wife, but she did not say it very loud.

"I will stay home, my husband," said Walks with the Sun, "and make the lodge ready for your return."

"And you will not break any of the pots we have worked so hard on," said the first wife.

"And you will not eat anything till we come back," said the second wife.

With all this Walks with the Sun agreed, though she would have loved to see the buffalo in their great herds and the men on their horses charging down on the bulls, even though they were Crow and not Cheyenne. She had heard that the sound of the buffalo running was like thunder on the great open plain, that it was a music that made the grass dance. But she kept her head bent and her eyes modestly down.

So Fifth Man Over and his two wives and most of the other hunters and their wives left to go after the buffalo. And the Arapaho went, too, for he was to take care of the horses along the way.

> Grandfather, a buffalo is not a bear, and you promised.
>
> There will be a bear.
>
> Buffalo do not eat bear. Bear eat buffalo. I prefer the bear.
>
> There will be a bear.
>
> There had better be.

But the young man returned the long way around, leaving his own horse in the timber outside of the camp. He came limping into the Crow village and the old people said to him, "Why are you here? What has happened to the people?" By this they meant the Crows.

"Nothing has happened to the people. They are following the buffalo. But my horse threw me and ran away and I have come back for another." He went to Fifth Man Over's lodge and saddled another horse and put two fine blankets on it, but not the best, because he was a slave after all. But before he mounted up, he went into the lodge and said to Walks with the Sun, "Now is your time. I have hidden my own horse in the timber down by the creek. You must take a large pot and go down later for water and you will find it there. Put your extra moccasins in the pot, for should you lose the horse, you will surely need them."

"What of you?" asked Walks with the Sun. "Surely you want to leave here."

"I have no other home," he answered.

"Then you shall come home with me," she said.

"I am poor and I have a bad leg and I am not a Cheyenne," he said. "But I will watch out for you, never fear."

He rode away, but in a different direction from the creek, so that no one would suspect that the two of them had spoken. And Walks with the Sun did as he instructed. Taking a large pot, she put the moccasins in. Then she went to the creek. There she found the horse, saddled, with two blankets. Swinging herself up into the saddle, she began to ride south, toward her home.

> I am still waiting, grandfather.
> Patience is a good thing in the young.
> I am not patient. I am impatient.

I did not notice. The bear, though, is coming.
In fact, grandson, the bear is here.
Here? Where?
In the story. But you cannot see it unless you
listen.
I see with my eyes, I hear with my ears,
grandfather.
You must do both, child. You must do both.

Walks with the Sun rode many miles until both she and the
horse were tired. So she got off, unsaddled it, and let the horse
feed on the new spring grass. Then she re-saddled the horse and
rode another long time past the Pumpkin Buttes. There she
made camp, but without a fire in case anyone should be looking
for her.

In the middle of the night she awoke because of a huffing and
snuffling sound and the horse got frightened and screamed like
a white woman in labor, and broke its rope. It ran off not to be
found again.

And there, near here, with the moonlight on its back, was . . .

The bear, grandfather.
The bear, grandson.

Walks with the Sun spoke softly to the bear, not out of honor
but out of fear. "Oh, Bear," she said, "take pity on me. I am only
a poor Cheyenne woman and I am trying to get back to my
own people." And then, quietly, carefully, she pulled on a pair of
moccasins and stood. Carrying several more pairs in each hand,
she backed away from the bear. When she could no longer see
the great beast, she turned around and ran.

She ran until she was exhausted and then she turned and
looked behind her. There was the bear, just a little way behind.
So, taking a deep breath, she ran again until she could barely

put one foot in front of the other. When she turned to look again, the bear was still there.

At last she was so tired that she knew she must rest, even if the bear was to kill her. She sat down on a hollow log, and fell asleep sitting up, heedless of the bear.

While she slept, she heard the bear speak to her. His voice was like the rocks in a river, with the water rushing over. He said: "Get up and go to your people. I am watching to protect you. I am stepping in your tracks so that the Crows cannot trail you, so that Fifth Man Over and his ugly wives cannot find you."

When Walks with the Sun awoke, it was still dark. The bear was squatting on its haunches not far from her, its head crowned with the stars. Awake, she did not think he could have spoken, so she was still afraid of him.

She rose carefully, put on new moccasins, and began her journey again, but this time she did not run. She walked on until she could walk no longer. Then she lay down under a tree and slept.

> You said he spoke in a dream, grandfather.
> I said he spoke while she slept, grandson.
> Is that the same as really speaking?
> You are sitting with me on the buffalo-calf
> robe. Do you need to ask such questions?

In the morning Walks with the Sun awoke and saw the bear a little ways off on top of a small butte. It did not seem to be looking at her, but when she started to walk, it followed again in her tracks.

So it went all the day, till she reached the Platte River. Since this was early spring, the waters were full from bank to bank. Walks with the Sun had no idea how she could get across.

She sighed out loud but said nothing else. At the sound, the bear came over to her, looked in her face, and his breath was hot and foul-smelling. Then he turned his back to her and stuck his great rear in her face. By this she knew that he wanted her to get on his back.

"Bear," she said, "if you are willing to take me across the river, I am willing to ride." And she crawled on his back and put her arms around his neck, just in front of his mighty shoulders. With a snort, he plunged into the water.

The water was cold. She could feel it through her leggings. And the river tumbled strongly over its rocky bed. But stronger still was the bear and he swam across with ease.

When they got to the other side, the bear waited while she dismounted, then he shook himself all over, scattering water on every leaf and stone. Then he rolled on the ground.

While he was rolling, Walks with the Sun started on. When she looked back, the bear was following her just as he had before.

So it went for many days, the Cheyenne woman walking, the bear coming along behind. When she was hungry, he caught a young buffalo calf and killed it. She skinned it, cut it into pieces, took her flint, made a fire, then cooked the meat. Some of it she ate, and some she gave to the bear.

The rest she rolled in the skin, making a pack she carried on her back.

> Did she feed him by hand, grandfather?
>
> By hand?
>
> Did she hold out pieces for him to eat?
>
> That would be foolish, indeed, grandson. He could have taken her hand off at the wrist and not even noticed. Where do you young people come up with such foolish ideas, heh?
>
> Then how did she feed the bear?
>
> She put it down on the ground a little way from her and the bear walked up and ate it.
>
> Oh.

They came at last to the Laramie River and below was a big village, with so many lodges they covered the entire bank.

"I do not know if those are my people or not," Walks with the Sun said. "Can you go and find out for me?"

The bear went up close to the outermost lodge, but someone saw him and shouted, and someone else, an old man whose hand was not so steady, shot an arrow at him. The arrow pierced his left hind foot and he ran back to Walks with the Sun, limping.

"Oh, Bear," she cried, "you are hurt and it is all my fault." She knelt down and pulled the arrow from his foot and stopped the bleeding with the heel of her hand.

When the people tracked the blood trail to them, she was still sitting there, holding the bear in her arms. Only he was no longer a bear, but a young man with a strong nose and straight black hair and a left foot that was not quite straight.

> The bear turned into the Arapaho slave, grandfather?
> That is not what I said, grandson.
> But I thought you said . . .
> Listen, grandson, listen.

Walks with the Sun took the buffalo hide, shook it out, and turned it so the hair side was outward. Then she wrapped the Arapaho in it to show he was a medicine man. Her people put great strings of beads around his neck and gave him feathers to honor him. Then they lifted him onto a travois sled and, pulling it themselves, brought him into the village.

He never walked as a bear again, except twice, when the people were threatened by Crows. Walks with the Sun became his wife and they had many children and many grandchildren, of which I am one, and you are another. The buffalo hide we are sitting on today is the very one of which I have spoken.

Is that a true story, grandfather?

It is a true story, grandson.

But how can it be true, grandfather? People can't turn into bears. Bears can't turn into people.

Heh. They do not do so today. But we are speaking of the time when the Cheyenne were a great nation and still in the north, when the land was covered with buffalo, and we passed the medicine arrows and buffalo hat from keeper to keeper.

And the buffalo hide, grandfather?

And the buffalo hide, grandson. This ties it off.

What does that mean?

That storytelling is over for the night. That it is time for children to ask no more questions but to sleep. Time for old men to dream by the fire.

This ties it off, grandfather.

WRESTLING WITH ANGELS

My father wrestled with an angel and, like Jacob in the Bible, was lamed in the match. It happened on Ninety-sixth, across the street from our building. I was just a little boy then, in a stroller, but I know the story is true. My father limped ever after.

But the angel is not the hero of my father's story. Not at all.

And maybe my father isn't, either.

He had been taking me out for some fresh air, if you can call what New York City has fresh. Or air. My mom was pregnant and having a difficult time coping with my noisy enthusiasms. So my father had promised to give her time for a much-needed nap.

We had just crossed the street into Central Park, and he was pushing the stroller along a path that winds past a small outcropping of rocks, when something large and dark fell from the sky.

My father's first thought was that the thing was a kite. Or a large bird. Or a piece of metal that had fallen off a plane heading for La Guardia Airport.

"Jeez, Jesse," he said to me.

I saw it, too, and reached out my hand for it. "Mine!" I said, as I said about everything in those days.

But the falling thing was heading straight toward a child playing ball on the grass.

Dad let go of my stroller and took off running toward the child. He was a New York cop in those days, and he had quick instincts.

He was fast, too, pushing the kid aside and out of harm's way. The big falling thing hit him instead, wrapping itself around him. It was only then that he realized that he had hold of an angel.

The angel was man-shaped, the color of old gold, with dark, almond-shaped eyes. Its wingspread was enormous. Dad often said that without those wings, he could have beaten the angel in that first fall—because though it was his size, it seemed to weigh very little, as if its bones were as hollow as a bird's. But those wings, Dad said, made up for its lack of weight. They simply wrapped around Dad's shoulders and head, nearly suffocating him.

All the while it wrestled with him, the angel sang. Dad said that it was years before he realized the angel had been singing a *Te Deum*. He didn't recognize it until he returned to the Mother Church.

How long the two of them struggled, Dad didn't know. But somewhere along the way, the angel got hold of his thigh and yanked hard, pulling it out of joint. A hold they teach in angel school, I guess, because it's the same one that's in the Bible, Genesis 32:25. I looked it up.

Dad screamed—a sound I hope never to hear again—and fell to the ground; but he took hold of the angel around the waist and carried it down with him. The minute the angel touched the ground, it screamed back, as if the very earth had wounded it.

". . . !" the angel cried in some unknown tongue.

"You're under arrest, damn you," Dad said. Even though he was not on duty, he carried handcuffs with him. Somehow he managed to cuff the angel's wrists behind; maybe—or so I am guessing—because Dad's curse had weakened it sufficiently. Or because, like the fairies in the old tales, its power was drained by metal.

Grabbing the angel's shoulder with one hand and pushing my stroller with the other, Dad took the angel down to the police station to book it. He limped painfully all the way.

"Mine!" I said, reaching out for the angel. It turned its dark eyes on me and I cried and looked away.

No one at the station could see the angel's wings. No one in the park had seen the angel falling toward the child. In fact, no one could even *find* the child, though they went door-to-door asking.

Some of the cops thought Dad had booked a very thin and very old man who spoke no English and looked perfectly harmless. Chinese, probably, they thought, looking away from the almond eyes. And no matter how much Dad begged them, they wouldn't weigh him.

"Jeez, Bernulli," the sergeant said to Dad, "of course he weighs nothing. He's just skin and bones. Comes from eating only rice."

The desk officer was sure Dad had been drinking. Dad had been known to throw back a beer or two on duty; he'd been reprimanded more than once. He and Mom argued about it all the time. I remember *those* fights vividly.

The cops finally had to let the angel go because there was no evidence. The angel disappeared right outside the door to the station. "Went to Chinatown," the sergeant said.

When Dad pointed skyward, his buddies laughed at him. He became the joke of the station. "Wrestling Jake," they called him. And sometimes, "Wings Bernulli."

Because of his bad leg, Dad was retired from the force within a few months, and then he really *did* start drinking. He saw angels everywhere after that. And imps and little pink elephants as well.

As for Mom, she had not been amused when he'd called her from the station to come and get me that day. It was a "last straw," she said. Though the real last straw didn't happen till five years later; that's when they got divorced.

I saw Dad as often as I could. He lived only a few blocks away, after all. But it was never very pleasant, what with his drinking. He wasn't a mean drunk, just a sloppy one. And he talked endlessly about angels.

No one took him seriously, of course, though every once in a while Mom would threaten to have him put away. But she couldn't do it. Not legally, not without his permission, since they were no longer married.

"I'm not so crazy as that, Jesse," he used to say to me. "You saw the angel, too. Don't you remember? Just a little?"

But all I remembered of that angel was in my dreams: a dark shadowy figure falling like a bird of prey from the sky in a sharp, perilous stoop. So I never really believed my dad's story. I mean—who could?

And then, quite suddenly, he quit drinking in a noisy conversion that included a baptism and a church where they did laying-on of hands. He changed his name to Israel because, he told me, it means "wrestles with angels."

The new name, the new church, didn't stop him from gabbing endlessly about angels. But these people liked his stories. If anything, he told more stories until, at last, he seemed to have talked himself out. Then he left that church and went back to Saint Mary's. Mom used to see him there at early Mass, and they would smile at one another, she said. Not old enemies any longer, but not exactly old friends, either. That was where he heard the *Te Deum* and mentioned it to me, not to prove anything (as if after all these years it could have been called proof), but just as if some curious itch had finally been scratched.

Then one night he was on the back porch of my house in Connecticut, where he'd come for a weekend. We were talking, reminiscing really. About the days when we had been a family on Ninety-sixth Street. Dad and Mom; my sister, Jeanie; and me.

I said, "Did you ever find out what it was that made you think that old Chinese man was an angel?"

"I drank a lot in those days, Jesse," he said. "I don't do that anymore." He said it like an apology. Like a prayer.

The air was suddenly heavy. Fireflies seemed to hang motionless between the porch and the back garden. Inside the house, where my kids were watching a program about dinosaurs, I could hear the TV; and from the kitchen, where my wife was putting the finishing touches on my father's seventy-second birthday cake, came the sounds of the mixer.

Suddenly something large and dark, like a meteorite, fell across the moon and down, down, down toward earth. Dad reached his arms up as if welcoming an old friend, and the angel's enormous golden wings enfolded him.

Dark fathomless eyes stared into mine for a second, just as they had so many years ago. And then the Angel of Death took Dad away, leaving only the husk of his body and a single wing feather behind.

HOW I FRACTURED THESE STORIES:

NOTES AND POEMS

How to Fracture a Fairy Tale

<u>The Thing About Fairy Tales</u>

The thing about fairy tales
is not the Once, but the After.
We all know about Once.
It is the start of our lives,
the mistaken old woman
of the wood, the one we forgot
to give half our sandwich,
all of our brisket,
most of the chocolate mousse.
It is the fox we did not brush,
the sparrow we did not save,
a lion whose thorny paw
we did not doctor.
The oven into which
we did not push the witch.

It all leads to the After,
which is not death,
but inconsequence;
not dancing in red hot iron shoes,
but living past our sell-by date,
hating the husband,
bored with the wife.
It is the princess growing fat,
the king unfaithful,
and no children write home
to ask us how we are doing,
only a postcard of need.

Snow in Summer

"Snow in Summer" is set in the 1940s in the small West Virginia town my late husband grew up in. Much of the setting is from the memories I have of so many visits there over the years, beginning in the early 1960s. Eventually I turned the short story into a fairy tale novel of the same name. There's a lot more happening in the novel, of course. And I love the surprise of the ending in my fracture. But it is the ending of the actual folk tale that both fascinates/bothers me because it makes no sense. In the oldest tale, the prince sees the girl in a glass coffin and pays the dwarfs gold for her. And off he goes on his horse, with his men carrying the coffin behind. (In some variants, they put the glass casket with the dead girl on a cart.) And for what reasons does he wants a dead girl in a glass coffin? I have three ideas, each one more disgusting than the last. I used some of those ponderings to make the poem, not the story. The poem was first published in *Asimov's Magazine*.

Prince Ever After

He paid the little men in gold,
their grubby hands greedy for more,
but his face remained stern with his refusal.
The casket's glass was well polished,
he had to give them that. No fingerprints
marred the view of the girl.

Lifting the box up carefully,
his seven chosen men set it on the wagon.
They made no hard steps, no joggles,
their boots—like the cartwheels—cushioned.
The last girl had woken up too soon
and had to be put down.

This one would make it to the castle
or chosen heads would roll. He felt for his sword,
burnished and sharpened in its leather sheath.
No one in the twelve kingdoms
would have a finer casket girl on display.
Of that he was certain.

The Bridge's Complaint

I was asked to contribute a story from a different POV to a fairy tale anthology and for some reason the idea of writing *The Three Billy Goats Gruff* from the bridge's POV came to mind. As an oral storyteller, I had great fun enlarging on the old Norwegian tale. But here it is a short version, perhaps because Bridge obviously has (trigger warning for pun-ophobes) a short attention span. My silly/sweet story became an excuse to be a

263

whiner for a couple of days. Did I enjoy doing it? Of course. I
will do anything for my art! So here's a poem that is a sadder
version starring a troll maiden—and yes, they do exist—in
Swedish and Norwegian folklore.

Troll Maiden on the Bridge

Water, as fleeting
as human life,
flows beneath her feet.

She cannot breathe deeply
because of the sorrow
that dams her soul.

Alone of her clan
she seems a human girl
as long as you do not look closely.

She has a tail, small and black,
that curls like a question mark
above her perfect buttocks

a small oak forest
of unbudded twigs pushing
through the skin of her back.

She is neither troll nor human,
but the bridge between,
which is why she sits there

letting the whole world
walk across her heart,
Her grieving heart.

The Moon Ribbon

"The Moon Ribbon" has a bit of Cinderella in it (stepmother and stepsisters being mean and greedy, plus Cinderella hiding the glass shoe in her pocket). It also has a bit of George Mac-Donald's *The Princess and the Goblin* (the magical grandmother). That book was published in 1892 and remains one of my favorite children's fantasy novels. But the rest of this fractured fairy tale is really mine. Well, maybe not a fracture but a mash-up? *Moon Ribbon* was the title story of my second fairy tale collection, published in the late 1970s, almost a hundred years after the MacDonald book. The poem is new and explains my fascination with strong-minded folk tale heroines.

<u>Learning from Those Other Princesses</u>

They are buried, those other princesses,
as deep in their tales, stone embroideries
mired by tradition. Even the folklorists type them
as just another pretty girl in waiting.

But see Rapunzel climbing down her own hair,
claiming the broken prince, as she was once broken.
The Finn King's daughter, digging through mounds
deep as diamond mines, without dynamite or hard hat.

We no longer wait for princes, rescuing ourselves
from those higher prisons, those darker palaces.
We pull on hobnail boots, kick down doors,
even the ceilings of the glass mountains.

Hand me my pickaxe, my pitons, my shears.
Stand out of the way, you gentlemen of leisure.
One princess coming through, one vote,
one tower, one castle at a time.

Godmother Death

This is a folktale (most often as "Godfather Death") that can be
found all throughout Europe. The Irish and Spanish versions are
the ones that most influenced this telling. No, scratch that—what
began this story was getting an invite from Neil Gaiman to do
a short story for an anthology he was editing for Vertigo/DC
Comics in which one of the characters from his comic Sandman
starred. As I read his invitation, I remembered the folktale and
got right to work. I was using Neil's character Death, in his
telling a wonderful, snarky Goth girl who is ageless and endless.
I finished the story and really liked it. (This is rare for me.) And
Neil really liked it, too. If you read that anthology, you will
know the story was never published there. Why? Because when
my agent and I read the contract, it said that that DC owned the
story till the heat death of the universe. Well, legal words to that
effect. I never sell all rights to anything I write. One never knows
. . . Watty Piper was the house name for a variety of people at
Platt & Munk Publishers. Mostly their young editors wrote the
stories for their board books under that name for a flat fee. And
one of them (we do not know who) wrote *The Little Engine that
Could*. I filed off the Sandman numbers, changed a few things,
and sold the story elsewhere. And the story has been reprinted
a number of times, thank you very much, Neil. (He was very
understanding and we are still good friends.) The poem is about
Death, too. In fact it's about some actual statues in a cemetery

where a couple, long-married but of two different religions, died. And the silly preacher and priest insisted each had to be buried in his/her own religious boneyard. The children and neighbors who knew of the couple's devotion, erected two stone statues on their graves, which reach across the wall that separates the religious areas, so they can defeat Death for eternity.

Stone Hand in Stone Hand: Norvelt Cemetery

Death could not separate them,
this husband, this wife,
as religion would have dictated,
preacher and priest approving
different heavens for each.
They reach across the wall
between the burial grounds,
going about familial visitations
like prisoners, a touch here,
a grasped hand there,
enough for stone,
enough for eternity.

Happy Dens or A Day in the Old Wolves' Home

Originally, I thought of this as a young children's chapter book with illustrations. Over time I came to see it was a gloss on wolves in fairy tales that—to a somewhat aging writer at the time (even older now)—also spoke to the warehousing of our elder citizens. So maybe *not* for little kids after all. But maybe a short story for adults, which is how it was first published, but then republished in both adult and young adult collections. Go figure. As for the poem, it is very political (I lean left) and not only has been published in one of my collections (*Last Selchie's Child*) but will also be in the upcoming CD from my band, Three Ravens. It's from a performance we do with music and poetry called "The Infinite Dark." I wrote the lyrics to the majority of the songs. My son Adam, who is the real musician in our family, told his kids, "Nana is in a band and she's seventy-nine!" His son asked, "What does she play?" And Adam answered quickly, "The audience."

Once Upon a Wolf

Once upon a time, there was a wolf.
But not a wolf.
An Other.
Whose mother and father were others
Who looked not like us—
Republican or Dem,
in other words:
THEM.
They were forest dwellers,
Child sellers.
Wife beaters,
Idol makers,
Oath breakers,
In other words:
WOLF.
So, Happy Ever After means
We kill the wolf,
Spill his blood,
Knock him out,
Bury him in mud.
Make him dance
In red—hot—shoes,

For us to win
The Wolf—must—lose.

Granny Rumple

I first thought about the character of Rumpelstiltskin being a
Jew when teaching a children's lit course (for seven years) at
Smith College. Eventually I wrote an essay about it: how in
the old tale the only character who does what he promises and
isn't lying is Rumpelstiltskin. The miller and his daughter lie,
and the king is motivated by greed alone. But the small man
with the unpronounceable name who lives outside the walls of
the kingdom and is allowed only one job—spinning straw into
gold—does not lie. Plus he helps the miller's daughter out of
a desperate position. So of course he must be a demon who
wants to use the (as yet unborn) baby prince in some disgusting
blood rite. *Blood rite.* That was when I realized the "demon"
was a stand-in for a Jew. Someone with an unpronounceable
name who is forced to live outside the city walls. Is allowed only
one job inside the kingdom—that of moneychanger. Plus the
canard that was current at the time of the fairy story in both
Germany and Russia: that Jews stole Christian babies to kill
them and use their blood to make matzo. So, I did what any
reasonable academic did—I published a paper/essay. But as I am
also a fiction writer (and poet), I wrote "Granny Rumple," which
was snapped up by a Datlow/Windling anthology. The poem
was written to be used with this story.

Spinning Straw

His hand moves so quickly
she cannot tell the wheel

from the wish.
Gold pours from somewhere,
already refined into coins,
enough to refinance a kingdom.

She tries counting them,
though her education ended at twenty.
Gold spills past that number.

She dreams of crowns like plates
on the heads of angels,
shoes the color of the sun.

But her small dreams
are barely adequate to the fortune
the money-changer spins.

The counting house in her head
has no way to know a hallmark
from a hatch mark.

Real gold from fool's gold.
Angel plates from gold plate.
A truth from a lie.

One Ox, Two Ox, Three Ox, and the Dragon King

"One Ox, Two Ox, Three Ox, and the Dragon King" is based on the fact that Chinese dragon stories (and the old beliefs about dragons) are much more positive than western dragon stories. The Eastern dragons are gods of rain and abundance, though they can occasionally (like any gods) act unpredictably if you do not follow the rules and do not have a good heart. In order to write this, I read several books of Chinese folklore, notably Eberhard's *Folktales of China* and Hackin's *Asiatic Mythology*. I worked on and off on the story for almost a year. This story takes various bits and pieces of Chinese folk characters and lore, but the way the Ox brothers solve their problem is really very Western and that is the real fracture. This was first published in my collection *Here There Be Dragons*, as was the poem.

'Story,' the Old Man Said,

looking beyond the cave to the dragon tracks.
"Story is our wall against the dark."
He told the tale: the landing, the first death, the second.
They heard the rush of wind, the terrible voice,
a scream, then another.
Beyond the wall the dragon waited
but could not get in.

Brother Hart

"Brother Hart" is based on the Russian/Grimms story of "Little Brother, Little Sister" in which the two children are forced out of their castle by their wicked stepmother, a witch. Their escape route takes them through an enchanted woods. The fracturing here is twofold—the point of view and how I inserted the love and protective nature that I had for my brother Stevie, who was four years younger than I. Of course we lived in a happy home, and didn't have wicked forests to travel through, though until we were fourteen and ten, we lived across the street from

Central Park in New York City and usually I was in charge out there. Not a lot of actual wolves, but still occasionally a place where we needed to be careful. The original tale is one of my all-time favorite fairy tales. The poem is about another brother/sister pair out in the wilds, only this time fairy children were brought into the world of humans. Based on an old English legend and published in my small book of fairy poems, *The Last Selchie Child.*

Green Children

Dazed they were, and scared
lying on the cold stones,
their arms and legs green.
Not the dark green of ivy,
not the yellow-green of apples,
ripe on the summer bough,
nor the deep green of the ocean
where it leans against its bed.
They were the green of leeks,
of new-furled feather fern,
of the early leaf breaking soil.
When they opened their eyes,
their eyes were green, too.
And the little hairs on their arms
were inchworm green.
They spoke a green language
which the trees and flowers knew,
but which we did not.

The boy died of a wasting,
the girl did not,
eating broadbeans,
forgetting her green tongue,

growing whiter with each day;
till she christened
and married and all, *all* white.
Not the white of milk
after the cream has been skimmed off,
nor the white of October snow,
nor the white of a spring lily,
waxen and still,
nor the white of sea pearls
formed within the shell.
She was the white of the old moon
that shines over the hall.

Sun/Flight

"Sun/Flight" is clearly a short fracturing of the Icarus story, done in two important ways—told from Icarus's point of view, and Icarus saved and pulled from the sea without memory instead of dying, as in the original Greek myth. Or at least I save him for a while. The gods cannot be fooled. This story—and the poem below—make four times I have used the Icarus myth in my writing: I also did a picture book, *Wings* (with the most achingly beautiful illustrations by Dennis Nolan), and a very short poem (six lines) published in *Parabola* magazine in 1977.

Icarus Fall

On feathered dreams,
sky his limit,
he was a child when he flew.

He fell as an adult,
down to the earth
to plow, and sow, and make do.

Yet still at night,
exhausted by seeding,
he feels the air

On his face, his arms,
under his feathers,
tangling his whitened hair.

Slipping Sideways Through Eternity

Yes, I wrote *The Devil's Arithmetic* which is a slipstream novel
that takes a Jewish girl back to the Holocaust when she opens
the door for Elijah at the seder. And yes, this story (which
was written years after *DA*) has a Jewish girl who goes back
into the past with Elijah. But other than that, the stories are
entirely different. Different kind of girl (this one older and
goes purposefully back in time, on a rescue mission) plus
an entirely different take on the role of Elijah in the stories
from Jewish tradition. Fractured and finished. The poem on
the other hand references both the Holocaust and "Hansel &
Gretel." Because once you say "oven" to a Jew, they either swap
recipes or Holocaust stories. There is nothing between. I have
written three Holocaust novels, a Holocaust picture book,
Jewish Fairy Tale Feast, and most recently *Meet Me at the Well*,
with Barbara Diamond Goldin, a book of feminist retellings,
history, and midrash about the girls and women of the Hebrew

Bible (aka the Old Testament), so I should know. The poem was published in my book of political poems, *Before/the Vote/ After.*

Ovens

> *". . . when cinders smart the eyes and we begin to spit soot."*
> —Simon Schama

The old witch's ovens never stop smoking,
that delectable house reeks of roast pork,
not a kosher smell, but tempting.
Along the property lines, a minyan of bones
dances the hora whenever another piece of meat
comes into sight, a warning never heeded.
There's only one word for what she does to them.
Speak it and you become a collaborator.
Just a shudder will do, and a curse,
even as your eyes turn red,
even as sooty spit pools
along with the candy

The Foxwife

There are many Japanese folk tales about foxwives, called *kitsune.* Some of the foxwives are sly and wicked, some are wise and loving. Shapeshifters all. I wanted the point of view character to be feisty, sharp, tender, and true. It's an easy voice for me to slip into. *That's* where the fracture comes—the point of view. I wrote this story in 1984 and it was later reprinted in the *Year's Best Fantasy* stories volume. Years later, Kij Johnson's achingly beautiful novel *Foxwife* (2000) came out. It is well worth looking for it.

<u>Foxwife</u>

I found him, my gentle scholar,
living in a ruined temple.
If he can stand my cooking—
the meat too rare for most—
and my rank smell,
if he can forgive the sight
of my red tail,
I will make him a good wife.
Beast or girl,
I pledge him a warm fire
and quiet for his studies
long into the night.
Any who disturb him
will know my teeth.

The Faery Flag

This story began when I first heard about the actual Faery Flag ("actual" being a wobbly word when you are dealing with legends in Scotland). It was on the wall in Dunvegan Castle on the Isle of Skye, ancient home of the McLeods. An unassuming and tattered piece of cloth, with a marvelous legend which was condensed to about three sentences beneath the flag. So fracturing this tale meant making up all of the interstitial parts of the story. My favorite thing to do! As for the poem . . . well, I

am a pacifist (mostly) and storyteller (always) which is why I had
to write it to accompany this fractured tale.

Carrying the Flag of Faery

We always win,
but some men die, some women,
for that glory.
The children, too,
only no one tells
that part
            of the story.

One Old Man, with Seals

"One Old Man, with Seals" is based on the Greek shapeshifter,
Proteus. But also, at the time I wrote it, I was beginning to
worry about aging. I was only in my early forties then—and that
was hardly old—but looking ahead. The story fits me much
more now that I am seventy-nine! This old story is fractured by
taking a Greek mythological character and bringing him into
the twentieth (at that point) century to interact with a single
American character instead of carousing with a bunch of Greek
heroes. I wrote this poem to go with the story in this book.

On Meeting a God

There is no preparation for it.
One moment you are on a St. Andrews beach,
the casual sun failing to warm you.
Or in a plane, touching down outside of Dallas,

a place you are going for business, never pleasure.
Or possibly standing arm in arm with an old beau
whose charms have not advanced with his years.
Maybe you are crossing a meadow full of wildflowers,
fording a stream, bagging a Munro.
Possibly you are in an armchair dozing.
And there is the Godhead, gender uncertain,
holding out a shining hand.

I have read the old stories, know the stern warnings.
There is no honor in these encounters.
The humans—even the lucky ones—always lose.
So why do I take that proffered hand,
follow the fast disappearing footsteps,
run on tiptoe trying to catch up?
Because curiosity—that human failing,
that human instinct, that human burden,
that human glory—makes us want to know things.
Even if it damns us to all eternity.
Even then.

Sleeping Ugly

"Sleeping Ugly" is actually a still-in-print easy reading book that a number of oral storytellers now have in their repertoire thanks to my friend and favorite storyteller Milbre Burch. This is a true fractured fairy tale, because of three things—I always thought that fairy tale princesses, being tall, blonde, and beautiful (even if they were peasants at first), often had no right to be picked by the prince. I was short, dark-haired, and somewhat cute. But no princes. Now that I am much older, still short, still dark-haired (with help), and look more like the old fairy, I still feel that way. So "Sleeping Ugly" is my way of righting that particular wrong by fracturing *Sleeping Beauty*. A lot! As for the poem—since my favorite character in the story is the old fairy, I decided she needed her own poem.

Old Woman by the Well

"Beware of old women who linger by the well, for they are usually fairies in disguise, and cranky. You've been warned." —Terri Windling

I'm standing by the local well, seventy-four years old,
growing crankier by the minute. I hate being kept waiting.
I check my watch, the sun overhead. We'd said eleven.
It's closer to noon.

A man riding a horse clops by, sees me, dismounts quickly, kneels.
He holds up a hand in supplication. I'm an American, a feminist,
not used to courtesies, prayers. On good days, we ask for things
through the ballot box, on bad days some of us use a gun.

Give me . . . he begins. I have no time for this. *I beg you*, he continues.
I dig in my pocket, find a zloty, a pound coin, a lire, a euro.
I throw them at his feet, He has the grace to look startled.
Enough! I say, and it is not a question.

Then I raise an eyebrow, a hand palm down,
and blast him to stone.

JANE YOLEN

The Undine

"The Undine" is mostly based on Hans Christian Andersen's "Little Mermaid" plus several French undine stories I read over the years. (In folklore, the Undine is a water nymph who becomes human when she falls in love with a man. However, she is doomed to die if he is unfaithful. Probably the basis of Andersen's story.) So my telling has French undertones though it is not set in any real France. It's sensual in its own way (if you like fish) and unromantic because the prince is, in his own way, as much of a swine as many men in power today. Remember—this story was written in 1982 for my collection *Neptune Rising*. So you shouldn't think it's a critique of modern American politics and Hollywood when you read it. Though of course you can. The Rusalka poem is almost the opposite—no passion but an abhorrent rape, written three years ago (ahead of, but not by much, the MeToo movement). Rusalkas are Slavic river mermaids. Also note, I am Jewish and my family lived in the Ukraine at the time of the Cossacks' raids. They came to America to escape that sort of thing, My father was seven years old, the second youngest of eight children.

Warning from the Undine

If you walk the beach at night,
  Driftwind tangles in your hair,
  Foam as fingers grip your ankles,
  Best beware, oh best beware.

Do not think that I am wave top,
Do not think that I am tow,
  I am ocean, up and under,

I am legion high and low.

I am whisper, I am roaring,
I am lullaby and scream.
I will find you on the shingle,
I am nightmare, I am dream.

I am tidepool in the shallows,
I am lace on top of wave,
I am shell and shifting sand steps,
I am undertow and grave.

Great-Grandfather Dragon's Tale

I was working on a book (the first of what turned out to be a series) filled with my dragon stories and poems: *Here There Be Dragons*. The problem was, I had neglected one of the most famous dragons of all—St. George's dragon. So I sat down to write it from the dragon's point of view. Why? At this remove I cannot remember. I just heard the rumble of his voice as he tells his great-grandchildren a bedtime story that may even be a memoir. The story is long for a fable and short for a novella, but evidently just right for his dragonlings.

St. George's Sword and Word

Not vorpal, but sharp enough
to cut through scales.
The blade slightly curved,
Damask style.
It had the heft of history,

the slight of mystery.
The handle fit just one hand.
George was destined
for canonization.
I'd like to think *killer*
was not a job description,
but a feint.

Maybe they had tea together,
talked borders, boundaries,
signed a pact,
including the length
of smoke, of fire.
A codicil detailing
the number of pigs
ready for the sacrifice.
Better than maidens who—
so it is said—taste like chicken,
and wear an annoying amount
of buttons, laces, furbelows,
and other indigestibles.

Green Plague

"Green Plague" is of course a satirical fracturing of *The Pied Piper of Hamelin*, a German legend about a town infested with rats and the Pied Piper who promises to get rid of the rats for a rather large fee. And when the town fathers refuse to pay his whole fee, he whisks the children away as well, using his pipe and descriptions of treasures they will find along the way. Only I have written a variant with frogs instead of rats, and set in a bucolic tourist town of today, because a friend who was doing a frog fantasy anthology asked me for a story. It works because small town politics haven't changed much. And neither have con men. As for the poem, I slammed one realtor who cheated us in a novel, have gotten back at other evil doers in poems, wrote an entire book of poems about the first year of President Trump's thievery. And so it goes.

To Be Paid

Musicians, writers, and poets
are often not paid,
not even the promised pittance.

The performance is over,
magazine or book printed,
yet still there is no reward.

We cannot whisk the children away,
cannot punish the innocent
for their parents' theft.

Cannot pull back the graft
on the internet
where people sing our songs.

But we can do this:
memorialize you in a lyric,
he's so vain, he knows this song
this poem, this character's about him.

Name me an artist, I will show you
Vengeance one song, one poem, one novel
at a time.

Thievery is for now.
Art hangs around forever.
You will thank me for the warning.

The Unicorn and the Pool

"The Unicorn and the Pool" is based on unicorn lore. The two pieces I have used are 1) That a unicorn's horn can cure disease and disperse even the foulest poison. (That is why in medieval times, kings used unicorn horns to test for poison in their food. And no, it didn't work because they had bought narwhale horns instead of unicorn horns. On the other hand, narwhales, at least, exist.) 2) Where a unicorn steps, flowers spring up. Probably why there are so many millefleur tapestries of unicorns picturing the creature sitting or standing in fields of flowers. And how did I fracture those bits of lore? Put them in a parable that suggests Jesus. Not an original idea on my part because the unicorn since early days was thought to be an avatar of Christ. Or perhaps Christ an avatar of the unicorn. Either way, I love parables from whatever religion or creed they develop. By the way—I wrote the poem in college, where I was an English major and a religion minor, and it was published in the college literary magazine my sophomore year. Two years later on at graduation (1960) I won all the poetry prizes the college had on offer. I have always wondered if some wandering unicorn had a hand . . . er . . . . hoof in getting me those awards!

Rhinoceros

Bloated relic of a past
Where hungry behemoths
In ponderous herds lumbered

Through the swamp-filled woods.
Behind the folds of unwashed poundage,
Behind that muted horn of plenty,
Pink eyes, myopic and small,
Strain into the African muds.

Preposterous nose,
Elephantine toes,
Cyclopian rear
Cumbrous ear,
Down to a wee-wispish,
Barely switch-tipped
Tail.

And yet the memory of a swift
And silken racer of the wind,
Golden horn rippling the pool
Of dreams, troubles my mind.
What alchemy of the last few worlds,
What lava-filled abyss
Transformed the silken fair?
Has the unicorn come to this?

The Golden Balls

"The Golden Balls" is a teaser of a story. And the fairy tale it comes from—*The Princess and the Frog*—has two interesting variants. In the English version the princess treats the frog (a Frenchman?) with haughty disdain and is ordered by her father the king to let him eat from her plate and sleep on her pillow. And what is her reward for barely keeping her promise? She wakes up in the morning to find a handsome prince sleeping by her side. And if that variant doesn't please you, try the German variant where the princess, ordered to take the frog into her bedroom, flings him against the wall. He slides down into a puddled mess and arises—yes, you guessed it—as a handsome prince. Dear Readers—they married and (presumably) lived happily ever after. (Possibly.) Perhaps had many polliwoggish royal children. What is the moral of either of those variants? Beats me. So, perhaps my little fractured tale is me trying to get to the (well's) bottom of the tale. Perhaps not. The poem speaks for itself!

Frog Meet Princess

You asked too much,
forgot to bow,
slurped your soup.
No wonder she denied you.
When she flung you against the wall,
Cook was appalled.
What a way to ruin Sunday dinner.

Sister Death

"Sister Death" comes from the Jewish tradition of both Lilith and the Angel of Death, stories that make Death female. And you thought Neil Gaiman made that up! You must have missed an older . . . (i.e. way before the Gaiman Sandman comics) story of mine called "The Boy Who Sang for Death" in my collection *Dream Weaver*. We writers have been stealing from tradition forever. This story fractures the Jewish tales in that Death is the sympathetic character. The keening woman of the poem is the banshee, of course, who lives in Gaelic folklore, most notably Irish and Scottish. Her wailing appearance warns a family that one of them will soon die. I like to think of her as Death's younger sister. The poem was written for this story.

The Keening Woman

She stands, birdlike,
over the cliff body,
dark robe her wings;
tremoring as if ready
to fly away from death.
But it is to death
she is beholden.
Her life, her living
bound up in it.

Her songs lift the spirits,
sets this spirit free.
We see it fly
like a kittiwake
high above us,
then below us,
skimming water
till it disappears
beneath a wave.

Oh, keening woman,
the wail in your mouth
devours our sins.
We fly up to Heaven,
leaving the dross
of our lives behind
till we are only
wind, waves, water
and a skein of memory.

JANE YOLEN

Sule Skerry

The fisherfolk who live in the Scottish islands of Shetland and Orkney and as far west as the Hebrides tell many strange and beautiful tales of the selchies, seals who can take on human form, usually by shrugging out of their skins. Often you see seals lying on the rocks (skerries) off the Scottish coast. So, first take into account that I own a house in Scotland where I spend four months a year. Next that I have read many selchie stories over the past fifty years. I have also written many selchie stories and poems about selchies, beginning with "Greyling," which I wrote when I was nursing my first child and she is now over fifty. Stir in my love of selchie songs: everyone in my birth family sang. Well, that is not entirely true. As I grew up, my mother no longer sang. She'd been a gifted contralto, or so she said, but her voice had hoarsened and changed. My father played guitar as if it were a ukulele, and sang cowboy songs. My brother and I were both musicians and singers, I a low alto. I have always loved folk songs, long and sad British/Scottish ballads especially. Among my favorites was "The Great Selchie of Sule Skerry," and this selchie story is fractured by being a modern version of the story. The poem is in my own voice after my husband died, looking back on my life.

<u>When I Was a Selchie</u>

"The cure for anything is salt water: sweat, tears or the sea."
—Isak Dinesen from *Seven Gothic Tales*

There was a time in my teens
when I was a selchie, changeable,
living by the dark waters
of Long Island Sound.

I danced on the sand,
almost always by myself,
playing alternate fairy tales
of acceptance, escape.

The waters of the Sound
sang their dark songs
threading my bones,
penetrating my dreams.

I thought I knew nothing then,
think I know everything now,
carrying those twinned dreams,
into every book I write,

into every new man who is not you
that I meet.

Once a Good Man

This is based on/fractured from a worldwide story. I have read both Jewish and Chinese versions. (In the Chinese the folks use long chopsticks to feed themselves, feed others.) I first heard a telling of this story at a Quaker summer camp when I was thirteen or fourteen, and it stuck with me for years. That was long before I had the writing chops for redoing such a story. (No pun intended.) When I began writing and fracturing folk tales, I wrote this story as a possible picture book. But it never sold. So when I needed an extra story for an early adult collection of my tales, I rewrote the story to take it away from its more childish telling, and published it there. As for the poem—you now know what I consider Heaven.

What Do We Need of Heaven

What do we need of heaven
when we have this outside the door:
millefleur tapestry of meadow,
throne of an old tree hewn by a storm,
choristers of birds singing hosannas,
huddles of hares waiting to perform,
Chinese paintbrush of clouds,
soft carpet of moss, leaves underfoot,
while the lullaby river, singing between banks.

Eden a step away.

Allerleirauh

There are three major variants of the Cinderella story, and in each one she gets the prince by dint of hard work, the goodness of her heart. And/or help from friends. The first is the one we all know best—mother dies, stepmother is a witch with two bossy/nasty stepsisters. She goes to the ball by hook or by crook or in special dancing shoes (the glass slippers are just a mistake in translation from the French, where the word for glass and the word for squirrel fur are very close in sound). The stepmother and stepsisters are embarrassed but otherwise unhurt at the end. There is a tougher version of the above (and probably older) where the stepsisters end up blinded by the helpful birds and maimed with their mother's help as they slice their feet up to be able to slip their feet into the glass shoes. (Disney ignored this part!) and the stepmother is killed. In the third—which is what Aller-leirauh is based on—is an incest variant. The princess's mother dies in childbirth, and the king makes her a dying promise that he will only marry someone as beautiful as she is. And when Allie is sixteen and comes to a ball dressed in one of her dead mother's party dresses . . . well, you can guess what happens. She runs away of course and finds a prince. But that's not the dark turn of my fractured tale. When I was getting my Masters Degree (in education), I did a paper on the variants, called "America's Cinderella." The poem accompanying this is much more positive than my fracture. I thought you might need it.

Cinderella in the Ashes

If you remember her weeping,
ash tears, fingers twining in sorrow,
you do not know the entire tale.

She bargains a dress from the tree
where her dead mother is buried,
gathering magic to her own breast.

Gives the rat coachmen a GPS,
rides off in a pumpkin, heedless of seeds.
Seduces a prince with small talk.

Dances in glass shoes
Imelda would have envied,
till the heels are only shards.

She lies her sisters into self-mutilation,
then rules the country on her own,
with an iron fist.

The Gwynhfar

"The Gwynhfar" is of course an Arthurian fracture, using the Welsh name for Guinevere. Plus the use of a horrific premise, that being the wholesale buying and selling of royal princesses to dukes and kings as brides, whatever their age, their condition, the princesses' own desires and needs. Or the king's. They were (as in this case) quite literally sacrifices to the royal bloodlines of the world. Not your usual Guinevere marriage tale. The poem, however, wants to speak of strong-minded, bloody-minded Princesses instead. To raise the flag for poor Gwynhfar.

<u>Not That Princess</u>

Not the one hid in the closet,
till almost midnight,
or the one who married a frog.
(Bad taste always did run in that family)
Nor the over-sleeper who woke
as the mother of twins.
No virgin she.
Not the ones who keep changing
into foxes, bears, snakes, wolves.
Hard to keep them anywhere but a kennel.
We have the goods right here, Majesty,
pure white, gleaming,
destined to keep her mouth shut,
legs open, do as she's told.
The best kind of princess.
Guaranteed for the life of your kingdom,
or your money back.

Just sign here, kick her tires,
and drive away.
She'll always be in the back seat,
keeping it warm for the kingdom.

Cinder Elephant

"Cinder Elephant" began as a companion piece to "Sleeping Ugly," and the editor finally turned it down because someone worried that it might hurt the feelings of overweight children. Honestly, I wrote it as a former overweight teen (and adult) myself who met and married a wonderful, handsome, and brilliant man who was—among many other things—an ardent bird-watcher who loved me for myself. If anything, I am a bit hard on very thin people in this story. (I apologize.) Actually I am really hard on mean people. It took years for the story to be published—not as a children's picture book but as a short story in a middle grade anthology. But when I wanted to put it in *this* book, I went back and made it a bit snarkier and older and added two extra morals. Because I could. (And just so you know, my mother was tiny and wore a size five-and-a-half shoe, triple-A heel. I wear size nine-and-a-halfs wide. So I got the whole family bit parts in this one. Years later than all of this, I was asked for a story for an anthology on "fat issues." I said I didn't have any ideas for a story, but I could write a poem. The editor said, "No poems." But I sent "Fat Is Not a Fairy Tale," and they made it the first piece in the anthology because they liked it so much. It got picked up by Poet Laureate Billy Collins for a teen anthology and has been reprinted many times since.

Fat Is Not a Fairy Tale

I am thinking of a fairy tale,
Cinder Elephant,
Sleeping Tubby,
Snow Weight,
where the princess is not
anorexic, wasp-waisted,
flinging herself down the stairs.

I am thinking of a fairy tale,
Hansel and Great
Repoundsel,
Bounty and the Beast,
Where the beauty
has a pillowed breast,
and fingers plump as sausage.

I am thinking of a fairy tale
that is not yet written,
for a teller not yet born,
for a listener not yet conceived,
for a world not yet won,
where everything round is good:
the sun, wheels, cookies, and the princess.

Mama Gone

"Mama Gone" is a straightforward vampire story except for two
fractures—the vampire is the girl's mother, and the setting is
(once again) Appalachia, an area I got to know well because

my husband was from a small mountain town called Webster Springs. This is one of the stories in *Fractured* that I love the most because of its tenderness, not something one usually associates with vampires. Maybe that's a third fracture. The story has been reprinted quite a bit. The poem was written especially for this book and this story.

The Vampire Regrets

There is blood on her fingers,
her mouth. Her eyes weep red tears.
She is at war with her own nature.
What nurture she once cherished
has been ripped from her.
No eternity is worth the price,
she thinks, sinking her teeth
into her child's throat,
his body still covered
with the blood of his birth.
There is no pact with evil.
None.

In this victory there will never be peace.

The Woman Who Loved a Bear

"The Woman Who Loved a Bear" is based on a Native American story. Trying to decide how a non-Native teller might fracture this story was to include a modern grandfather telling it to a grandchild. I hope I did honor to the original tale. It was published in an anthology called *Tales from the Great Turtle* in

1994. The poem comes as a response to the original story, and was published first in *Mythic Delirium* magazine in July 2017.

Marrying the Bear

When they found me,
with my broken basket,
I saw their true nature,
wanting it for my own.
That is how I married
the prince of bears
bore him two sons,
each with his dark hair
and long nose.
They are a powerful people
dreaming long and true
in the stretch of winter.

With my new basket
I bring them many berries,
teach them to make fire,
roast turkeys, make jam.
I would have lived happily
with my husband forever,
but my brothers found us,
burned his bones.
The ash will make more life.
But not in me.
Never again in me.

I miss his arms
strong, hairy, comforting.
Miss his small grunts
when we lay in the dark together.

There is a dirge here,
but I shall sing it in a major key
so all women who would marry bears
can dance.

Wrestling with Angels

"Wrestling with Angels" was written for a story-and-poem collection of mine called *Here There Be Angels*, one of five collections, the others being *Dragons*, *Unicorns*, *Witches*, and *Ghosts*. This story harkens back to the Old Testament (Hebrew Bible) where Jacob wrestles with the angel and is lamed (Genesis 32:22–23). Only I set this in modern times, and the point of view is very human. The poem was written to accompany this story.

Jacob's Regret

My hand on his thigh,
his hand on mine.
I hope he has something more in mind
than merely wrestling.
But I hear the sound of the break
before I feel the pain.
It is always thus,
when wrestling with angels.

ABOUT THE AUTHOR

Beloved fantasist Jane Yolen has been rightfully called the Hans Christian Andersen of America and the Aesop of the twentieth century. In 2018, she surpassed 365 publications, including adult, young adult, and children's fiction, graphic novels, non-fiction, fantasy, science fiction, poetry, short-story collections, anthologies, novels, novellas, and books about writing. Yolen is also a teacher of writing and a book reviewer. Her best-known books are *Owl Moon*, the How Do Dinosaurs series, *The Devil's Arithmetic*, *Briar Rose*, *Sister Emily's Lightship and Other Stories*, and *Sister Light, Sister Dark*.

Among Yolen's many awards and honors are the Caldecott and Christopher medals; the Nebula, Mythopoeic, World Fantasy, Golden Kite, and Jewish Book awards; the World Fantasy Association's Lifetime Achievement Award, the Science Fiction/Fantasy Writers of America Grand Master Award, and the Science Fiction Poetry Grand Master Award. Six colleges and universities have given her honorary doctorates.

Yolen lives in Western Massachusetts most of the time, but spends long summers in St. Andrews, Scotland.